HIS CAPTIVE LADY

Carol Townend

MILLS & BOON®
Pure reading pleasure™

® and T... ...re trademarks owned and ...ed by the trademark ...wner and/or it... ...censee. Trademarks marked ...with ® are register...with the United K... ...dom Patent Office and/or ...or Harmo...sation in the Intern... ...Market and in ...

First pub...shed in Great Britain 2009
Harlequi... Mills & Boon Limited
Eton Hous...18–24 Paradise Road, Richmond, Surrey TW9 1SR

© Carol Townend 2008

ISBN: 978 0 263 86775 6

Set in Times Roman 10½ on 12¾ pt.
04-0409-78455

Printed and bound in Spain
by Litografia Rosés S.A., Barcelona

Carol Townend has been making up stories since she was a child. Whenever she comes across a tumbledown building, be it castle or cottage, she can't help conjuring up the lives of the people who once lived there. Her Yorkshire forebears were friendly with the Brontë sisters. Perhaps their influence lingers…

Carol's love of ancient and medieval history took her to London University, where she read History, and her first novel (published by Mills & Boon) won the Romantic Novelists' Association's New Writers' Award. Currently she lives near Kew Gardens, with her husband and daughter. Visit her website at www.caroltownend.co.uk

Recent novels by the same author:

THE NOVICE BRIDE
AN HONOURABLE ROGUE

Author Note

In the eleventh century heraldry was in its infancy—the devices of the various noble houses did not start to develop properly until the second quarter of the twelfth century. However, flags and pennons may be seen on the Bayeux Tapestry. They were used in the Battle of Hastings to convey signals as well as to reveal identity. Thane Eric of Whitecliffe's battle pennon is similar to these.

Many thanks are due to my editor, Joanne, for her thoughtful (and always tactfully phrased!) suggestions. She is worth her weight in gold.

Chapter One

Captain Wulf FitzRobert sat waiting on a stool by the fire in the middle of King William's cavernous new barrack-hall. Waiting, waiting. It was an exercise in patience, he told himself, but even so, he was unable to keep his keen blue eyes from straying to the top table where the great lords were in conference. He was hungry for his next commission.

The freshly whitewashed walls around him displayed a formidable array of shields and lances, which winked in the fitful candlelight. Thick beams arched above Wulf's head, beams that had been cut so recently that he could smell sawn timbers, could see the marks of the adze. While Wulf kicked his heels and mastered his impatience, a troop of foot soldiers tramped in and headed for the wine jugs.

Glancing down at the worn brown tunic that stretched across his broad chest, at the shabby and barely ser-

viceable grey hose that barely covered his long legs, Wulf
noticed a rip in the weave and grimaced. His clothing
needed to be replaced and he could ill afford it. Advancement, that was what he craved, more advancement.

Under the high table two wolfhounds—a grey and a
brindle—were snarling over possession of a bone.
Wulf's mouth twisted. So it was with those lower in the
ranks, he thought, lifting his gaze once again to the
noblemen and commanders clustered around the board;
that is what we are reduced to, fighting over scraps
dropped by those above.

Parchments were scattered across the tabletop—
maps, most likely. Wulf knew what the lords were
about: they were busy slicing up lands won in the recent
conflict. Estates that had once belonged to Saxon
noblemen were being parcelled out among King
William's most loyal supporters. Campaigns for suppressing rebellion were being planned; offers were
being made for the most wealthy of the Saxon widows
and heiresses.

Just then, the brindle hound lunged amid a flurry of
growling and snapping. The grey yelped and dropped
the bone and in a moment it was all over. The brindle
darted into the shadows with the bone fast in its jaws,
while the loser slunk away, tail between its legs.

Was time running out for him? Wulf thought.
England had only so much land; there were only so
many titles. If he did not get a decent commission, there
might be nothing left to win, neither land nor title nor
heiress. Not that Wulf had ambitions for an heiress—no,
the shadow over his birth meant he could not look so
high. He was illegitimate. But lands and a knighthood,

yes, he certainly had ambitions for those. And with no noble family to sponsor him, Wulf must shift for himself.

The lords had wine cups at their elbows. Of delicate imported glass, they were a world away from the clay goblet Wulf had warming by the fire. As well as the maps, there were several jugs of sweet red wine on the high table; wine that Wulf knew had only that morning been shipped in from Normandy. Briefly, Wulf spared a thought for the merchant willing to risk his ship to a winter crossing, but then this was King William's hall, so doubtless the man and his crew would have been well rewarded. Wulf propped his chin on his hand. Rewarded as he hoped to be, when he was given a good chance to prove himself…

One lord in particular held Wulf's gaze: William De Warenne, his liege lord. As one of the King's most trusted commanders, De Warenne had recently been granted estates on the coast south of London, near a place called Lewes. Wulf had heard that his lord was also in the running for more land, land in the remote east of England, somewhere in the fens. Wulf had never set foot in the fens, nor did he want to. If what he had heard was true, the fen country was marshy and waterlogged even in high summer. And at this time of year, in mid-winter, the fens would be frozen solid.

Wulf wound lean fingers round the clay cup and lifted it to his lips. He took no more than a sip; he wanted a sober head on him when his lord called him over.

Perhaps, if he were lucky, he would be granted a commission in those southern lands so recently acquired. Two days, Wulf thought, for two interminable days he had been whiling away the time here, kicking his heels while the commanders discussed tactics and jostled for power and position.

A lock of dark hair fell over Wulf's eyes; impatiently, he shoved it back. He *must* get his hair trimmed, it had grown so much he looked more Saxon than Norman, and the last thing he wanted was for the lord of Lewes to think he was favouring the Saxon half of his heritage.

'*Captain!*'

Wulf's blue eyes narrowed and his fingers tightened on his wine cup. His heart thudded—De Warenne was looking directly at him. *At last!*

'My lord?' Setting his cup down, Wulf rose and approached the high table.

'FitzRobert, isn't it?'

'Yes, my lord.' Wulf stood, feet planted squarely apart, and waited.

'FitzRobert.' De Warenne unrolled one of the maps and weighed it down with a jug and a candlestick. 'Take a look at this, and tell me what you see.'

Ignoring the curious gazes of the other men sitting in council with De Warenne, Wulf peered at the candlelit parchment. Thankfully, he had made it his business to interpret maps; it was lettering he struggled with.

'It is England.' Leaning in, Wulf put his finger on the spot which he knew represented London. 'We are about here, my lord. See where the river is marked? And here, this is where Lewes lies.'

'Excellent. Now show me Normandy.'

'Normandy?' Wulf blinked. 'This map is not large enough to show Normandy, my lord. If it were, it would lie down here, somewhere past the Narrow Sea.' He indicated a knot-hole on the table, a couple of inches below where the parchment ended.

Nodding, De Warenne smiled and lifted a meaningful brow at one of his companions, Count Eugène of Médavy. 'I repeat, Captain FitzRobert is the man for this job.'

'Hmm.' Eugène of Médavy scrutinised Wulf with a soldier's eye, noting his height and how much weight he carried, assessing the strength and width of his shoulders. Wulf knew without vanity, for it was a fact, that by that measure he would not fall short. He had been born with a large, healthy body, and years of training had made it the body of a warrior. He was big, but he carried muscle rather than excess flesh. As a warrior Wulf did not disappoint, but the Saxon blood in his veins was quite another matter, never mind the shame of his illegitimate birth…

To Wulf's astonishment, the Count began addressing him in English. 'Captain, have you any knowledge of this land to the north of London?' The Count's accent was thick, but his English was intelligible, which was rare, *very* rare, in a Norman lord.

Hastily, Wulf closed his mouth and looked where Count Eugène's blunt finger was pointing. East Anglia. 'That's marshland,' Wulf said, replying in English, for this was doubtless some kind of test. A *frisson* of excitement ran through him. The fens might not exactly be the South Downs, but if they could bring him the preferment he sought, he would learn to love them. 'Here is Ely, my lord,' he continued in English. 'I have not been there, but I have been told that there is more water thereabouts than land. The fens are criss-crossed with waterways rather than roads, and the fen folk use boats to travel from one place to another.'

'The wenches there have webbed feet,' Count Eugène said, on a laugh. 'And people use poles to vault from island to island.'

Wulf shrugged; he, too, had heard the tales, but he doubted that half of them were true. 'Perhaps.'

The Count watched him, a small smile playing about his mouth, and Wulf's heartbeat speeded up. Giving one last glance at Wulf's over-long hair, the Count of Médavy grinned at De Warenne and pushed himself to his feet. 'Captain FitzRobert certainly has the looks, William, and he speaks the language like a native. He could well be our man, but he will have to be quick-witted, because he will not have long to learn the lie of the land.' Picking up his gauntlets, Eugène of Médavy nodded at Wulf and sauntered to the door. Without turning, he snapped his fingers and the brindled hound detached itself from the shadows with its bone, and trotted after him. The Count's voice floated back. 'I shall leave it to you to arrange, De Warenne, since the King was making noises about granting you more lands there.'

A general scraping of benches announced that the other noblemen took this as their signal to leave, but Wulf scarcely noticed. His attention was all for his liege lord, though he fought to keep the eagerness from his expression. 'I can be of service, my lord?' At last. At *last*.

'Aye, I think that you can. FitzRobert—' De Warenne broke off, scowling.

'My lord?'

'*Merde*, you cannot use that name, we shall have to give you another.'

Some of Wulf's elation began to drain away. 'What, precisely, is my commission?' He kept his expression blank and reminded himself of a lesson he had learned years ago—if he wanted to avoid disappointment, he should not expect too much. Likely he was being given this commission because it was too distasteful for a Norman nobleman to consider. Wulf set his jaw. Well, he was not proud, he was not noble. But he *was* ambitious and he would do whatever his lord asked, provided it brought him advancement.

'Saxon outlaws have been reported hiding out in the fens,' De Warenne told him. 'We need good intelligence as to their number and strength. Any threat to our King's rule must be eliminated.'

A spy. Ignoring the sudden griping in his belly, reminding himself of that knighthood that had been his goal for more years than he could count, Wulf straightened his shoulders. 'What is it you would have me do, my lord?'

'You must pose as Saxon. It should prove easy enough—you speak the language like a native.'

'I am a native,' Wulf said softly, 'at least, half of me is.'

'Ah, yes, your mother, I recall. You were brought up not far from here, were you not?'

'Aye, in Southwark.'

De Warenne's gaze sharpened. 'The Godwinesons had a hall in Southwark.'

'I know it well, or I did.'

De Warenne reached for his wine. 'Not a plank standing,' he said, oblivious that his words evoked yet more conflicting feelings in Wulf's chest.

Wulf remembered playing in that hall as a young boy. He had even met King Harold long ago, when Harold had been but a young earl. And this man, this man sitting at the trestle in the new king's barracks with the map of Harold Godwineson's kingdom unrolled before him, now held title to a large slice of Harold's lands around Lewes. Lord, Wulf thought, how the wheels do turn.

'So, FitzRobert,' De Warenne was saying, 'these Saxon rebels—you are to track them to their lair in these marshes. Infiltrate their band. Our sources speak of a leader known as Thane Guthlac. An outlaw now, of course, as are those who ally themselves with him. Word has it that this Guthlac has built up a sizeable force, but so far none of our men have managed to come back with precise numbers.' Wearily, his *seigneur* scrubbed his cheeks. 'Nor can we pinpoint the location of his camp. Which is damned odd, since one of my scouts reported hearing a rumour that the man had built a castle out there.'

Wulf's brows rose. 'A castle in the fens? That seems unlikely.'

'Nevertheless, that is the rumour.' De Warenne took up the wine jug and filled a couple of glasses. Taking one, he slid the other towards Wulf. 'Take a seat, Captain, we still have to discuss the question of your name. I hardly think that FitzRobert is suited to a Saxon.'

Wulf groped for the bench, trying to will away the knot that was forming in his belly. Finally he was being offered the chance that he had longed for, but where was the elation, the triumph that he had expected to feel? 'I am to be a spy.'

'Locate Thane Guthlac's encampment. Worm your way inside, we need to know how much of a threat they pose. It could be that there are just a few stragglers hiding out with him—we have no idea and we must know. Now, about your name—'

'I could use my other name, my lord.'

'*Other* name?'

'Saewulf Brader.'

For a moment his lord gazed blankly at him, before understanding lit his eyes. 'Oh, I take it Brader was your mother's name? You used it before your father had you brought to Normandy?'

'Yes, my lord.'

'Saewulf Brader,' De Warenne repeated, slowly examining Wulf's features. 'Yes, that will do, it has an authentic ring to it. Don't bother to get your hair cut either, it will help you look the part. And, if I were you, I might consider growing a beard. Damned hairy, these Saxons.'

Wulf took a sip of the wine. It was rich and sweet, smoother by far than that served lower down the hall. 'No, my lord, I do not think a beard is for me, I have grown accustomed to the Norman fashion.'

De Warenne raised a brow. 'You will raise their suspicions.'

Wulf grinned. 'I could say I ran into some Normans and cut my beard off to disguise myself.'

'Suit yourself. I leave the details to you.' De Warenne met Wulf's gaze directly. 'Do a good job, Captain, and I won't forget. There will be preferment for you.'

'Thank you, my lord.' Understanding that he was being dismissed, Wulf rose. 'When do you want me to leave?'

'As soon as you can. Oh, and one thing more…'

'My lord?'

'You have a horse?'

'Aye.' Not that his lord would call his poor Melody a horse; Wulf was a long way from affording a knight's destrier. One day, perhaps…

'You will have to leave him behind.'

Wulf nodded. A horse might also raise suspicions, since Saxons did not use them as much as Normans. But, in any case, from what Wulf had heard, horses and fenland did not sound compatible.

'Put him in the stables here in the charge of my groom. I'll see he knows to take care of him.' De Warenne picked up a pouch and lobbed it towards him. 'Here, this will help buy anything you might need.'

'Thank you, my lord.'

Tossing back his wine, Wulf turned to go. His mind was spinning. Finally, he was being given the chance that he burned for! He would not have chosen to spy on his former countrymen—in truth, his commission was far from pleasant. Some might call it a dirty task. Certainly it was not a task for a noble Norman. And this was, of course, exactly why it had been given to him. De Warenne and the Count of Médavy could flatter him all they wished by referring to his aptitude, to his fluency in English, to the length of his hair, but Wulf knew the real reason he had been chosen.

Wulf was not noble, Wulf was not even legitimate, Wulf was a bastard. A bastard of a commission for a bastard of a man. That had been the unspoken undercurrent in the entire discussion. No highborn knight would even consider such a commission.

Reaching the weapon stack by the door, Wulf picked his sword out of the pile and stood for a moment staring at it. It was a plain sword. With its wooden scabbard and its hilt bound in cowhide, it was the sword of a plain man. It might have a keen edge and Wulf might be able to wield it as well as any knight, but he had no noble family to sponsor him. And there, too, was another reason the Lord of Lewes had selected him to go to the fens. If by chance Wulf were killed, there would be no aristocratic friends calling for vengeance, there would be no noblewomen weeping at his graveside.

Rolling powerful shoulders, Wulf shrugged off his dark thoughts and buckled on his sword. He glanced around the huge hall filled with King William's soldiers. He could not afford to be churlish, not when he was being given his chance. He might not choose to spend the winter in the fens, but the sooner he was gone, the sooner he might return. So, distasteful though this commission might be, he would do his best. As he saw it, those rebels, outlaws, call them what you will, were fighting a lost cause, and the sooner they came to realise that, the sooner the bloodshed could end. The sooner England could be at peace.

If there was one thing that Wulf had learned from his liege lord, it was that peace was not something that happened by chance. No, in the winter of 1067, peace had to be *made*. And if Wulf could play his part in bringing about that peace, and at the same time earn preferment for himself, then so much the better…

Chapter Two

East Anglian Fens—January 1068

Even when clad in green homespun and a simple matching veil, Erica of Whitecliffe presented a queenly figure. Night had fallen, and she was sitting by the fire in the rough reed-thatched shelter that was her latest refuge. Someone had actually found a chair for her. Incongruously it reminded Erica of a throne, and she was able to prop her chin on her hand and stare into the flames. Ranged about her on stools and benches, hugging close to the hearth, were the men she had chosen as her personal escort.

Ailric, his fair hair tied out of the way with a leather thong, was bent over his sword, sharpening it, and the gentle rasp of a whetstone on steel formed a backdrop to her thoughts, thoughts which went back and forth as she struggled to find a way out of their predicament. Morcar's cough—it was worsening—brought a worried frown to her brow.

Outside the cottage the temperature had plummeted. And it was going to get worse, of that Erica was certain. It was early January; the coldest weather might yet be round the corner.

She was in exile, they were all in exile. And they could not live like this much longer, as that persistent cough was reminding her.

When they had fled her father's hall at Whitecliffe in the south, Erica had prayed it would be a temporary exile, and that soon they would be home again with the world set to rights. But her father was dead and her people divided. Some had insisted on remaining with her while others, almost a hundred warriors, had taken refuge elsewhere in the marshes. When there was the slightest chance of harrying the Normans, the warriors took it. She longed for them to be together once more; she worried about the wives and children left behind in Whitecliffe.

Morcar, one of her father's oldest housecarls, smothered another cough. She held down a sigh. Morcar was too old to be living the life of an outlaw, his chest was weakening. And there was Hrolf, with that leg wound that refused to heal—Hrolf needed good food which she could not give him, and rest and… Daily, Erica prayed to return home. This was no place to live, this was no life. But William of Normandy had fast hold of southern England and was not to be ousted, it would seem.

What could she do?

'The bloodfeud with Thane Guthlac must end,' she said and braced herself for the inevitable barrage of objections.

The whetstone stilled and Ailric spoke up. 'My lady, you are not serious?'

'I have never been more so.'

Ailric's brow furrowed and the moment he set his sword aside, Erica knew she was in for an argument.

'Ailric, look at us. We need to pool our resources with others, we need allies. Our very survival is at stake.'

'The bloodfeud will never end,' Ailric said. 'It is a matter of honour and—'

'The bloodfeud *must* end.'

'There are other ways.'

'No, Ailric, you are wrong! We ran out of choices months ago, but were too blind to see it. The bloodfeud with Guthlac must *end*. I have made my decision.' Erica clenched her fists and stared fiercely round the ring of bearded faces that gleamed in the firelight. Her father's housecarls were loyal, and it went without saying that they would sacrifice their lives for her. As they would have done for her father, had he not died at Hastings. But loyalty had never prevented them from disagreeing with her. Unfortunately.

The fire guttered and an icy draught cut through Erica's cloak while she marshalled her arguments. There were dozens of cracks in the slipshod planking and the fenland wind knew its way into every one of them. Suppressing a shiver lest it be mistaken for weakness—and she would die before one of them thought her weak— Erica dragged her cloak more firmly about her shoulders and drew in a deep breath. Loyal her father's housecarls might be, but that would not put an end to their dissent. She was, after all, a woman, and some of them had difficulty taking orders, even from her. And in the matter of the bloodfeud they were stubborn as mules.

'I am sorry, Ailric.' Erica made her voice hard, trying

for that tone that her father had used when he would brook no contradiction. 'But I disagree most strongly. What can we few do from here?' A wave of her hand encompassed not only her personal guard, but also the cruck-framed cottage, pitifully small and stark compared to the luxuries of Whitecliffe Hall. 'On our own we are as nothing, we are but a candle in the wind, we need allies.'

Scowling, Ailric hooked his thumbs round his swordbelt and tossed his blond head; Hereward shifted on his bench and opened his mouth. Erica silenced them with a look.

'We are nothing,' she repeated, frowning through the smoke. 'Think, all of you. Here we have, what, a couple of warriors young enough to be worthy of the name? Hereward, Ailric, yes, you I count as warriors.' She softened her voice before directing her gaze at two of the older faces round the fire. Men with greying hair and scarred, weather-beaten faces, men in their late forties, men who were weak with old age and infirmity. 'But it is time to face reality. Morcar, Siward, you are fine warriors, both of you, but age is no longer on your side. Luck was with you at Hastings, and you know it.'

Siward's grizzled head shook as Erica had known it would. But Morcar simply stroked his beard and lowered his eyes to the leaping flames, misery in his every line. Erica had also noticed the difficulty Morcar had had hoisting himself in and out of the boat as he patrolled the waterways.

'These marshes are not good for a man with stiffness in his joints,' she murmured.

Morcar coloured and muttered into his beard, and

that told Erica all she needed to know. Morcar had had enough. Time was when Morcar would have leaped to his feet to deny the slightest weakness, but now, in this bitter fenland winter, he sat by the fire like an old man, muttering about the damp getting into his bones, trying not to cough. At night, they listened to him wheezing in his sleep. Morcar *was* an old man, she realised with a jolt. And if she did not try to protect him, Erica did not know who would.

'If we are to mount a decent campaign against those who took King Harold's throne, we must link up with our warriors and join forces with *other* Saxons. If we do not…' Erica lifted her shoulders. She did not have to finish the sentence, every man around this fire understood what she was saying. They needed allies, if they were to stand a chance of success. But Erica realised it was worse than that, they needed allies, if they were to *survive*.

Ailric nodded tersely at Hereward, who jumped to his feet. 'Lady Erica,' Hereward said, dignifying her with the title that was her due as the only child of a thane. 'Lady Erica, none of us would argue with your plan to join forces with others against the Norman bastard. But *Guthlac*…' Hereward's face distorted and he spat, most eloquently, into the fire before thumping back onto the bench. Some of the fierceness left his expression as he sent her a sad smile. 'This outlaw's life is not for women, my lady. It has addled your brain.' He shook his head and his temple-braids swung with the movement as Erica struggled to muster the tart response that was necessary. Hereward's lip curled. 'Treat with *Guthlac*? If your father had caught wind of such a suggestion, he would have had you in the stocks.'

'On the contrary, my father would have agreed with me. Thane Eric was a warrior, but he was also a practical man. Divided, we Saxons stand little chance of overcoming the Normans. And with our warband depleted and our best warriors deep in hiding…' She shook her head. 'Hereward, we *need* Thane Guthlac. He is the only Saxon with a half-decent force in this area, and if he accepts us as allies, then I can recall the warband and at the least our household will be reunited.' Erica transferred her gaze to the housecarl who, in better times, her father had thought to see her wed. 'Ailric, you said in your last report that you had located Thane Guthlac's camp, that he, too, has taken refuge in East Anglia.'

'Yes, my lady. Guthlac has kept his warband together and his encampment…' His voice trailed off.

'What of it? Where is it?'

Ailric shrugged and a brooch at his shoulder gleamed gold in the firelight. 'It is not so much an encampment, but a castle.'

A ripple of surprise went round some of the men. Erica, too, was startled. Whoever had heard of anyone building a castle in this watery world? But Ailric was nodding.

'A castle, my lady. Oh, to be sure it is a wooden one, it is not built in stone, but it is imposing none the less. Guthlac has had it thrown up on one of the larger islands; there is a palisade, and even a mound, and the main hall is built on that. From the distance you would think it a tower, a wooden tower.'

Erica's forehead puckered as she struggled to imagine it. 'In the Norman style?'

'Very like. It resembles the ones that William of

Normandy built in London and Winchester, before he brought in his Frankish stonemasons.'

'And Guthlac has used wood throughout?'

'Aye. It is…' Ailric's eyes lost focus as he recalled the details. 'It is as well built as any I have seen. The palisade looks impenetrable and there are walkways and sentry posts around the tower. It dominates the marshes for miles around.'

Hereward grunted. 'Guthlac always was a prideful fool, to draw attention to himself by such means. Soon every Norman in East Anglia will discover its location. Ailric tells me that by night the place blazes with more lights than King Harold's palace at Bosham ever did.' The housecarl gave Erica a straight look. 'You cannot mean that we should ally ourselves with such as he?'

'Indeed I do.' Erica stiffened her spine. 'Guthlac is our only hope.' She made herself smile at Ailric, and prayed that he would not sense the doubts in her. 'Ailric, you will accompany me, tomorrow at dawn. You will take me to Guthlac's…castle, where we will discuss the terms of an alliance.'

An appalled silence filled the cottage. It was broken only by the popping of willow logs on the fire and the wind combing the reeds outside. And then Hereward and Siward bounced to their feet, the young housecarl and the old, united in their horror at what she was proposing.

'Tomorrow? No, my lady!' This from Hereward.

'Lady, *no*, you *cannot* forget the feud!' This from Siward. His gnarled hand had gone straight to his sword hilt.

Rising to move round the fire, Erica put her hand on

Siward's and gently peeled it from his sword. 'The time has come for us to put it to rest.'

'But, my lady!' Hereward was practically spluttering into his beard with outrage. 'The feud is as old as I, older! It was old in my father's time.' Glaring at Erica, his eyes were hard and indignant. 'You cannot simply dance into Guthlac's lair and expect such a feud to be ended. I told you,' he muttered in Siward's direction, 'that to pass Thane Eric's authority on to his daughter was a mistake. The woman does not live who understands the sacred nature of a bloodfeud.'

'Sacred? *Enough!*' Erica made a chopping motion with her hand. Her jaw was as set as the jaw of the young man quivering in front of her, her determination was as grim. It had to be, for this, she was convinced, was the only way forwards. She drew herself up to her full height. 'Hereward, you forget yourself. I know full well the import of the bloodfeud—have I not grown up with it? Did I not lose my cousin to it? I will not waste breath discussing the futility of his death to a fellow Saxon on the very eve of the Norman invasion. I know how you men…' she looked into each and every silent face around the fire and poured scorn into her voice '…do value this…squabble. And squabble it is, however you might choose to glorify it. You say it is a matter of honour. *Honour?* I call it *pathetic*. One of Guthlac's men slighted one of ours, and in revenge one of our men slighted one of their women, on and on and on it goes. Why, this feud stretches back in time so far—'

'Theirs was the first slight,' Siward said confidently.

Erica looked coldly at him. 'Was it? You were there yourself, were you?'

'We…ell, no, my lady, not exactly, but I do remember Maccus telling me that Hrothgar's father—'

'Siward, be silent! This feud between Guthlac's family and mine has run for generations. Be honest, no man living can remember the original slight.'

Solveig, Erica's maid and companion, and the only other woman in their camp, stepped quietly out of the shadows. 'I was told that some years back it re-ignited when Waltheof despoiled Guthlac's mother.'

Erica drew her head back. *That* she had not heard, but it could not be true—surely someone would have said something to her, if such a dreadful thing had indeed happened. 'No, *no*.' There was no one here who might testify to the truth. A distant relation of Erica's, Waltheof had been killed at Hastings alongside her father.

Solveig's soft voice continued. 'Whatever the original cause of the feud, my lady, if such a thing did happen to Thane Guthlac's mother, Thane Guthlac would have little reason to love you.'

Ailric took Erica's hand. 'Solveig is in the right. Erica, if you walk into that…that den—I cannot allow it.'

The wind rattled the reeds outside. Erica looked down her nose at the man she might have married and slowly withdrew her fingers from his clasp. If she was to have her way in this, she must draw on her authority. And she *must* have her way on this, if they were to survive. '*You* cannot allow it? Ailric, who are you to command me?'

Again, Ailric reached for her hand, but she twitched it away, hiding in her skirts. 'Erica, think.' His voice cracked. 'Do not make me do this. It is not what your father would have wished.'

Turning her back on him, Erica stared into the heart of the fire where the bright flames flickered like pennons. Her skin was icy—why could she not feel the heat? 'Ailric, you forget yourself,' she murmured, for his ears alone. 'I am not your betrothed for you to command me in this manner, I am not your chattel.' Putting strength in her voice, she lifted her head to address the entire company. 'My mind is fixed. Tomorrow at first light, we go to treat with Thane Guthlac.

'Remember, Guthlac Stigandson is himself a survivor. Like us he is Saxon. Even Thane Guthlac cannot but see the sense in our two parties uniting. Together we will overcome these invaders, our Norman enemies. I declare that the feud between my family and Thane Guthlac's,' she said, ensuring she caught Siward's eye, 'is *ended*. And I will personally geld the man who resurrects it.'

Chapter Three

Thane Guthlac's hall door slammed and the ashes on the clay hearth shifted in the sudden draught. Wulf shivered. A faint light was showing through the crack at the bottom of the door. Dawn. And, since his report for De Warenne's man was ready, it was the last he would see in this hall. Come noon, he would be gone from here, thank God.

Wulf's pallet, as one of Guthlac Stigandson's rawest recruits, had been unforgiving, and his every limb creaked. He might as well have slept on the bare boards. Suppressing a groan, he flung back the cloak he had been using as a blanket and sat up. He had barely slept, partly owing to his position at the draughty end of the hall, and partly because being a spy made for an uneasy night. He glanced regretfully at the dead fire. He would have preferred warmth while he had tossed and turned all night and dreamed…ah…impossible dreams…

Dreams that warded off memories of his half-sister, Marie. Dreams that gave him a position in society, when slights to his family would no longer go unpunished.

Dreams of being knighted and of owning a plot of land for which he could do knight service to his lord openly and above-board, instead of having to meet men and smile and talk with them and know that, one day soon, he might have to betray them. He had even dreamed of a lady who stood tall and proud at his side…hah! There was no room for a woman in his life. What fools we are in the middle of the night, Wulf thought, what dreams we dream to block out reality.

While he eased his broad shoulders, working the stiffness from his muscles, it occurred to Wulf that it mattered not whether one sided with Normans or Saxons—in both camps raw recruits invariably got a rough deal. That mattress—Lord.

He groped for his boots. It was a bitter morning; even inside the hall amid so many sleeping men, his breath made smoke. Grimacing, Wulf tossed his hair out of his face; it was not getting any shorter, but neither was it long enough to tie back—in fact, it was a damned nuisance. He wished he could shave, too, but that would have to wait until later. De Warenne had been in the right, his lack of beard had been a point of concern when he had first arrived at the castle. A visit to the barber would definitely *not* have helped. Wulf had been accepted as a rebel purely on account of his childhood links with Southwark. It was his good fortune that Guthlac Stigandson himself remembered him from those days.

Taking up his sword and belt, Wulf moved lightly to the door so as not to disturb anyone fortunate enough to have bagged a softer pallet. The oak door was heavy. Pushing through, he went out onto the platform. The torches on either side of the entrance were guttering, sending up an evil black smoke that the wind whisked away.

Here, where the platform girdled the tower, there was a commanding view of the fens. In full daylight one could see a broad expanse of water—water that at this point was large and wide enough to be known as 'the lake'. The lake was surrounded by low-lying land on all sides, but in this dull pre-dawn light visibility was poor, the colour leached out of everything.

Wulf remembered his first sight of Guthlac's castle as it reared out of the mist. Its sheer size meant that he was bound to stumble across it sooner or later, for the wooden tower and its motte dwarfed the local alder and ash trees. Guthlac might well have fled to the fens from the south, but not even his worst enemy could accuse him of skulking.

A water-butt stood on the walkway immediately outside the main door. As the door latch clicked shut behind him, Wulf found he had not quite shaken off the melancholy that had gripped him from the moment Marie had entered his thoughts. Two years his senior, his half-sister would have been twenty-four had she lived. And her child—Wulf's heart squeezed—her child would have been nine.

Wulf thrust aside the image of Marie; he must not think of her. Lifting the lid of the water-butt, he splashed his face, hissing through his teeth as the icy water hit him. He washed quickly and dried his face on his sleeve. The wind scoured his cheeks. Thank God he was leaving today.

The marshes were still shrouded in gloom, but by the bank beyond the palisade he could make out a thin skin of ice at the base of the reeds. Guthlac's island was fringed with many such reeds. Wulf had made a point of memorising the lie of the land for miles around; it would be of great interest to De Warenne. Farther out, the water was black, shiny and apparently fathomless.

And there, over in the east, a glow—the glow that heralded dawn. Uneasy for no reason he could put a finger on, unless remembering what had happened to Marie had left him out of sorts, Wulf ran a hand round the back of his neck. No, that glow could not be the dawn; that was not the east. That glow…he frowned…it was in the *west*.

Attention sharpening, Wulf reached for his swordbelt, buckled it on, and was off down the walkway, boots ringing loud on the boards. Had the sentries seen? Until he left here, he must be careful to act his part; he must behave precisely as Guthlac and his rebels would expect him to behave.

With a start, the man on watch dozing over his bow snapped upright. '*Sir!*' Beorn, if Wulf remembered his name aright. He had long flaxen hair and he eyed Wulf uncertainly, doubtless wondering if he was to be reprimanded for sleeping at his post.

Wulf pointed out across the fen. 'Is that what I think it is?'

Beorn stared, frowned, and went pale. 'God in Heaven, a boat!'

Wulf's brow furrowed, too. As the darkness lifted, the boat slid closer. A yellow light shone in the prow, the light that moments ago Wulf had mistaken for the rising sun. He shook his head, glancing askance at the sky, a sky that had been determinedly leaden ever since he had arrived in East Anglia. As if the sun would actually shine in this place. This was the fens, a low, flat land where everything was grey and wet and cold and—an icy gust bit into his neck—no doubt snow would soon add to their joys. God grant that once he had delivered his report, De Warenne, who might yet be in Westminster, would have him despatched to London or Lewes, to anywhere but here.

Beorn bit his lip. 'I…I am sorry, sir. I…I will raise the alarm.'

'Do that—I shall stand in for you here.'

'My thanks.' Beorn clattered down the walkway, clearly happy to escape a reprimand. Wulf's nostrils flared. The man had to be thinking that Thane Guthlac's new housecarl was a walkover, but he didn't give a damn what he thought. Wulf was not going to be among these rebels long enough for discipline to become a problem. Come sunset, he would be gone.

The door slammed.

While Wulf waited for the uproar that he would bet his sword was about to ensue, he watched the oars of the approaching boat lift and fall, lift and fall. His eyes narrowed. It was a small craft and it contained two…no, three, people. One of them looked to be female; she wore a russet cloak. Curious, wondering if he had seen this woman elsewhere on the waterways, Wulf strained to make out the colour of her hair. But the woman had her hood up and her hair was hidden. She sat perfectly still, hugging her cloak against the January chill. No great threat there, surely? They might be pedlars working the waterways, though Wulf could not see anything that resembled stock in the bottom of their boat: no barrels, no crates, no bundles of merchandise wrapped in sailcloth.

As the boat glided ever closer, an unnatural quiet held the fen. There was no honking of geese, no men shouting, there was not even the sound of the oars creaking in the rowlocks.

Abruptly, the hall door bounced back on its hinges and Guthlac Stigandson erupted onto the platform. 'Maldred! *Maldred!*' The outlaw wrenched his belly into his swordbelt. 'My helm, boy, and look sharp!' Guthlac's hair was straggling free of its ties, hanging in grey rats' tails, his beard was uncombed and he was so exercised by this intrusion into his territory that his mottled cheeks were turning purple.

Maldred ran up. Guthlac snatched his helm and slapped it on his head. He stomped up to Wulf at the sentry post, golden arm-rings rattling. 'Saewulf? Report, man.'

Wulf waved in the direction of the small craft. 'It is as Beorn has no doubt told you. One boat only, my lord, three passengers, I doubt they present much of a threat.'

Hrothgar, Guthlac's right-hand man, was peering over Guthlac's broad shoulders. Other housecarls crowded behind.

Guthlac elbowed Hrothgar in the ribs. 'Let me breathe, man.'

'My lord.' Hrothgar stepped back, waving to clear a space. His bracelets gleamed in the morning light, valuable gold bracelets that showed he was his lord's most favoured housecarl.

Guthlac's battle-scarred hands grasped the handrail as he scowled down at the water beyond the palisade.

'They must be Saxon,' he muttered. 'No Norman would dare to venture this far into the fens.'

Wulf's stomach tightened, but he kept his expression neutral.

'A woman, eh?' Guthlac's eyebrows rose.

At that moment the breeze strengthened and something fluttered in the stern of the boat. A pennon. Guthlac stiffened. 'That flag, Saewulf…' he frowned, peering in such a way that Wulf realised the outlaw's eyes were not as keen as his '…can you make out the colours, does it bear a device?'

'No device, my lord. There's a blue band above a white ground with green below.'

Guthlac's fingers tightened on the handrail. 'A white ground, you are certain? Is the green straight edged?'

Wulf narrowed his eyes and the pennon lifted in the breeze. The green band met the white ground with a jagged edge. 'No, my lord, it is dancetty.'

Eyes suddenly intense, delight spreading across his face, Guthlac struck the rail with his fist. 'At last, I have her! At least I hope to God I have her… Tell me, is the woman fair or dark?'

Both the question and the febrile excitement struck a jarring note. The little boat was close to the jetty, so close that it was drifting out of their line of sight behind the palisade. 'I couldn't swear, my lord, she has her hood up.'

A grin that was as much grimace as it was grin was spreading across Guthlac's face. Wulf felt a distinct prickle of unease.

'It *is* her. She has come crawling at last! I knew this moment would come when Hrothgar told me one of her men had been sighted in Ely.'

Wulf stared at Guthlac, and wondered why his dead half-sister Marie had chosen this day of all days to walk in and out of his mind. He also wondered why cold sweat was trickling down his back. 'Her?' His sense of unease was growing by the second. The sooner he was out of here, the better.

'Eric's daughter—it must be Lady Erica of Whitecliffe!'

Whirling round, Guthlac elbowed through his house-carls and stormed down the stairway to the bailey, tossing orders as he went. 'Beorn!'

'My lord?'

'Have them lift the portcullis when they have disembarked.'

'They are to enter, sir?' Beorn's voice was more than startled, it was stunned.

'Certainly.' Thane Guthlac's harsh voice floated back to Wulf, still motionless by the sentry post. 'The woman at least.' There was a brief pause as Guthlac leaped the last few steps into the bailey. 'And her men, too, provided they disarm.'

'Yes, my lord.'

Moments later, Wulf stood alone at the watchpoint, frowning. Lady Erica of Whitecliffe? Who the devil was Lady Erica of Whitecliffe?

And then it came to him. Of course! The bloodfeud, the damn bloodfeud.

Wulf had only been in Guthlac's warband for a few days, but already he had heard enough about the bloodfeud to last him a lifetime. For years, Guthlac Stigandson's men had been hurling insults, and worse, far worse, at the men loyal to another Saxon thane. Both thanes had apparently held land attached to his own lord's recently acquired holding in the south, near Lewes. The feud had run for generations.

A cold hand clutched Wulf's gut as he recalled that the last insult had been apparently to Guthlac's own mother. Some of the men who had talked about the bloodfeud had used the word seduction, others had muttered darkly about rape.

And, Lord, there was Marie's face again, swimming into focus in front of him, pale as the ghost it was. Her eyes were glassy with tears.

'Hell,' Wulf muttered, and before he knew it he was striding down the walkway, gesturing for another man to take his place at the watchpoint.

In the bailey, the chapel stood to one side of the port-cullis. It was an unpretentious wooden building with a thatched roof and topped with a reed cross. A reception committee was gathering by the door: Thane Guthlac, Hrothgar, Beorn, Maldred, Swein….

That woman, Wulf thought, recalling the slender figure sitting proud and still in the prow, that poor woman. He shook his head, hoping to hell that Lady Erica of Whitecliffe had something damn good up her sleeve. The way that Thane Guthlac's face had twisted every time her name had been mentioned…

More cold sweat broke out on his back. He must remain cool. This woman was a total stranger—what was it to him if she got hurt? And if she was indeed Erica of Whitecliffe, then she should know better than to march into her enemy's stronghold like this, she deserved to get hurt. Wulf could not get involved, par-ticularly since he was on the brink of leaving…

Saints, there was Marie's face again. Shoving his hand through his hair, Wulf tried to eject his half-sister from his thoughts. He succeeded, but not before it came to him, that if someone had helped Marie when she had needed it, she would still be alive.

'Hell.' How in God's name was he supposed to aid the woman when he was here under false colours himself? He had his commission to think of, he must not disappoint De Warenne.

'Problem, Saewulf?' Hrothgar asked, pale eyes watchful.

'Not at all.' Wulf forced a smile and reminded himself of the land that he longed for, of the knighthood that he hoped to win. He must not fail now. Tonight he would be away from here—God willing, he would be on the London road.

Maldred and Swein were applying themselves to the windlass. The portcullis creaked, and Lady Erica of Whitecliffe appeared under the arch. Her two companions stationed themselves either side of her. Gowned in purple beneath her russet cloak, she was tall and dignified, composedly nodding her agreement while her companions were divested of their arms. Men in their late twenties, housecarls by the look of them, Saxon warriors who handed their swords over to Maldred without a murmur. But they did not like it; their eyes and their stance betrayed them.

Guthlac Stigandson swept the woman a mocking bow. 'Greetings, Lady Erica.'

She dipped her head in acknowledgement. 'Thane Guthlac?' Her voice was low and even.

'At your service,' murmured Guthlac.

Wulf took stock of her. Yes, she was tall, and she had a stately air, and when she flung back the russet hood of her cloak, he bit back a gasp. Close to, with her dark hair gleaming in the growing daylight and with her startling green eyes, Erica of Whitecliffe was beautiful—breathtakingly, radiantly beautiful.

Lady Erica glanced swiftly round the compound, tipping her head back to take in the tower perched on its mound. Her quick eyes ran over the sentry points, the palisade, the outbuildings, and, finally, lingered on the chapel.

While she nodded briefly, unsmiling but polite, at each man in the compound, Wulf was disconcertingly aware that his heartbeat was less than steady. She was his very image of beauty. Not that that signified anything. Although when her eyes met his—they were a particular shade of green, which brought to mind the woods near Honfleur on a sunny spring day—Wulf felt a distinct jolt in his belly. She nodded at him and her gaze moved on, to Hrothgar, Beorn, Maldred. He could see by the sudden stillness that gripped Guthlac and his housecarls that they, too, had been struck by her beauty. And who would not be?

The Lady Erica had pale skin, which was clear and unblemished; her brows and eyelashes were dark; she had a straight nose with a scattering of freckles across it; her lips were red and full and tempting and there was not a wrinkle anywhere, not even around those remarkable eyes. Wulf caught the gleam of gold—her cloak fastening was patterned with interlocking snakes. Two thick dark plaits trailed down to her waist, their ends caught in finely wrought golden fillets.

Thane Eric's daughter must be about his age, perhaps a little older. If pushed, Wulf would say she had been born at about the same time as his half-sister. Those glossy plaits were black as a crow's wing. Her carriage was proud and straight, and though that cloak hid her bosom, it could not entirely disguise the full curve of her breasts. Briefly Wulf shut his eyes. Thane Eric's daughter was beautiful enough to steal any man's breath. He remembered what had happened to Thane Guthlac's mother, and he feared, he very much feared, that this woman's beauty was about to be her downfall. *Merde.* It was not his business. Particularly since De Warenne was awaiting his report.

The rebel leader was giving her another of his mocking bows. 'You will take refreshment, my lady?'

Regal as a queen, she inclined her head. 'My thanks.'

Wulf had scarcely set eyes on the woman, yet even as she picked up her purple skirts and made to precede Guthlac into his hall, he knew, without shadow of a doubt, that she understood that Guthlac Stigandson's courtesy was false. Oh, yes, she knew. Those bright eyes ran swiftly, searchingly, over Guthlac's features, those white teeth worried her lower lip for an instant, then she straightened, turned her gaze ahead and calmly continued towards the wooden stairway that led up the mound and into the tower.

'Saewulf?'

Wulf started. 'My lord?'

'See to it her men rest here.'

'My lord, I...' Wulf thought quickly. He did not want to be stationed down here by the chapel, not if she was going to face Guthlac on her own—the force of his feelings, akin to desperation, confounded him.

Luckily Thane Eric's daughter had other ideas. Pausing at a landing halfway up the mound stairway, she rested a slender white hand on the handrail. Bracelets to rival Guthlac's chinked at her wrist, emphasising her high status. Finger-rings glinted. 'My men, too,' she said, voice clear as a bell and every inch her father's daughter. 'Ailric and Hereward are more in need of refreshment than I; it was they who sat at the oars.'

Wulf glanced questioningly at Guthlac. 'My lord?'

Impatiently, Guthlac waved them on. 'Let them come, Saewulf, they are unarmed.'

Pleasantly surprised at Guthlac's malleability in the face of his enemy's request, Wulf motioned for the two housecarls to follow their lady.

Chapter Four

The rebels were eating their evening meal, and Wulf was—much against his better judgement for he should be at the rendezvous with Lucien—still in Guthlac's hall. He peered through the stinking haze of tallow candles towards the head of the trestle and wished he had been party to the negotiations between Thane Guthlac and the Lady Erica. They had talked from dawn to dusk and it was impossible to tell from their manner how they were progressing. Wulf could hear nothing of note over the clatter of knives and the guffaws and the general babble of conversation. He had to get closer...

Meals in this fenland castle were taken very differently to meals in King William's barrack-hall at Westminster. Here, no weapon stacks bristled with arms by the walls; instead, men wore their arms to table. They sat with their swords jutting out behind them, an ever-present hazard for servers approaching the benches with dishes and ale jugs. The continual bearing of arms by every able-bodied man in the camp reminded Wulf, if reminder were needed, that he was breaking bread with outlaws. To a man they were poised to jump to arms at a moment's notice. If they suspected that he served another master, a *Norman* master, a dozen swords would be at his throat.

'More ale, Saewulf?'

The lad Maldred was at his elbow, jug in hand. Smiling, Wulf nodded and held out his cup, but his attention never wavered from the top of the table. A sense of unease had sat with him since the morning—and it irked him, because he knew it was not connected with the Saxon outlaws and his commission for De Warenne. Rather, it was centred on Lady Erica.

Wulf should have met De Warenne's man this afternoon. With every moment he lingered here, the risk of discovery grew. But he could not leave, not yet, because the lady… *Merde!* Thank God he had thought to arrange a second, fall-back meeting a few days hence. That one he would not miss.

Lady Erica was hemmed in on the one hand by the rebel Guthlac and on the other by Hrothgar. Guthlac's wife Lady Hilda sat close by, but Wulf had yet to see the two women exchange words with each other. Like the other men, Guthlac and Hrothgar were wearing their arms; indeed, Hrothgar sat so close to Lady Erica that Wulf wouldn't be surprised to learn that the scabbard of his dagger was digging into her side.

The only men *not* wearing arms were the lady's housecarls. They were glowering from a side-table, under guard but uncowed. Their eyes barely left their mistress for a moment, as if by watching her they could protect her. Wulf followed their gaze, even though looking at her made him uneasy. So startling was Lady

Erica's beauty that he found her hard to look on, and he did not wish her to think that he was ogling. Not that any of the outlaws seemed to hold with such scruples; both Hrothgar and Beorn had been openly drooling ever since she had stepped into the bailey.

Her gown was an unusual shade of violet, with silver embroidery at the neck and hem. The silken side lacings were designed to emphasise a figure that was as fine as her features. Lady Erica had a high bosom, a narrow waist, and gently curving hips. That gown, Wulf thought, with that hint of purple, could have been the gown of an empress. Her white silk veil must have been imported from some exotic land in the east, Byzantium most likely. Wulf frowned as he looked at the gold bracelets winking on those slender wrists, at her finger-rings. Purple was worn by royalty; the bracelets and rings were worth a fortune—following Saxon custom, she was wearing her status the same way a man wore armour when he went into battle. In her finery, she looked like a queen.

Just then, the man next to Hrothgar rose and headed for the door that led to the privies. A moment later Wulf had taken his place, nodding to Hrothgar as he eased onto the bench. Better, he thought, *much* better; at last he might hear something of interest.

The bloodfeud was none of his business, yet Wulf feared for the lady's well-being. She and Guthlac had been dancing round each other since she had arrived, so why had no conclusion been reached? Guthlac Stigandson did not strike Wulf as a patient man, quite the opposite, in fact. Why, the day before yesterday, Guthlac had had a body-servant beaten to within an inch of his life for laying out the wrong tunic; a serving wench had seen the flat of his hand for accidentally spilling some wine in Lady Hilda's lap. What was the key point in these drawn-out negotiations?

The rebel leader hated Lady Erica. Wulf could see it in his eyes; he could see it in the over-polite way Guthlac handed her a piece of fish on the end of his knife, apeing the fine manners of a courtier in King William's palace at Westminster, when all the while his face was set like stone.

So, Wulf thought, swallowing down some ale, why the delay? Why spend hours dancing around the lady and her demands? She wanted her men—outlaws like these, Wulf reminded himself—to enter into an alliance with Thane Guthlac. It made sense in military terms, but Wulf did not think that Guthlac had the first intention of forging an alliance with Erica of Whitecliffe. Guthlac's eyes glittered with loathing; they were hard as glass in the flare of the torches. He was toying with her and she knew it.

The fish was settling uncomfortably in Wulf's stomach. Guthlac's eyes were warning him that the feud between his housecarls and Lady Erica's was far from dead; the man was biding his time.

And Hrothgar? Eyeing the lady's bosom. Lord, the entire warband was eyeing her body.

Erica of Whitecliffe leaned forwards and murmured at Guthlac's wife. Lady Hilda gave a weak smile of ac-knowledgement, but a sharp look from her husband had her ducking her head to pick at the fish on her trencher.

Wulf's sense of frustration grew. Thane Guthlac sat like a king at the head of his hall, downing measure after

measure of ale, offering the lady yet another portion of
fish, of eel. And all the while, Wulf's indigestion got
worse. What the hell was Guthlac waiting for?

Tired of waiting for Guthlac to end the game, tired
of wishing his stomach was not in knots and of wishing
that William de Warenne had sent him anywhere but to
this bleak corner of England, Wulf was glowering into
a candle flame when a scraping of stools and benches
told him the meal was over.

His stomach cramped. Lady Erica's face was white
as snow and she was staring at Guthlac as though he had
sprouted horns. Into the sudden hush, her voice came
clear. 'You cannot mean it.'

Guthlac's smile was empty. 'I assure you, I do.'

'No, my lord, this feuding must *end*!'

Guthlac thrust his face into hers. 'Easy for you to say,
my dear, since you have been foolish enough to put
yourself in this position. But would you have spoken up,
I wonder, before my mother was…disparaged?'

Never had Wulf sat through a silence so profound in
a hall full of men who had just eaten and drunk their fill.
He was not sure he understood what Guthlac was
talking about but, dimly recalling the mutterings of rape,
he had his suspicions. No one so much as breathed.

One of the lady's men lurched towards her, desperation in his eyes as his hand went to the hilt of his
sword—the sword that was not there because he had
been disarmed.

The lady held him back with a calm, 'Ailric, *no*.'

'But, my lady,' her housecarl protested as, at
Guthlac's nod, two men leaped to restrain him, 'he
means you harm!'

'Ailric, be still.'

'Ailric?' Guthlac Stigandson looked with calculating curiosity at the lady. 'This man means something to you?'

Ailric strained against his captors. 'I should hope that I do, Thane Eric said I was to marry Lady Erica before…before…'

'Before the Norman bastard came and killed him?'

'Aye!'

A slender, beringed hand came to rest on the outlaw's sleeve. 'Thane Guthlac, the feud *must* end.'

Guthlac ground his teeth, and got heavily to his feet. 'No, my lady, not yet. The bloodfeud is a matter of *honour*. Its continuance is as vital to me as the duty a thane owes to his liege lord. Know this: your father was my sworn enemy in the matter of the feud between our families. But he and I fought shoulder to shoulder for Harold at Hastings. And though Thane Eric was my enemy, I honour him. He died an honourable death, fighting for his king.'

'Then surely, my lord—' Lady Erica's steady voice carried clearly to every corner of the hall, a hall that to Wulf's mind was filled with an increasingly ugly air of expectancy '—you could find it in your heart to end this bloodfeud? You honour my father as a warrior, and I know he honoured you in the same way, but—'

'Silence!' Guthlac's fists clenched. He turned to face his wife. 'And you, woman…'

Lady Hilda's lips tightened, but she answered meekly, 'My lord?'

Guthlac jerked his head in the direction of the door. 'Out! I will see you later, when this business is concluded. Wait for me in our chamber.'

'Yes, my lord.'

The atmosphere was thick with tension, and was almost suffocating. Wulf's skin crawled. Whatever Guthlac had planned for this Saxon lady, he doubted she was ready for it. At the edge of his vision, Hrothgar wound his fingers round his swordhilt, bracelets flashing in the candlelight.

Lady Hilda pushed back her stool, dropped a quick curtsy at her lord, and sent Erica of Whitecliffe a pitying look. Waving for her ladies, she scurried with them from the hall.

Guthlac stared coldly at Erica of Whitecliffe, now the only woman present. Gripping her by the arm, he hauled her to her feet. His words were slightly slurred from all the ale. 'So, daughter of Eric, *you* are to make reparation for the slight your family did to mine.'

Lady Erica stood, slim and straight as a wand next to Guthlac's solid bulk. She tossed her white veil out of the way, a veil of so fine a weave that her dark braids were visible beneath the fluttering silk. Her cheeks were pale, her expression composed, but the hem of that veil was trembling. Her composure was a mask; she knew what was likely to happen to her. The bile rose in Wulf's throat.

'I will do it,' Hrothgar said, getting up to seize the lady's other arm. His mouth twisted. 'Seeing as you are a married man, my lord.'

One man made a lewd remark. Another spluttered into his ale.

'My lord!' Wulf scrambled to his feet. He was not certain, but he feared that the Lady Erica was about to face the same fate as his sister. With his commission, the last thing he needed to do was to draw attention to himself, but he could not stand by and let this happen. 'You cannot sanction this…it…it would be rape!'

Great green eyes fixed on him, wide and startled—Wulf felt their impact in his core. Then Lady Erica seemed to draw calmness about her person like a cloak and her features went blank. It was as though she had somehow absented herself from the hall.

'Rape?' Guthlac Stigandson was shaking his head and several around the board murmured their agreement. 'Not rape, but reparation, Brader, *reparation*. Since you have not been long of our number and are unfamiliar with this feud, I will explain. If one of my men disparages Thane Eric's daughter, then our honour will be satisfied. In view of what was done to my beloved mother, such an act is not rape, it is merely reparation.'

Wulf edged his sword free of its sheath. Hrothgar was watching him like a hawk. 'No, my lord.' For his part, Wulf did not take his eyes from Guthlac. Wulf did not want a fight, not here, not over this woman, but in memory of his poor sister, he could not see her hurt. 'Call it what you like, but if a woman is bedded against her will, it is rape.'

Lady Erica's bosom heaved. 'I think, sir, I would be willing—' her tone was distant, her sang-froid astonishing '—if I knew *for certain* it would finally put an end to the bloodfeud. That is why I am here, to end the bloodfeud.'

Appalled, Wulf stared. She was obviously personally innocent of any wrongdoing and yet she could *accept* such barbarism? The man she had called Ailric could not; on the other side of the trestle, the veins were bulging in his temples as he struggled vainly to wrench free of his guards. The lady looked directly at Wulf, but her green eyes had lost their luster; they were dull as they had not been when she had first walked, head high, through that portcullis. The Lady Erica's body might be here in this hall, but her mind and her soul had fled. It came to Wulf that already, though hardly a finger had been laid upon her, this woman was being scarred by what was happening.

But surprised?

Wulf gritted his teeth. No, the lady had definitely not been ignorant of the revenge that the Saxon leader might demand, she had *known*. Oh, she could not have been certain of the revenge Guthlac would exact on her, but she had recognised that her ravishment was a distinct possibility.

She had hoped, perhaps, that Guthlac Stigandson would relent, but she had known the possibilities and—with stunning bravery—she had walked into this stronghold fully prepared to offer herself up so that the bloodfeud might end. She was desperate, so trapped she was prepared to be the sacrificial lamb.

Stepping carefully round her, Wulf looked directly at Guthlac. The man's gaze was as cold as fenwater. 'My lord, I realise I am but a newcomer here, but I am bound to say that, however you dress it, this is not an honourable act.'

Hrothgar's lips curled. 'Woman.'

Wulf was not about to be distracted by such a crude attempt to draw his fire. 'My lord?'

Guthlac sighed. Now that his wife and her ladies had left the hall, some of the tension seemed to have left him. Perhaps all was not lost. Was it possible that the

man possessed a shred of decency? Had he been
ashamed to sanction such an act before his wife?
Guthlac wanted his revenge, to be sure, but perhaps on
one level he did not have the stomach for it. He had
openly admitted to a grudging respect for the lady's
father…and yet, as leader, he could not back down
without impugning his honour.

The leader of a warband would not want to lose face
before his men. And Wulf recalled that it had been
Guthlac's *mother* who had apparently been—what was
the term they had used?—disparaged. Had she really
been raped? Dear God, did two wrongs make a right?

'Saewulf Brader…' Guthlac released Lady Erica to
Hrothgar and reached for his ale '…as you have not
been long of our number, I shall once again overlook
your questioning me. But let me assure you, the feud
between Thane Eric's family and mine is an honourable
one. Why, even a man born by the docks in Southwark
as you were, must have heard of such bloodfeuds.'

Wulf nodded. 'Indeed, my lord, but surely the honour
that is satisfied in harming an innocent young woman
is a pretty poor sort of honour.' The image of his sister,
pale as she lay on her bier, took form in his mind's eye.
No bloodfeud had caused his sister's death, that had
been an individual act of violence, one person on
another, but in Wulf's mind rape was rape. This
woman's tribe might sanction her sacrifice, but he could
not. Lady Erica would not suffer hurt tonight, not if he
could help it.

Eyes narrowing, Thane Guthlac raised his ale cup.
He drank deep, set the cup down with deliberate
slowness and wiped his mouth with the back of his

hand. 'Aye, *boy*,' he said, managing with one word to emphasise his seniority in both rank and age, 'so you might think. But what say you to the honour that saw one of her father's housecarls abduct my mother and take her against her will?'

Wulf's heart thudded as he realised the enormity of what he was up against. 'One of Thane Eric's men did violate your mother—it is true, then?'

'Just so.' Guthlac's lips thinned and his voice became soft, but no less dangerous. 'Her blood cries out for vengeance, so stand back, Saewulf Brader, let honour be satisfied.'

Somehow Lady Erica was keeping her composure. Tall and stately, she stood with lowered eyes and with only that almost imperceptible quivering of her veil to show the agitation that she must be feeling. Wulf ought to step back, De Warenne would wish it—his commission was of the first importance. But Wulf could not do it. The memory of his dead half-sister had kept him in this place when he should have gone hours ago, and now it drove him on. 'My lord—'

'*He* wants her.' Hrothgar's mouth became ugly. 'That is what this is about—Saewulf fancies the girl himself. What's the matter, Brader, wouldn't Maude oblige last night? Never mind, *boy*,' he sneered. 'Since we are, as my lord has explained, honourable men, I will fight you for her.'

Wulf's mouth went dry. He thought quickly. He did not want to fight Hrothgar, but if he did fight and if he won, he might be able to keep the lady safe. He swallowed; he might be one of the rawest of the housecarls in this place, but he had trained shoulder to shoulder with De Warenne's knights, and his swordplay was strong. Hrothgar had no idea what he was up against. When Wulf had 'enlisted' with the rebels, he had naturally been tested in combat, but he had held back, misliking that these men should know his true measure.

Lady Erica waited, apparently meekly between Wulf and Hrothgar, while Hrothgar held fast to her arm. *Remember why you are here*—Wulf felt the anger rise within him—*remember your commission. You should not be drawing attention to yourself.* But Wulf could not tear his eyes from the large hand crushing the purple cloth of the lady's sleeve and he knew that, whatever the cost, he could not see Erica of Whitecliffe ravished as Marie had been. Clenching his fists, he struggled for control. A hot head would not help him here; he must use his anger, not be used by it.

The lady's head came up and those green eyes fastened on him. There was a slight crease between her brows. Tall Erica of Whitecliffe might be, her height equalled Hrothgar's, but she only reached Wulf's shoulder.

Wulf smiled. She did not return his smile, but her eyes ran over him, assessing him as she would a thoroughbred. Wulf felt oddly naked and hoped he was not flushing. Resigning himself to a hard, bloody fight, he was opening his mouth to accept Hrothgar's challenge, but the lady forestalled him.

'My lord?' Erica darted a swift look under her lashes at the tall young warrior who was apparently prepared to risk life and limb to save her from the attentions of Thane Guthlac's right-hand man. Thane Guthlac had referred to him as Saewulf Brader. He was, as Hrothgar had pointed out, some years Hrothgar's junior. Why,

Saewulf Brader might even be younger than herself. His hair was thick and dark and a deal shorter than most of the men's, and while he was not exactly clean-shaven, he wore no beard. Perhaps it was the lack of beard that gave him his youthful appearance. Erica was twenty-four years old, and, if put to it, she would judge Saewulf Brader to be a couple of years younger than her.

Her mind raced. His youthfulness would not necessarily be a disadvantage in combat; he was big and solidly built, with strong muscles that showed clearly beneath that worn brown tunic. His hands were oddly at variance with his calling; they were beautifully shaped for a warrior, long fingered and fine-boned but—Erica frowned—no arm-rings jingled at his wrist. Had he won no prizes for his skill at arms? How odd, when a warrior was so strong he usually had any number of arm-rings…

For a moment their eyes met and her heart stuttered. His eyes were blue, bright and clear as the sky above the South Downs at harvest time, and framed by thick dark lashes. Saewulf Brader, Erica thought somewhat breathlessly, was physical perfection. No, not quite perfection; there were shadows under his eyes that hinted of fatigue, there were lines of tension, too…but, that aside, he was physically perfect—the man looked every inch a lady's champion.

If she could but trust him.

Saewulf was apparently a newcomer to Thane Guthlac's band and he did not hold with the bloodfeud, but did that mean Erica could rely on him? The lack of arm-rings was a worry, too…maybe he was not as adept as he looked.

'Lady Erica, you had something you wished to say?'

Guthlac's tone warned her that he was startled at her interference, but Erica took heart from his continuing use of her title. For even if Thane Guthlac was planning to force her to lie with one of his men as his price for ending the bloodfeud, he was still paying lip-service to the courtesies. Provided she showed herself to be amenable, he would not beat her or force her in that way. A wave of nausea threatened to overwhelm her.

Provided she was amenable.

Another stolen glance at Saewulf Brader, a briefer one at Hrothgar, whose fingers were gouging holes in her arm and who had roused an immediate and instinctive loathing in her, and Erica had made up her mind. 'Might I choose, my lord?'

Thane Guthlac's brows climbed, and on the benches someone groaned, 'No, my lord, a fight, give us a fight!' Other men, loathe to lose what was speedily becoming the best night's entertainment in years, joined in the chorus. 'A fight! Give us a fight!'

Wrenching herself free of Hrothgar, Erica clasped her hands at her breast. 'Please, my lord, let me choose. What sense in permitting two of your finest to wound themselves? We shall need *every* man in the coming conflict, when we fight as one.' Beside her, the warrior Saewulf shifted, but he said nothing. The warmth of his body was oddly comforting.

Hrothgar snorted. 'My skin is not at risk, my lord. This *boy* is all ambition and no staying power.'

Thane Guthlac exchanged grins with his champion. Ice trickled down Erica's spine—she was certain her request was about to be denied. 'My lord,' she rushed into speech, 'I do not relish the thought of Saxon blood being spilled on my account. If I agree to your terms, why make them fight? The bloodfeud will have ended, your honour will be satisfied, and your men and mine will have new allies against the Normans.'

'Who would you choose?' Thane Guthlac scratched his neck, his tone so casual, so idle, it was nothing less than an insult.

Swallowing down a rush of rage, Erica reached blindly for the brown homespun of Saewulf Brader's tunic. 'This one,' she murmured, praying her instincts were not letting her down. As her fingers curled into the fabric, they closed on hard muscle beneath. 'I would choose this one.'

Chapter Five

'He is not nobly born, my lady,' Hrothgar hissed in her ear.

Erica shrugged. 'I care not. If I am allowed a choice, I choose this man.'

'Oh, but it is worse than that, my lady.' Hrothgar's lips curled and he shot the young man standing stiffly at Erica's side a disdainful look. 'Brader is a bastard.'

Saewulf Brader's jaw tightened, but he did not refute Hrothgar's accusation.

It certainly was shocking, in a day when to produce a child out of wedlock was deemed one of the greatest sins a woman could commit. Erica's breath caught as it struck her that, after tonight, that might be her fate. She sent another prayer winging heavenward that, whatever happened tonight, she must *not* conceive. And another, that Thane Guthlac would give her to the younger housecarl. Saewulf Brader's birth was nothing set against her desire, her very *strong* desire, that she should *not* be given to Hrothgar.

Dimly, Erica was aware of more muttering down the table, more calls of, 'Let them fight! A fight!'

She kept her gaze pinned on Guthlac Stigandson. 'Please, my lord, for the respect you felt for my father, I ask you in acknowledgement of the respect he had for you. Let me choose.'

Her thoughts moved swiftly. *And now*, she told herself, *no more words, lest you begin to beg*. For she misliked the look of Thane Guthlac's right-hand man. Neither in his words nor his manner did Hrothgar appear to be someone who would consider a woman's feelings. But this other whose tunic she could not seem to release...this younger man who, though low in the pecking order, had spoken up for her. It was little enough to judge a man by, but what else had she to go on? The ridiculous realisation that, even in this hall, on this most hideous of nights, she found Saewulf Brader attractive? Those thickly lashed blue eyes seemed to be the only eyes in the hall to see her, to really see her; his wide shoulders suggested that here was a man strong enough to share her burdens; the fine-boned fingers clenching and unclenching on his swordhilt hinted at a sensitivity she would not have looked for in a warrior loyal to Thane Guthlac.

She must be losing her wits. For even in the midst of her humiliation, she found herself drawn to this Saewulf Brader.

Thane Guthlac was stroking his beard, making much of coming to a decision. Erica swallowed down a bitter taste. She was only too conscious of the men on the benches holding their breath, awaiting his judgement. Her fate, the question of whether she was to be given to Thane Guthlac's champion or his rawest recruit, was little more to most of them than an evening's entertainment. A minstrel or a dancing girl would have been received with like interest and with as little concern.

Biting back a tart response, Erica gripped Saewulf Brader's brown homespun for all she was worth. She lowered her gaze, for, if Guthlac Stigandson saw the anger that must be burning in her eyes, he would surely give her to Hrothgar. She wanted to fly at her father's old enemy, kicking and screaming; she wanted to turn tail and run. But one thing weighed more than her anger at Thane Guthlac—her determination that Morcar, Hrolf and the others should not rot in that noisome cottage. Add to that her hatred of Normans and her vision that the two warbands should unite against those who had stolen her father's lands…

She stood firm, it was all she could do. Erica of Whitecliffe was at the mercy of Thane Guthlac's whim. And to think that the men watching so avidly were fellow Saxons…

Thane Guthlac pushed up her chin. 'Lady Erica, you are a brave woman, you do not weep and wail, you are a daughter a man could be proud of—a peace-weaver.' He waved at Saewulf Brader. 'Take Thane Eric's daughter—this night a true-born lady is yours.'

A sigh rippled round the hall like the wind in the reeds, but Erica barely heard it. She dragged in a breath.

At her side the dark head bowed briefly. 'Thank you, my lord.' Saewulf Brader spoke quietly and without triumph. Her heart warmed to him. Then blue eyes were looking into hers and he offered her his hand. The palm was callused from much swordplay and for a moment she blinked at it. 'Lady Erica?'

Erica managed to release the death grip she had on his tunic and strong fingers closed on hers.

'No! *No!*' Ailric renewed his struggles with his captors, but a sharp elbow to his stomach had him rolling in the rushes, gasping for breath like a landed fish.

Thane Guthlac grinned briefly in Ailric's direction before transferring his attention back to Saewulf Brader. 'You may…rest in the storeroom tonight.'

Saewulf Brader's grip tightened and he led her towards a small door to one side of the hall. Laughter erupted behind them. The blood rushed in Erica's ears.

'My apologies, Hrothgar,' she heard Guthlac say. 'Despite the feud, I find I have some liking for that girl. She is courageous—for a woman.'

Hrothgar let out one of his snorts and signalled for more ale. 'I care not. Truth be told, the wench is too tall for my taste anyway.'

In a daze, in which Erica could not have told whether relief or trepidation held the upper hand, she watched Saewulf Brader's lean fingers reach for the door latch. The storeroom door swung open, a dark space opened out before her, and he gestured her inside. Thane Guthlac's laughing response to Hrothgar, the retching noises Ailric was still making, and the noise and babble in the hall faded.

Blackness, shadows. Erica held down a groan and her steps slowed—she had a hearty mislike of the dark.

The wooden lintel was so low that Saewulf Brader was ducking his head as he followed her in. He glanced frowningly around the ill-lit, cramped space, which was almost entirely taken up with barrels and narrow-necked clay jars, before his gaze ran slowly over her face.

'Dark,' Erica muttered, hugging herself, and hating that he should see this weakness in her. 'Too dark.'

'Wait here, my lady, I will bring light.' The shadows retreated as he opened the door and stepped back into the hall. When he closed it behind him, they advanced again.

Erica stared through the gloom at the rectangular sliver of light around the edge of the storeroom door. Her heartbeat was erratic, her hands were shaking. She curled them into her skirts.

Wait here? Where else might she go? she wondered, wildly. Hysteria was a breath away. Staring at the cracks of light, she strove for calm. He would not hurt her, not this one. Might he hurt her—had she misread him? But, Sweet Mother, how she hated the dark.

In the hall a dog yelped, another snarled. She heard the murmur of voices, muffled by the door, the scrape of a stool leg on the floorboards. She could no longer hear Ailric.

Calm, Erica, calm. He does not seem cruel. He—

The door swung back and a broad-shouldered form stooped to enter—Saewulf Brader with a flickering oil lamp and a bundle. Another, slighter shadow darkened the doorway, and a thin pallet was heaved onto the floor, next to a barrel.

'My thanks, Maldred,' Saewulf Brader said.

The door shut, cutting off another burst of laughter.

He set the lamp on top of the barrel along with a couple of tallow candles. 'We will save those for later.'

Later. Erica's breath froze. Later.

He faced her. Smiled. There was so little room that he was scarcely a foot away from her. He was very tall, this man to whom she had been given, his head almost touching the planked ceiling. And, now that he stood close, Erica could see that he did indeed look young. She clung to the thought that she was most likely his senior, by a couple of years at least. How ridiculous that this thought should give her ease. Saewulf Brader's skin was smooth and his eyes were clear, the blue rimmed by a charcoal-coloured ring. And he was, she realised with a start, examining her with equal attention. Convulsively, she swallowed.

'Do not fear me. You are safe,' he said, softly.

'I…I thank you.' Absurdly, she believed him.

'Do you reckon the ale will spoil if I shift this? We need elbow space to sleep in.' He nudged a barrel with the toe of his boot, and, without waiting for her reply, set about moving it to one side. His voice took on the edge of laughter. 'Guthlac will have me pilloried if I spoil his ale.'

Strong muscles bunched and shifted under his tunic. A tunic that, now Erica had leisure to study it, she saw was simple in design, a brown worsted with no embroidery either at cuff or hem. A straightforward weave, it had once been of a reasonable quality, but it had seen better days. His belt was wide and simple, had no fancy pattern chased into the leather. His chausses were grey. Long boots hid most of his cross-gartering, but she saw a flash of blue. But why did he have no arm-rings?

Erica backed against another barrel to give him room to manoeuvre. Saewulf Brader was, she recognised as she swallowed hard on the lump in her throat, the image of health. He should have won at least a couple of trophies. But his lack of arm-rings was not uppermost in her thoughts. Young men, healthy young men were, in Erica's admittedly limited experience, not entirely reliable where women were concerned. This she had learnt from listening to Ailric and Hereward. Even when Ailric had hoped to become her betrothed, he had visited the tavern girls by the docks in Lewes.

Until today, Erica had led a sheltered life—her high status had protected her. Physically, at least. Politically, of course, she was far from sheltered. A favoured only daughter, many was the night that she had sat at her father's board listening to his men; many a time she had joined in their debates. Which was how her father's housecarls had come to heed her counsel when news had come of Thane Eric's death. Physically though, she remained naïve. Even though Erica had fled Whitecliffe with her father's men, and had been living the life of an outlaw ever since, they remained extremely protective of her. Not one of her housecarls would dream of laying a finger on her. Physically, she was as chaste and innocent as a nun in an enclosed order.

Today that had changed. Erica had come to Thane Guthlac to end the bloodfeud. She was the sacrifice and she must personally make reparation for the slight suffered by Guthlac's mother.

Silently, she stared at Saewulf Brader's broad back as he worked and wondered what was running through his mind. He might have no arm-rings, but tonight he *had* been given a trophy. Her. Could she take him at his word? Could she trust him not to…touch her? He was— she must remember—Guthlac Stigandson's man.

'Saewulf?'

He ceased rolling a barrel closer to the wall, and glanced across. 'Hmm?'

'Wh…what have they done with Ailric?'

'Locked him up with your other man,' came the brief answer. Turning away, he continued clearing their sleeping space.

'Thane Guthlac would not harm them, would he?'

Again the blue eyes met hers. A shrug. 'I think not.' He rested an elbow on the barrel. 'This Ailric,' he asked quietly, 'you were to marry him?'

'I…I…at one time. Not now.'

'But there is…affection between you?'

Erica twisted her hands together. For her part, she had never felt anything more for Ailric than for any other of her father's housecarls. Ailric, on the other hand, had been wont to act as though she belonged to him. Not that that had prevented him from visiting those tavern girls with Hereward.

Guthlac's man smiled, and his expression softened. Erica's pulse quickened—he was extraordinarily well favoured when he smiled.

'Ailric certainly appears possessive where you are concerned.'

'Yes.'

'He will be angry after tonight.' A thoughtful look came over him and he sighed. 'I dare say he will wish to kill me. Such is the nature of a bloodfeud, so it continues, feeding on itself like yeast in a brew-tub.'

Erica bit her lip and glanced at the door. 'But you said that you would not…that you…you swore you would n-not…'

'Peace, my lady.' The blue gaze was steady. 'I will keep that vow. At dawn you will leave this chamber as pure as you were when you entered it.'

Again he smiled, and again Erica's heart warmed towards him, for taking care to reassure her. His mouth was beautiful, she thought, disconcerted. One could see more of a man's expression when he was not hiding behind a beard as was the Saxon fashion. And certainly in Saewulf Brader's case, the lack of beard was far from unattractive. The curve of his mouth and the shape of his jaw—strong…

Presenting his back to her, he rolled one of the barrels in front of the door, grunting with the effort. 'And before you object…' His voice was amused, though how on earth Erica could tell that she could not say. Saewulf Brader was Guthlac's man, a stranger, yet already she knew when his voice was smiling. 'Before you object, my lady, I am putting this here to ensure that you may sleep in privacy this night. It is not there to keep you imprisoned.' Straightening, he dusted his hands on his thighs.

'Saewulf?'

He came close, so close that she had to tip back her head to look up at him. 'My friends call me Wulf.'

'Wulf.' Erica gave him a shaky smile and broke eye contact. Wulf. It suited him. And, since January was *wulf-monath*, the month of the wolves, it was fitting somehow. Sweet Lord, but he was tall. Having inherited her father's height, Erica was unaccustomed to looking up at a man; it made her feel…shy. And Wulf's proximity in the cramped storeroom made his physical presence seem overpowering. It was not simply his height; it was the width of his shoulders, the intensity of his gaze. If he wanted to, he would have no trouble in forcing her. But, thankfully, he did not appear to have any such intention. Her guardian angel must have been watching over her this night. This particular wolf was not of the ravening sort.

'Wulf…' she swallowed '…how apt.' The name Wulf was, however, a timely reminder. Here she was, a lone woman among a pack of wolves, and he was one of them—she must not forget that. However personable Seawulf Brader appeared, she must keep in mind that he was Thane Guthlac's man.

'Apt? Oh, I see, of course, you would think that. It is *wulf-monath*—you must feel you have been flung into a den of them.'

Erica's jaw dropped—he could read her so easily? She looked at the pulse beating in his neck and frowned. 'Wulf, I…I do thank you for your help. But I wonder…'

'My lady?'

'It is just that I am not certain why Thane Guthlac gave me to you and not to…to…that other one—his name escapes me.'

'Hrothgar.'

'Yes. Why did he give me to you when you made it clear then that you had no intention of…?' She tried unsuccessfully to hold down a blush and would have turned away, but a light touch brought her face back to his.

'That is easily answered. After tonight, my lady, you will find that your status has changed—no one will believe that you are chaste. It will matter not that I have not touched you, everyone will assume the worst. And because—' his hand fell away and steel entered those blue eyes '—because I am what I am, your disparagement will be the more certain, your fall from grace the more precipitate.'

'How so?' Erica's chest was tight; there was not nearly enough air in this storeroom.

Seeming to sense her discomfort, he eased back a pace, though his eyes remained cold. 'Did you not hear Thane Guthlac and Hrothgar? Not only am I new to the warband and untried in battle, but I…' He gave her a mocking bow. 'Thane Guthlac recalls me from my childhood in Southwark. He knows I am Winifred Brader's illegitimate son, and he has made sure that every man sworn to him knows me for what I am—a bastard, a *low-born* bastard.'

His cheeks had darkened and he was no longer meeting her gaze. Erica did not think it was shame that made him look away. *He imagines he will see scorn and dismissal in my face.* 'Wulf?' She made her voice as gentle as she could. 'You could not help the circumstances of your birth.'

'Lady, did you not hear me? My parents' union was unsanctified. A bastard will share your sleeping quarters this night. That is why Thane Guthlac permitted you to choose me.' He smiled, but his smile was bitter, and her heart ached.

'Your birth does not trouble me,' Erica said, frankly. 'I chose you over…?'

'Hrothgar.'

'Yes, him. Of the two of you, I knew at once who was the man of honour.'

Wulf shook his head and his dark hair gleamed in the lamplight. 'Lady, we are strangers.'

'I know you,' Erica said firmly. 'And you, Wulf Brader, will not hurt me. That tells me all I need to know.'

With a sigh, he stooped for the pallet, dragged it to

the space he had cleared and flung his cloak over it. 'Lady, your bed.' Drawing his own russet cloak from the bundle he had brought in with him, he handed it to her.

'And you? Where will you sleep?'

'Here, by the door.'

The spot he indicated was small for a man of his proportions. 'There is little room.' Immediately, Erica blushed, and wished the words unsaid. They sounded almost like an invitation.

'There is room enough.'

Retreating to the pallet, she sank down on it and drew her cloak to her chin. She tried not to look his way. The cloak that she was lying on—*his* cloak—was thick and double lined, but there was no disguising that the mattress under it was thin and lumpy. For a moment Erica felt a longing for the fat, down-filled mattress of her box-bed at Whitecliffe, but she pushed the thought aside, and closed her ears to the harsh rustle of straw as she shifted on her crude bed.

It would be an uncomfortable night, Erica thought, recognising with something approaching astonishment that fear no longer gripped her. Her judgement of this man had been sound—she *could* trust him. He might be illegitimate, but there was no denying that Wulf Brader was an honourable man. Honour, she was fast learning, was not confined solely to the aristocracy.

She raised herself up on an elbow, bracelets jingling. 'Wulf?'

'Mmm?'

He was sitting on the floor, leaning against a barrel, pulling his boots off. Briskly he unbuckled his belt and set his sword close to hand. Erica's stomach lurched as he began unwinding the blue cross-gartering. She had never slept alone with a man. And Wulf's dark, almost sinful good looks, were having a strange effect on her; it would seem that they made improper thoughts leap into her head, unseemly thoughts that an unmarried Saxon lady had no business thinking, particularly since she had barely escaped ravishment at the hands of Hrothgar.

But Erica could not help herself, the thoughts kept coming. Thoughts about what it would be like to kiss such a man, one with penetrating blue eyes and a well-shaped mouth that had softened more than once when he had looked at her, a powerful man with a peculiar hint of sensitivity about him. Erica had never kissed a man, not intimately. Once, Ailric had attempted to steal a kiss in the Christmas before the Normans had come, but he had come to Erica with the reek of the ale-house on his breath and she had pushed him away very quickly. Her position as thane's daughter had spared her other men's attentions.

As Erica watched Wulf Brader prepare for sleep, the disconcerting intimacy of their situation stole her breath, and for a moment she forgot her question. Then she remembered. She was curious about him, his background, and not just what it might be like to share a kiss with him. It was quite ridiculous that she was having carnal thoughts and most unlike her. Still, it had to be better than dwelling on her current plight—hostage to the whim of Guthlac Stigandson.

'Wulf, you say you are but newly recruited—how came you to join Thane Guthlac?'

For a moment it seemed he was not going to respond, then he shifted and said, 'I was brought up in the port of

London, near Earl Godwine's house in Southwark. That was where, as a boy, I originally met Thane Guthlac.'

Erica's eyes widened. 'Did you meet King Harold, too?'

Again, Wulf took his time answering. In the hall, the noise was lessening, save for the clatter and bang of trestles and benches as they were pushed back to the wall to make room for sleeping.

'Yes, but I do not like to talk of those days,' he said in a closed voice, and bent over his cross-gartering.

Erica nodded. She understood; she felt the same way herself. She also had met King Harold, both when he was an earl and, later, when he had been king. And, yes, it was indeed painful to recall former times, when a Saxon king sat on the throne of England, and when William of Normandy was but a minor princeling on the other side of the Narrow Sea. 'We all wish King William in hell,' she said. 'What loyal Saxon would not?'

Wulf shot her an impenetrable look and set the leg bindings aside. 'Goodnight, my lady.'

'Goodnight.'

Settling down once more on his cloak, Erica composed herself for sleep.

Chapter Six

Erica drifted awake some time in the dead of night, uncertain as to what had woken her. The lamp was smoking, its light was feeble, but there was enough of it to ward off her fear of the dark. Indeed, it was surprising that she had actually slept, for sleep had been elusive since coming to the fens. She had been ill at ease every moment since leaving Whitecliffe, even when among her men, yet sleep had taken her here in the heart of Guthlac's castle; it was very odd.

The smoke from the lamp was twisting upwards in a lazy spiral when she became aware that the barrel was no longer blocking the storeroom entrance and the door was ajar. She was alone!

Heart in her mouth, Erica bolted upright, clutching her cloak to her breast. Soft footsteps approached. The door creaked wide and a tall, broad-shouldered figure stooped to enter.

'Wulf!' The relief was so intense she almost laughed. 'Where have you been?'

'Did you think that I had abandoned you?'

Slowly she shook her head.

A dark brow lifted; it told her he thought her a very poor liar. 'You have my cloak, I was cold,' he said, showing her the blankets he was carrying. 'Go back to sleep.' He rolled the barrel back in front of the door.

'I was right to choose you, Wulf Brader,' she murmured as—wonder of wonders—sleep came to take her a second time.

Wulf stared into the flickering half-light created by the lamp. God, but these boards were hard as iron and just as cold, he thought, as he tried to find a more comfortable position. The lady considered that she had been right to choose him. Hah! If only she knew what she had chosen. Never mind that she was apparently bedded down with one of Guthlac's men—how would she react if she knew the whole truth? If she knew that Wulf was a Norman captain? What had she said—that she wished King William in hell? Hell indeed, Wulf thought, wearily scrubbing his face.

He wished he were a thousand miles away or, at the very least, back at the temporary Norman garrison that had been thrown up at Ely. He wished he had been given another commission, *any* commission, as long as it did not involve betraying Saxons or meeting a brave and beautiful thane's daughter who compelled him to help against his better interests.

Thankfully, with Lady Erica saved from real disparagement, he should be able to report to De Warenne's man and, with luck, return to the Norman base at Ely. Archers, he had decided, archers would be key to any successful attack on Thane Guthlac.

Meanwhile Lady Erica lay happily ensconced in

his cloak, a small bump in the gloom, her breathing soft and even. Heaven help her, she trusted him. Given the precariousness of her position as the daughter of Guthlac's sworn enemy, that was nothing short of miraculous. He permitted himself the luxury of savouring that thought. She, a Saxon noblewoman, trusted Saewulf Brader—now there was a novelty. It was too dark for him to make out her features, but they had been engraved on his mind from the moment he had first seen her: that pale, delicate skin, the dark hair, so dark as to be almost the colour of jet, the straight nose, the freckles, the gentle curve of her mouth, the rosy lips. A beauty.

And brave, too.

He could imagine how her body would feel if he were to draw her into his arms. She would be warm; she would have long, straight limbs and her skin would be smooth and—

Enough! The Lady Erica might have reacted with calm courtesy to the fact of his lowly birth, but he had sworn not to touch her. If he did in truth touch her, doubtless her reaction would be quite different. Wulf must not delude himself, he must remember who he was and what he was doing in this noisome fen. He pulled the coarse blanket tightly about him. How those green eyes would fill with scorn if she discovered his real purpose here, if she knew where his true loyalties lay.

Casting a last look at the figure a few feet away on the floor, Wulf closed his eyes. The lady thought she knew him. In the gloom his lip curled. Lady Erica of Whitecliffe would not exchange the time of day with him if she truly knew him.

Not only was he a low-born bastard, he was a low-born *Norman* bastard; if that beautiful bundle of womanhood got wind of that, she would no doubt take to her pretty heels and, bracelets a-jingle, run screeching from the room.

Willing his muscles to relax—Saints, lying on these boards was a penance—Wulf's thoughts melted into one another. There was no point worrying what the Lady Erica would think of him once she realised his true role in Guthlac's entourage; there was no point already beginning to dread the look of hatred that would distort that lovely face.

He had come to East Anglia to discover the strength of the Saxon resistance; he had come to win favours for himself and make his way in the world. His gut clenched. Yesterday he had not known of Lady Erica of Whitecliffe's existence. Other men must surely answer to her—other outlaws, perhaps large numbers. *Merde.* He must find out, it would surely be useful for De Warenne to know. Because of her he had missed the first rendezvous, but, since he had missed it, he might as well make the most of things by discovering what he could about her people, they were rebels, too. That was why he was here; he must focus. And don't forget about those archers, he reminded himself, think about training for the archers…

The next morning on the platform outside the hall, Erica splashed her face in icy water from the butt. Wulf stood like a sentry at her side, wreathed in the clouds made by his breath. With a sinking feeling it occurred to her that she would be hard pressed to tell whether he was there for her protection or to prevent her from attempting to escape. It is still *wulf-monath*, she reminded herself.

In the bailey below, a long-robed priest was walking towards the wooden chapel, hands folded into the sleeves of his habit against the cold. He vanished inside. Erica eyed the adjacent buildings, one of which was apparently being used as a lock-up for Ailric and Hereward. The hut closest to the chapel had no windows, and guards were posted outside, stamping their feet in the chilly morning. That hut, she thought, that must be where they are.

The portcullis was firmly lowered and, from Erica's vantage point on the walkway at the head of the stairs, it was impossible to see whether their boat was moored at the jetty. The lake had iced over during the night, but a navigable passage remained in the centre of the waterway, a slim dark line dividing the frosted surface in two.

'Good morning, my lady.' Hrothgar's sneering voice broke into her thoughts. Erica's stomach lurched.

Thane Guthlac's second-in-command was leaning his shoulder on a doorpost, arms folded across his chest, watching her with an unsettling air of expectancy. Nodding at him, conscious of Wulf's hand hovering over his swordhilt, Erica dabbed her face with the edge of her veil and prepared to push past him.

Hrothgar shifted to block the hall doorway. 'You may no longer enter.'

'I…I beg your pardon?'

'You cannot return to the hall.' A pause, then, as an insolent afterthought, 'My *lady*.'

'I need to speak with Thane Guthlac.'

'He is busy. Get you into the bailey.'

Erica blinked. 'But...I do not understand. Our agreement...'

'What agreement?'

Gripped by a return of the nausea she felt whenever she stood in close proximity to Hrothgar, Erica swallowed. 'Th...that our people should come to terms. If I...' She shot a sideways glance at Wulf, whose blue eyes were fixed intently on Hrothgar's, and collected herself. 'Guthlac said that once the affront to his mother had been avenged...'

Hrothgar shook his head. 'Thane Guthlac has changed his mind.' Glancing at Wulf, he gave a thin smile. 'Perhaps my lord thought one night with a low-born bastard who had openly claimed he would not touch you was not enough disparagement.'

The nausea rose in Erica's throat and for a moment she could not speak. 'No! *No!* Thane Guthlac said—'

Hrothgar lifted his massive shoulders in a careless shrug. 'He changed his mind.'

Rage took her and she lurched forwards. 'You are loathsome!' Curling her hands into claws, she resisted the urge to rush at him, but Wulf must have read her first impulse, for he caught her arm.

'My lady.' Wulf's voice was calm and restraining, but Erica was not to be restrained.

'I must speak with Guthlac!' She shook Wulf off.

Hrothgar reached behind him and shut the door with a bang. 'I repeat, he will not speak to you.' He jerked his head towards the bailey. 'Go, Erica of Whitecliffe, there will be no collaboration between Thane Eric's housecarls and Guthlac Stigandson's.'

The blood thundered in her ears, her head throbbed. He meant it. She had lost her reputation—oh, Wulf Brader had not laid a finger on her, but it was as he had warned her: Wulf had not had to touch her for her to have been despoiled. When word got out that Lady Erica of Whitecliffe had spent the night closeted in a storeroom with a virile young warrior like Wulf Brader...and add to that the fact of his lowly birth, his *illicit*, lowly birth...

Briefly, she closed her eyes. No man of honour—she managed not to look at the prison hut across the yard—no, not even Ailric, would have her now. Stiffening her spine, reminding herself whose daughter she was, she glared at Hrothgar. 'Do you mean to tell me that what happened last night was for *nothing*?'

'Exactly so, my lady. You made a tactical error when you agreed so easily to your disparagement.'

Erica blinked. 'An error?'

An infuriating smile lifted Hrothgar's lips. 'Let me give you a hint. You should have struggled a little, or perhaps screamed—you weren't seen to suffer enough.'

Erica put her hand to her head. 'This is insane. Hrothgar, step aside. Let me speak to Thane Guthlac.'

'No.'

She darted a glance at Wulf, no, at *Saewulf* Brader. He was no friend of hers if he was complicit with this...this...

It was one thing to agree to be humiliated if it ensured that her warriors could at last unite with Guthlac's against a common enemy; it was one thing to have been humiliated if it brought the rest of her people to safety—but for it to have been for nothing, *nothing*...

She chewed the inside of her cheek. But that, of course, was what Hrothgar was saying. For Guthlac's mother to be truly avenged, Erica's humiliation had to be complete, her degradation absolute. Even though she had not wanted to be degraded, the fact that she had agreed and had *chosen* Wulf, this had in some way diminished Thane Guthlac's act of revenge.

Wulf's face was unreadable, but the knuckles of his hand were white on the hilt of his sword. The tension in the air was palpable—Guthlac's two housecarls had a hearty dislike of one another and made no secret of it. But this was not the moment to dwell on the petty jealousies of Thane Guthlac's housecarls…

She sucked in a breath and repeated her questions. 'Last night was *truly* for nothing, then?'

Hrothgar's smile widened. 'Quick, aren't you?'

'And you knew this, last night?'

At Hrothgar's shrug, she rounded on Wulf. 'And you, what about you? Did you know Thane Guthlac had no intention of honouring our agreement?'

The blue eyes were fastened on Hrothgar, but he answered readily enough. 'I did not know, my lady, but since it has happened, I cannot say I am surprised.'

Staring at his profile as he watched Hrothgar, Erica wished she could believe him. Last night she had thought Wulf honourable. Last night she had thought to end the feud that had blighted her family and Guthlac's for generations. Last night, she acknowledged, she had been a hen-witted fool.

Dragging her cloak from the guard-rail, she flung it on. 'Very well. I shall leave,' she said, making her voice as cold as the wind that blew across the fens.

Hrothgar's eyes were equally cold as, slowly, he shook his head. 'Leave? I do not think so.'

Erica clenched her jaw; her cheeks were hot despite the frost in the air.

'I am come to escort you to the lock-up. Count your blessings, my lady, you are about to join your men.'

Stunned at Hrothgar's—at Guthlac's—perfidy, Erica's feet would not move. 'If I am Thane Guthlac's prisoner,' she managed, 'he is utterly without honour.'

Hrothgar simply stared.

This could not be happening, Erica thought wildly, she could not be held here. If she became Guthlac's prisoner, who would see that Morcar was cared for? And what about Solveig? And Hrolf? 'No, no, I have to return, my people need me!' They needed Ailric and Hereward, too. Without their boldest warriors, her diminished household would not survive the winter. Not when her father's other housecarls were hiding out deep in the fens…

'You should have thought of that before you came visiting. Now you must await my lord's pleasure.'

Hrothgar made to take her arm, but Wulf got there first. '*I* will escort the Lady Erica.'

In a daze, Erica felt firm fingers on her arm, as Wulf led her to the top of the stairs. She looked over her shoulder at Hrothgar. 'My people will not forget this,' she said, trembling with rage.

'Doubtless, they will not. Oh, and, my lady, one further point…'

Erica raised a brow.

'While you are waiting on Thane Guthlac's pleasure, think on this. Your father's death has done you no favours. Your position as leader of his men is untenable. Guthlac bids me ask you what lord worthy of the name would permit a *woman* to dictate terms to him? Think on that, my lady, before you question my lord's honour. Think on that while Thane Guthlac decides your fate.'

Choking down her fury, Erica turned away before she struck him. At the top step she gathered up her skirts and reached for the handrail. Wulf's touch on her elbow was steadying, but she only acknowledged him when they had gained the yard. 'My men?' she asked, in as haughty a tone as she could muster.

'In here, my lady.'

The prison hut was indeed the one next to the chapel.

And the chapel was barely a yard away.

One short yard, Erica thought, her heartbeat speeding up. Wulf was not looking at her, he was nodding at the two guards by the prison hut, gesturing at them to unbar the door.

Her mind raced. *One short yard to the chapel. She could claim sanctuary in the chapel! One yard.* Her heart thudded. She held back until Wulf had relaxed his grip on her arm and was waving her into the prison hut.

Quick as lightning, she whirled on her heel and darted in the opposite direction, into the chapel. Two candles burned on the altar, either side of a silver cross. The faint smell of incense lingered in the air, but there was no time to register more. Erica pelted up to the altar, skirting the priest. She glimpsed a gaping jaw and goggling eyes and dodged behind the altar table, chest heaving.

Wide shoulders filled the doorway. Wulf. He strode past the priest, boots loud on the beaten earth floor. Lean warrior's fingers reached past the cross. 'My lady…' his eyes glittered in the candlelight '…you cannot hide here.'

'No violence!' The priest stepped closer. 'No violence, sir!'

Wulf flung him a cold glance. 'None is intended.' He looked back at Erica, and flexed his fingers. 'My lady?'

Erica backed until her shoulders hit the planks of the east wall, and shook her head. 'I will not come, and you cannot force me.'

'No?' Wulf's voice was low and dangerous, his expression hard as granite.

She lifted her chin. 'Sanctuary, I claim sanctuary! Neither you nor Thane Guthlac can evict me from this chapel.'

'My lady…' Again, Wulf reached for her.

She batted his hand away and looked to the priest for support. 'You cannot force me, not now I have claimed sanctuary. Tell him, Father, tell him!'

Tossing back a dark lock of hair, Wulf frowned at the priest. 'Is this true?'

'I…I…yes, yes, indeed it is.' The priest's bald head gleamed. 'No one—not even a king—may violate sanctuary. She may stay here as long as she wishes.'

'My lady, think.' Wulf held that long-fingered hand out, palm up as he had done in Guthlac's hall. 'If you claim sanctuary here, you will be just as much Guthlac's prisoner as you would be in the prison hut.' Blue eyes searched hers. 'The only difference that I can see is that you will be alone. Come, take my hand, let me escort you to the lock-up. At least there you have your men to keep you company.'

Erica shook her head and her veil rippled about her. 'There is another difference, *Saewulf* Brader,' she said, stressing the formal version of his forename to distance him from her. Last night, she had thought there might be a measure of amity between them, but after Guthlac's perfidy, she could not bring herself to use the more familiar version.

'And that is?'

He must realise she would never go with him, for his hand withdrew and he tucked his thumbs into his belt. Erica straightened her shoulders. 'It is an important distinction. Here in sanctuary, I am imprisoned on my terms, not Guthlac's.' She gestured imperiously. 'Go. Tell Thane Guthlac where I am, and be certain to emphasise why I have chosen to claim sanctuary here rather than imprisonment with my housecarls.'

Glancing pointedly about the chapel at the narrow window slits, at the rough-planked walls, Wulf leaned towards her. For a moment Erica imagined she read genuine concern in his expression. 'My lady, please think again, there is barely any light here.'

Erica waved at the altar candles, at the sanctuary flame. 'There is enough.'

'It is bitterly cold and like to snow any day. There is no fire. Nor is there any sanctuary rule that I know of that guarantees you sustenance. There is food and water in the lock-up, but here there will be none. Thane Guthlac will think nothing of starving you out.'

'Let him try.'

'My lady, it is January, you will not last long.'

'Go. Tell Thane Guthlac I have claimed sanctuary. We shall see then if he will speak to me.'

He held her gaze a moment longer before turning to the priest. 'Father, you are certain I may not remove her?'

'Not now she has claimed sanctuary, not unless you want to risk your immortal soul.'

Wulf nodded his understanding, shot one last look at her and headed for the door.

Biting her lip, Erica watched him leave.

The moment the chapel door clicked softly behind him, she shivered. She felt very alone, she felt—how ridiculous—as though she had been abandoned. *Stupid*, she berated herself, *stupid*. She made herself smile at the priest. *Look, you are not alone. And be thankful for the small mercies—there is light in here, there is light.*

The priest's eyes were wary. *He looks at me as though I may sprout wings*, she thought. *No, it is far more likely he thinks I will grow a forked tail.* Conscious that her hands and legs were shaking, Erica's eyes fell on a convenient stool by the wall. Dragging it towards her, she collapsed onto it.

'Are you all right, my lady?'

'Yes, thank you. Father, what is your name?'

'Father Agilbert.'

'Father Agilbert. Well, Father, if you do not mind, I will rest here until Thane Guthlac…until…'

'Thane Guthlac is a proud man. He will not appreciate your summons.'

Raising her head, Erica met his gaze straight on. 'Do you know who I am?'

'Aye, you are Lady Erica of Whitecliffe. I know you are well intentioned, but your attempt at reconciliation is doomed.'

She sighed and rested her head against the chapel wall, watching him through half-closed eyelids. 'You should not be saying that, Father Agilbert. For surely that is tantamount to saying that Thane Guthlac will never treat with me and my people, that the bloodfeud will never come to a close.'

'That is what I believe.' Father Agilbert heaved a sigh. 'Much as I might pray otherwise. I think, my lady, that I am a realist where Guthlac Stigandson is concerned.'

'And I am not?'

The priest spread his hands.

'Father, will Thane Guthlac respect sanctuary?'

'I believe so.'

'Thank God.' Erica closed her eyes and leaned her shoulders against the wooden planking. She was Guthlac Stigandson's prisoner, but it was also as she had told Wulf—no, *Saewulf*, his name was *Saewulf*—here in the chapel, she was imprisoned on her terms, not Thane Guthlac's. There was comfort in that thought. True, it was watery gruel, but at that moment watery gruel was all there was.

Chapter Seven

At dusk three days later, Wulf was rowing back across the lake *towards* the rebel castle, cursing the fact that he was not rowing in the opposite direction. He needed to get De Warenne's archers to their practice butts, with all speed. What he was planning would be challenging enough in full daylight, but at night…

As he pulled on the oars, a heron looked across at him from the reed-fringed bank and, wings beating heavily, launched itself clumsily into the air.

Wulf was on borrowed time. Having missed the first meeting with De Warenne's man, Lucien, he had but one chance to make the next. De Warenne wanted the fens cleared of rebels as soon as possible—he would not thank Wulf if his intelligence was delayed. Like a warhorse with the smell of battle in his nostrils, De Warenne was champing at the bit…

That morning Wulf had left the rebel stronghold on Guthlac Stigandson's orders. 'Patrol the waterways, Saewulf,' Guthlac had said. 'Nose around. Keep a sharp eye out for enemy activity.'

Wulf had used the time he should have been patrolling to gather together supplies at a disused fisherman's hut. The hut stood on a small spit of land at the end of one of the lesser-known waterways. Some days earlier, Wulf had stumbled across it by accident, and the hut's relative inaccessibility had made him pick it for the meeting point. Lucien should be there at dawn tomorrow. Wulf could not afford to miss this rendezvous, which meant he must leave the castle soon. Thank God.

Except that—Wulf glowered at the approaching jetty—except that he could not help but wonder how Erica of Whitecliffe was faring in her sanctuary. It was none of his business, but his conscience would not let him rest until he had ensured there was no risk of her suffering the fate of his sister, Marie. And, of course, there was that other matter. What had happened to the rest of Thane Eric's warband? There had to be more than the two housecarls Lady Erica had brought with her—where were the others? It must be possible to use the lady to gain yet more information about them. Guthlac's outlaws were not the only Saxons in the fens who were plotting insurrection. Wulf's brow creased. These were the matters he ought to be considering; politics was his first priority, not the safety of a reckless Saxon noblewoman.

Tying his boat up at the end of a line of other, similar rowboats, Wulf vaulted onto the jetty. Lady Erica's vessel was still there, firmly secured in the middle of the line. Her pennon no longer fluttered in the stern, but, as he walked past towards the portcullis, he glimpsed it lying forlornly across one of the seats. Striding under the portcullis and through the palisade, he greeted the guard. 'Am I the last to return?'

'Aye.'

Outside the chapel, Wulf's pace slowed. Three days. He could not afford to be concerned about her personally, but he had not so much as glimpsed Lady Erica for three days, and as far as he was aware the only person to have spoken to her was the priest. The outlaw Guthlac had, as Wulf had anticipated, refused to treat with her. Not only that, but Erica of Whitecliffe had been forbidden food and drink. Was she cold? She must be.

As he stood rubbing his chin outside the chapel door, it swung open and Father Agilbert emerged. 'Good evening, my son.'

'Good evening, Father. Father…?'

'My son?'

'Lady Erica…is she…?' Wulf stumbled to a halt. What could he ask? Was she cold? Assuredly. Was she hungry? Certainly. But it would be her thirst that would be the worst. In the last three days, Wulf had spent more time than he could spare worrying about her when he should have been concentrating on his commission. The Lady Erica of Whitecliffe was a distraction, one that he ought to ignore, especially given that his time here had run out. Except that…except that…*where was her warband*?

Father Agilbert's mouth curved, and he held open the door. 'You may speak to her, my son. Thane Guthlac has not forbidden her visitors.'

Startled, Wulf met the priest's eyes. Kind eyes, he realised, not pompous and self-righteous, but eyes that were used to looking at human beings and seeing them, frailties and all. 'He has not?'

'Of course, since her two housecarls are under lock and key, no one has in fact been to see her, but…' the priest held the door an inch wider and lowered his voice '…it might help her if you went in, for I do not think she will back down. I fear that in her quiet way Lady Erica is as stubborn as Thane Guthlac. Do try to persuade her to come out. I have failed utterly.'

Nodding, Wulf stepped over the threshold. The latch clicked as the priest left.

Oddly, it felt colder in the chapel than out on the fen. The silence was unnerving, and the place was hung with shadows as what was left of the daylight squeezed through the narrow window-slits. A faint glow lit the east end, where in front of the sanctuary light Father Agilbert had left a couple of rush lights. Her dislike of the dark, he thought, she must have communicated it to him.

But where was she?

Rounding the altar table, Wulf drew up sharply. She was asleep, more beautiful even than his memory had painted her, lying amid an exotic tumble of church vestments and altar cloths. Her veil had been set to one side and her hair was tied in a loose braid—several tendrils had escaped and were curling about her temples. Her cheeks were pale as alabaster, her lips were parted, but her forehead was clear. Her pallor aside, she looked as though she did not have a care in the world.

Curiously reluctant to disturb her slumber and bring her back to reality, Wulf hooked a three-legged stool closer and sank onto it. Leaning his forearms on his knees, he linked his fingers and waited for her to waken. The vestments she was lying on were rich, encrusted with gold and silver embroidery. She has a bed fit for a queen, he thought wryly. She was almost too beautiful. As Wulf watched, something deep within him twisted.

After a time, she stirred, sighed and swallowed. Grimacing, she put her hand to her throat and opened her eyes.

When she saw him she bolted upright, bracelets jingling. 'W…Wulf! That is…I mean…*Saewulf*!' Hand still at her throat, she blinked and swallowed again.

Her throat had to be dry as dust. Three days and not one drop of liquid had passed those pretty lips. 'My lady—'

'Wh…what are you doing here?' she whispered hoarsely. 'I did not think to see you again.'

The thought was not a good one. Wulf caught himself wondering whether she would have wanted to see him again. What foolishness, to allow her to distract him like this…politics, he reminded himself, think of the politics.

'How are you?'

'Parched,' she admitted, continuing to massage her throat.

Wulf had taken a goatskin bottle out on patrol and had some weak ale left. With a swift glance in the direction of the door, he unhooked it from his belt. 'I have watered ale, my lady.' Carefully, he set it down on the floor by her feet. 'Yours, if you wish.'

She looked at it, licked her lips and swallowed. Then she nudged the waterskin back at him with her foot—it was a stockinged foot that peeped out from under the vestments, she had removed her boots and tucked them neatly under the altar. 'No, no, put it away, I must not drink.'

'My lady, you are pale. It is midwinter and you will be weakening fast. Please drink.' He nudged it back.

She shook her head and more of her hair broke free of its braid. Dark silk in gorgeous disarray. His mouth went dry. Was it as soft as it looked? Curling his fingers into his palms, for it was not for a Norman captain to discover the softness of Erica of Whitecliffe's hair, Wulf kept his voice even. 'No one will know, I will not tell.'

'No! If I drink, I will break the rule of sanctuary.'

Wulf's brow creased. 'I am not sure that is so, my lady. I am certain I have heard of friends bringing food and drink to those who have claimed sanctuary. And I have already told you, you might find a friend in me.'

Leaning forward, he took her hand and immediately felt such a *frisson*, he almost dropped it. It went clear to his toes. He frowned. In his entire life, a simple touch like that had never evoked such a response. Distraction indeed.

Their faces were but a foot away from each other. Her eyes were wide and she seemed to have stopped breathing. Wulf was having difficulty himself. She looked at his mouth and heat rushed to his groin. Wulf held down a groan. She was a lady, a Saxon *lady*. He must not think of her in this way. And of all the times to feel lust…Lord. He was disgusted with himself, it was wrong. Wrong woman, wrong time, wrong place…

He shuffled uncomfortably on the stool, and forced himself to concentrate on getting her to drink. In that at least he could be a true friend. 'Let me help you, my lady. Please drink.'

Her mouth was set in a stubborn line. Her eyes flickered briefly to his waterskin. Her throat had to be dry as desert sands, it had to be. Driven by some emotion Wulf could not begin to name, save that the thought that was uppermost in his mind was that Lady Erica *must* drink, he moved without warning.

Dropping to his knees amid the gleaming muddle of altar cloths, he pushed at her so she half-lay against the altar. Brutally, he pinched her nose, so she had no choice but to open her mouth. Her body he held in place with his knee.

Her mouth opened; nails dug into his wrist; and bracelets, warm from her body heat, chinked against his skin. 'Get off me, you oaf! Get off!'

Ruthlessly, he kept her head still, thrust the bottle at her mouth and tipped. The ale ran down her chin, darkening the rich purple of her gown. She spluttered, choked and swallowed; he definitely saw her swallow. He leaned over and tightened his grip. The tiny gold flecks flashed in her eyes. He tipped again.

More spluttering. More choking. More flailing about amid increasingly crumpled vestments.

'Why, you b—'

'Bastard?' Grimly, Wulf lifted one side of his mouth. 'As you say.' Gritting his teeth, he upended the water-skin again.

She swallowed again and again; it was either that or choke. And then, unexpectedly, she capitulated. It was as though, having tasted the watered ale, she could not help herself. Her grip shifted; her nails were no longer tearing the flesh from his wrist; she clutched at the neck of the bottle and drank deeply.

Removing his knee from her belly, Wulf rocked back on his haunches and let out a sigh. It troubled him that he had had to overpower her, but he had got some liquid down her and that was a relief. More of a relief than it ought to be. With a sigh, he pushed his hair out of his face.

She lowered the goat-skin and wiped her mouth on the sleeve of her gown. 'You *are* a bastard to force me,' she said, her voice falling quietly in the dim chapel.

He shrugged. 'It is dangerous to go too long without

water.' Reaching out, he plucked the bottle from her fingers. 'It is also dangerous to drink too much at one sitting when you have been fasting. You may have more, later.'

Levering herself up to a sitting position, she leaned against the back of the altar. Three days and no food, she had to be weak.

'Are you dizzy? Faint? Do you have a headache?'

She looked away, jaw set. 'I will not eat when I am in here. Try to force food down me and I swear I will choke.'

'You will need your strength, for your people, perhaps. How can you help them if you are weak? Is that not reason enough to eat?'

Green eyes narrowed. 'Why should you care, Guthlac's man? Your lord made it plain that he will never treat with my father's men, so what possible interest could you have in the welfare of me or my people?'

More than you think, Wulf thought. Your people, though you do not know it, ought to be in the care of my real lord, William De Warenne. And they would be in his care, if they were back where they belonged at your father's holding near Lewes. De Warenne is not the devil you might think him, he looks after his own. But you, my lady, you and your people have become outlaws. And it falls to me to discover their intentions…

Wulf's heart felt like lead. He did not like keeping secrets from this woman; he did not like having to mislead her. Squaring his shoulders, he pushed himself to his feet. Mislead her he must, if he was to carry out his orders for De Warenne. And it was not merely his knighthood that was at stake here, as the mess that the Lady Erica had got herself into was proving so poignantly.

Wulf wanted peace. He wanted an end to the conflict between Saxon and Norman—his mixed blood cried out for it. He looked bleakly at the beautiful, bejewelled woman lying like a pagan queen amid the glitter of gold and silver embroidery, and knew that that was not the sum of his wants.

The bloodfeud had shown him that he also wanted an end to the feuding between Saxon and Saxon. And more than that, he wanted… Wulf turned his gaze away from the slender, well-shaped limbs partially concealed by Father Agilbert's altar cloths and shook his head. There, he could not go. 'This feud—'

Her face grew hard. 'Thane Guthlac will not parley, the matter is out of my hands.'

'You came here to end the bloodfeud. Were your people in full agreement?' Wulf posed the question idly, as if the answer was of little importance, but he found himself holding his breath, waiting for her reply.

'My people will follow my lead.' She waved a dismissive hand. 'But this conversation is pointless, since Thane Guthlac will never end the feud.'

Shivering, she drew an altar cloth over her legs and tucked it about her feet like a blanket. It was green and matched her eyes, green flecked with gold, the Trinity cloth.

Lifting a brow, Wulf set the waterskin at her side, lest she need it later. 'Isn't it sacrilegious?'

'What?'

'To sleep amongst the church vestments.'

'Father Agilbert did not think so, it was he who brought them out of that coffer, he said my cloak was insufficient to ward off the cold.'

Wulf nodded—yes, that fitted, Father Agilbert would want to help her. Damn it, he himself wanted to help her, which was, of course, given his priorities, nigh on impossible. There was something about Lady Erica that made a man want to help, something about that independent, responsible, yet fragile spirit.

Hell, Wulf thought, as he turned to go. This is the last time I shall accept a questionable commission. Back in King William's barrack-hall at Westminster, he had thought he could not afford to turn it down, but today he was beginning to think he would in some way be impoverished if he completed it. He wanted to help Lady Erica of Whitecliffe and he could not, it was as simple and stark as that. Unless…

'Would you eat, if I brought you food?'

'No.'

'And I cannot persuade you to join your men?'

'No.'

'Goodnight, then.'

'Goodnight, Guthlac's man.'

Erica awoke some time between midnight and dawn, wondering what had disturbed her this time. Both the rush lights and the sanctuary light had gone out and the chapel was as black as ink made from an oak gall. Nothing, she could hear nothing, she was back to sleeping badly again, it seemed. And in the dark, which she hated. But she must be safe, surely, in God's house?

As she dragged the vestments more closely about her shoulders and tried to convince herself that she was not afraid and that the dark was not total, she heard a quiet laugh and the murmur of male voices. The guard that

Guthlac had stationed at the chapel door must be talking to the guards outside Ailric and Hereward's lock-up.

Shuffling deeper into her makeshift bed, Erica was telling herself it was safe to close her eyes when another, more alarming sound reached her. The chapel door was fixed on leather hinges so they did not creak, but a soft scraping told her someone was lifting the latch. The hairs rose on the back of her neck.

Quiet footsteps approached.

'Who's there?'

No reply. The blackness was impenetrable. Childish fears crowded in on her, fears that peopled the chapel with monsters, monsters usually conjured by poets reciting in her father's hall, but which now emerged dripping from the lake outside. Long talons reached towards her…Grendel, Grendel's mother…

The blood drummed in her ears. With fingers turned into thumbs, Erica groped for a candlestick she had hidden under the covers and gripped hard. It was a poor weapon, but, since her dagger had not been returned to her, it was the only one to hand.

Biting her lip, straining eyes and ears, she fought to control her breathing. Something fell with a clunk on the beaten earth and she heard a muttered curse.

Gripping the candlestick for all she was worth, Erica ignored the ice in her belly and the goose-bumps on her arms. She prayed for courage.

There was a swift whisper of sound, a faint huff of cold air as a shadow whisked round the altar and then the inky dark seemed to fly at her, more solid than it had any right to be.

A small whimper betrayed her position before she

had time to prevent it. *Idiot!* she told herself, even as a hard hand clamped round her mouth.

'Be silent!'

The voice was male, and harsh. Blindly, she flailed out with the candlestick and connected with…something.

Her assailant grunted and shook her like a terrier with a rat. 'Stop that!' The candlestick was ripped from her grasp. It thumped to the floor and rolled away.

Erica sank her teeth into that suffocating hand and a metallic taste burst on her tongue.

A grunt. Another jaw-rattling shake, but he did not release her. A cloth was forced into her mouth. She kicked out, stubbed her toe, let out a muffled squeak and choked. The pressure on the gag eased, enough to give her breath, but not enough to let her break free. A violent jerk snapped her head back and the gag was pulled fast. Ruthless fingers caught painfully in her hair. Tears stung her eyes.

What was happening? Was she about to be raped? Had Guthlac honoured the custom of sanctuary only long enough so that lack of food would weaken her? Was she about to be disparaged in truth?

Her arms were forced behind her. Tied. The bonds cut into her wrists.

She was whirled back to face her assailant, and then felt another whisper of air as he bent closer. She thought she heard the words, 'Forgive me', but knew she had imagined it because in the next moment something— scratchy, like sacking—was dragged over her head.

The gag stopped her screaming, but she heard a pathetic gurgle and to her shame knew that it was she who had made the sound. She was lifted, held by arms that gripped like iron bands.

Blindly, unable to scream, scarcely able to draw breath because of the sacking over her head, cold to her bones with terror, Erica fought to keep her wits about her. *Control*, she told herself, *control. He has not really hurt you.* Her mind was skittering all over the place, like a child slipping on ice. Would she be killed? Tortured to reveal the whereabouts of her camp? *Control, Erica, control. Concentrate.*

Somehow she kept the monsters at bay. Her captor was carrying her, taking purposeful strides, she could hear his boots striking the earth floor. He seemed to bend down, she was shifted, and then bent double. He had thrown her over his shoulder.

The door latch clacked. Icy night air fingered the back of her neck, reaching her skin through a gap in the sacking. More goose-bumps. Breathing hard, he took quick strides. *Serves you right*, Erica thought, with a flash of grim humour, *I am no featherweight*. Her bosom was squashed against his shoulder.

He strode on, paused, shifted to one side. An owl hooted. And then he was moving again, his boots making a different sound, ringing hollow as if on wood. The jetty? Erica fought to breathe through the itchy sacking. If only there was more air; if only her hands were free.

The side of her head cracked against something and she let out a muffled cry.

A hand steadied her head, rubbed the spot. 'I am sorry.' His voice was low, unrecognisable. He was *apologising*?

He was out of breath. He grunted and altered his grip and somehow she was in his arms and for a couple of seconds he was holding her so close she could hear the pumping of his heart. Another grunt and she was deposited—dropped might be the better word—on the ground.

Except that the ground was rocking. A splash. He cursed under his breath. More rocking. She was trussed up like a chicken in the bottom of a boat and he was joining her…

Wood knocked against wood. The boat swayed, less violently. And then came the softer sound of oar blades dipping into fenwater, the scraping of oars in rowlocks and, farther off, the hushing of the wind in the reeds.

Catch your breath, she told herself. *Make the most of the time*, think. *Thane Guthlac cannot be behind this.* Her abduction from the chapel where she had claimed sanctuary was nothing less than sacrilege. And her father's old enemy would not break sanctuary. As Thane Eric's daughter, she was no longer in any doubt that Thane Guthlac loathed her and negotiations with him were out of the question. But would Guthlac risk his immortal soul by breaking her out of sanctuary? Never. Guthlac Stigandson's sense of honour would not permit him to commit such an act. For someone to break into sanctuary and steal her away, they would have to be utterly without honour, they would have to be utterly beyond the pale.

A pair of charcoal-ringed blue eyes flashed vividly into her mind. Saewulf Brader? He had not been long of Guthlac's number and he was a bastard, and that, in most people's eyes, put him well beyond the pale.

The ribs of the boat pressed hard against her cheek. Icy water had pooled on the planking, it was seeping into her clothes. Shivering, Erica twisted, testing the ropes that pinioned her arms. They held firm. She let her muscles go slack; it was pointless wasting precious energy with futile struggle. Wulf had been right in that regard, she thought ruefully, she had little strength after her fast. Perhaps if she had let him bring food she might have been able to break free.

Erica cast her mind back to the moment when her abductor had come into the chapel. He had used stealth, which implied further that Guthlac was not behind this. Yes, he had been quick to silence her and quick to bind her, but her abductor was no thief, he had made no attempt to strip her of her finger- or arm-rings. Not yet, at any rate. He had not set out to hurt her either, not deliberately, for when she had cracked her head, there had been that hand that had rubbed her throbbing scalp through the sackcloth, that gentle hand. Perhaps she had not misheard that muttered apology.

Wulf, her abductor had to be Wulf. The man was a mass of contradictions. He was no noble, yet in his dealings with her he had been innately gentle, innately courteous. In the short time that she had known him he had shown himself to be more considerate of her feelings than most men. Relief flooded through her as the certainty gathered power, Wulf Brader was her abductor. Though why he should do this when he answered to Guthlac was a mystery. She tried to speak, but through the gag it was impossible.

Wet and uncomfortable, Erica lay in the bottom of the boat while her captor rowed. *Please, God, let it be Wulf,* she prayed, *let it be Wulf.* Surrendering to the motion of the boat, an almost imperceptible swaying, she wished he would remove the hood—it itched like the plague. Her skin crawled. And her boots were back in the chapel; her feet were freezing, her toes going numb. Shivering, she thought longingly of the great fire at Whitecliffe Hall, and blinked back a rush of tears. Gone, those days were gone and would never return. Her tears soaked into the sacking.

Half an hour passed, perhaps an hour—she lost track of time. Then, without warning, the boat juddered. More splashing. The boat tilted, there were various creakings and grunts and she was urged to a sitting position.

She mumbled into the gag. The sacking was snatched from her head and an intense cold bit at her cheeks and ears. Starlight—no, not stars, but light leaking from an iron lantern, which had stars cut into the shutter. A broad-shouldered figure crouched beside her. She was pulled unceremoniously against a wide chest and quick fingers untied the gag.

Chapter Eight

Spitting out bits of sacking, Erica jerked back and rubbed her cheek on her shoulder to get rid of stray threads. 'Wulf!' Relief made her weak, and angry. 'What in hell are you doing?'

'Rescuing you, I think.'

There was amusement in his tone, damn him. How *dare* he laugh at her—did he not realise how much he had frightened her? 'Rescuing me?' Shuffling round on her knees, she presented him with her bound hands. 'Did you have to bind me so tightly? Release me, for pity's sake.'

In a moment her hands were free and she was facing him again, rolling aching shoulders, rubbing sore wrists. 'Why?'

Dark brows drew together. 'I did not trust Guthlac with you.' He sounded guarded, but a wave of his hand had her focusing on her surroundings rather than his tone. 'You are free now.'

The sky must be overcast, for the only stars that Erica could see were the stars shining from the lantern. There was no moon and a cold wind was shaking the reeds. She shivered. 'In breaking me out of sanctuary, you imperil your mortal soul.'

His shoulders lifted. 'There were…more important considerations.'

'More important than the state of your soul? Father Agilbert would take issue with you there.'

Another shrug. 'There are many who would say my soul is of little account—I am damned by my birth, remember. Besides—' his voice warmed '—I did want to see you out of there.'

'You felt impelled to be my champion? Why? Thane Guthlac will have you flogged when he finds out.'

'Thane Guthlac would do more than that if he knew the whole,' came the cryptic response.

Erica did not have the first idea what he was talking about. She peered into the night, but the light from the starry lantern did not reach far and she could only make out a shrubby shoreline fringed with ice, and a dark shape that might be a fallen tree. 'We seem to have run aground.'

'Aye.' Wulf shoved his hands through his hair. 'Damn waterways are like a maze, especially in the dark.'

'Lost your way, did you?'

'I know where we are, at least I hope I do.' With a sigh, he rose and the boat shifted. He picked up a bundle and offered her his hand.

He was dressed for travelling, with those wide shoulders swathed in a fur-lined cloak Erica had not seen before and sturdy knee-length boots that hid most of his cross-gartering. And he was armed—when his cloak parted, she glimpsed the hilt of his sword. A pair of gloves was tucked into his belt.

'Come, my lady, let us see if we can find shelter. If we are where I think we are, there's a hut nearby. Take the lantern.'

Slowly, for her stockinged feet were clumsy with cold, Erica let him help her scramble out of the boat. He looped the mooring rope round an overhanging branch, gripped her free hand, and led her inland.

After a couple of minutes of stumbling through trees and of tripping over rocks, a tree root and Lord knew what else, he came to a halt. 'Here it is.'

Erica's toes were so numb she could barely stand, her fingers throbbed. Lifting the lantern, teeth chattering, she saw what at first glance seemed to be a couple of reed-thatched hurdles lashed at an angle to each other. A leather flap took the place of a door. 'This?' She fought to keep the scorn from her tone. 'I would think twice before keeping swine in it.'

His face became closed, the grip on her hand relaxed. 'It might not be what you are accustomed to, my lady, but it is all we have.' He waved her in. 'Ladies first.'

She did not like it, but since she could barely move she was disinclined to argue. Wulf's 'shelter' was nothing but a hovel, but surely it would keep out the worst of the frost? Ducking her head, keeping careful hold of the lantern, she kilted up her skirts and scurried inside.

The earth floor was covered in hide and the roof was so low that the only place you could sit without bowing your head was at the centre, beneath the apex.

Wulf followed, crowding her in the confined space before settling down cross-legged. Erica placed the lantern on the hide between them and hoped he couldn't see her shivering. The lantern made starry patterns on his tunic and cloak, on the shadow of his growing beard.

His gaze ran over her, and he swore softly. 'Lord, my lady, I forgot your feet!'

Her stockings were in ribbons. Erica made a half-hearted attempt to pull her feet out of sight under her skirts, but a swift hand reached out and her protest was ignored as he pulled them onto his lap and began chafing them.

The warmth stung at first, but Wulf's capable warrior's hands continued chafing, chafing, infusing warmth back into her and then, gradually it became heaven. She ought to protest, she really ought. It was not fitting for Wulf's fingers to be moving over her in this way. It was too intimate, far too intimate, but the intense cold seemed to have stolen her will. And his hands…so firm…so careful. Warm. What heaven. Erica curled her toes into his palms until, blushing, she recalled herself. This would not do. Not only was Wulf a stranger, he was one of Guthlac's housecarls…

This time when Erica made to draw her feet back under her, Wulf let her have her way.

'I did bring your boots, you should have reminded me,' he said.

'And when might I have done that?' Embarrassment made her sharp. 'When you shoved a gag in my mouth perhaps, or when you dragged a sack over my head? Should I have spoken *before* you carted me out of the chapel? Against my will, I might point out.'

'I had to gag you, you would have brought the guards down on us.' Wulf reached into the bundle and tossed her boots at her. 'Here, my apologies. I forgot about them in the rush to escape.'

Escape? What an interesting choice of word. But Wulf's hands had found her feet again, snapping off the tenuous thread of her thought, as he resumed kneading the life back into them. As the cold eased, Erica bit back a moan of pure pleasure. 'Ladies don't generally sleep with their boots on,' she muttered. In a minute, she would tell him to stop. In a minute...

'They do not?' His teasing voice. Their eyes met and he smiled and Erica did not quite understand it, but much of her embarrassment seemed to dissipate. 'I am glad to know this,' he went on softly. 'My experience of...ladies...has been somewhat limited, I fear.'

Something told Erica that while Wulf Brader's experience of ladies might be limited, his experience of women in general was far from limited. Though why such a ridiculous distinction should interest her was beyond her. Wulf Brader's experience or lack of it with women of any station was none of her business.

Mercifully releasing her feet before Erica shamed herself completely by melting into a puddle of bliss, Wulf reached into the bundle and produced a woollen blanket. 'Wrap this round you. And since you are no longer in sanctuary and are out of Guthlac's hands, I thought you might enjoy these.' He drew out a smaller bundle and passed it to her. 'Unless you have any more objections, that is?'

Erica tore off the cloth. 'Bread!' Her mouth watered. 'Cheese! And...oh, Wulf, roast chicken, I don't remember when I last had chicken!' Her stomach growled; it was shamingly loud. On impulse, she leaned forwards and pressed a swift kiss to his cheek, catching, as she did so, the subtle fragrance of soapwort, mingled with the musky male scent that was Wulf. 'Thank you!'

He drew back, touching his cheek as Erica sank her teeth into the bread. Soft wheat bread, fresh-baked that evening if she were any judge. She could hardly chew quickly enough.

With a crooked smile, Wulf set a wineskin in her lap. 'I need to beat the bounds outside, I won't be long,' he said, lifting the leather flap that served as a door.

With her tongue savouring the rich flavours of chicken roasted with chives and wild thyme, Erica nodded.

Wulf gave her time to finish eating before he returned. 'It is only I,' he said, lifting the entrance flap and ducking his head through the opening. 'There is a fire pit out here and I have got a small fire going.'

Erica had put her boots on and the blanket was draped about her shoulders on top of her cloak. No, Wulf reminded himself, he must not think of her as Erica. She was *Lady* Erica. *Lady Erica of Whitecliffe.* He must keep his distance from her. And, for his own peace of mind, he must keep her out of his thoughts as much as possible, even though it was coming home to him that, since he had freed her from Guthlac, he was honour bound to consider her welfare.

Her face was pinched with cold, but her eyes brightened. 'A fire? Is there hot water?'

The question disconcerted him. 'My lady, this is not a hostelry.'

'I had noticed.' Bringing the lantern with her, she crawled to the entrance. Outside, she gathered up her purple skirts and began marching in the direction of the boat.

'Not that way!' Wulf snatched the lantern from her, closed the shutter and steered her away from the water. 'Please be careful, my lady, the light may betray our position.'

'Who are we hiding from? Thane Guthlac or the Normans?'

Wulf grimaced. He did not think anyone had followed them from the castle; the guard he had relieved would not have returned for some time, and he had rowed like the very devil. But when Guthlac discovered that Saewulf Brader had removed Erica of Whitecliffe from his clutches…there was no knowing how the man would react.

'In any case the lantern is small,' she said, eyes downcast as she picked her way through the murk. 'And you said you had lit a fire—surely that will act as a beacon?'

'The hearth is in the remains of an ancient fire-pit, my lady, the flames are concealed by the pit walls. I think the fisherman whose hut we are…borrowing must have used it as a smoke-house. If ever there was roof, it has long gone, but—'

'Show me,' she said, imperiously, using tones that only a thane's daughter would use.

Flicking open the shutter, Wulf angled the lantern so the light fell onto the path in front of them. Taking her hand, bitterly aware that if she knew he was a Norman captain she would refuse to speak to him, let alone touch him, he led her into the clearing where the fire-pit was. He did not know what it was about this woman, but she gave him the most inappropriate ideas. Warming her feet like that had been a bad mistake. Most inappropriate, but she had been so cold. And now he was noticing that her fingers were like ice, just like ice, and he had to quell another inappropriate impulse. He wanted to chafe them, too.

When Wulf had taken Lady Erica from the chapel he had remembered to pick up her boots, but her gloves— Lord, they might be anywhere.

Her quick eyes were scouring the area. 'The fisherman has left his cooking pot behind.' She pointed at a three-legged cauldron lying on its side by the trunk of a leafless willow. Blackened with use, it all but blended into the night. In its pit, the fire glowed like a sunset; it sent out a surprising amount of heat.

Despite himself, Wulf's lips twitched; it was not hard to guess the trend of her thoughts. 'Hot water,' he murmured. 'I see you are set on it.'

Nodding, she stood at his side, hair bedraggled and unravelling, dishevelled by the sack he had flung over her head, but in some mysterious and ladylike way maintaining her dignity. Her gown was dark with water at the hem, and her eyes were enormous in the light of the lantern and very green. 'Wulf, *please*.' Bracelets chinking, she reached for the cauldron. 'Three days in sanctuary, three days without water to drink, let alone to wash in. Surely you would not deny me hot water?'

Shaking his head at the foolishness of a Norman captain who could not resist a request from a woman who had sworn to rid England of all Normans, irritated beyond measure at how pleased he was that she was again calling him Wulf rather than the more formal Saewulf, Wulf took the cauldron and trudged back to the fen to fill it for her. Women, he mused, they are the same the world over, Norman, Saxon, it matters not. Water slopping over the sides, he returned to the clearing and set the cauldron on the fire. 'I will be back in a moment.' He reached for the lantern.

She sent him a sharp look. 'You would not leave me, not here?'

On impulse, he picked up her hand and dropped a kiss on the back of it. 'Never.' It was best to ignore the way his heart lifted when she did not repulse him. 'I have some soap and a comb in my pack, I thought you might care to use them.'

When she stared at him, a pleased smile lifting the corners of her mouth, it warmed him to his core. *Merde.* Abruptly, Wulf turned and strode back to the hut, leaving her to toast herself by the fire while the water heated. He shook his head. *Wrong, wrong, this is wrong, she is your sworn enemy.*

On his return, Wulf stood guard with his back to her while she washed and tidied herself to her satisfaction. He was surprised that she did not take long, not half as long as he would have expected a thane's daughter to take. Notwithstanding, in the short time that she had been out of the hut, the ground had frozen. White crystals gleamed in the lamplight, and as they made their way back to the shelter, hoar-frost crunched underfoot.

After the glow of the fire, the fisherman's hut seemed twice as damp and dark as it had before, but there was a roof, which was a blessing. It was cold enough for snow. Tempting though it might be to sleep by that fire, they could not risk lying out in the open.

Shivering again, Erica—no, damn it—*Lady* Erica

took up her position on the floor, hugging her cloak
about her like a shield. Her re-braided hair hung loosely
over one shoulder. 'I…you…there is not enough room.'

Wulf's eyes narrowed. 'There is plenty of room,
my lady. Surely you are not afraid I will…take advan-
tage of you?'

A beringed hand fluttered towards him and was still.
'No, of course not, I recognise an honourable man when
I see one. You are not like Thane Guthlac or Hrothgar.
It is simply—' she eyed the scant inches between them
'—there is less space than there was in Guthlac's storeroom, and to lie so close to a man who is not of my
blood, I…I am unaccustomed.'

Wulf jerked his head at the leather flap doing duty
as a door. 'If you think I intend to freeze my
boll…backside off out there, you have another think
coming. Here, you had best take charge of this.' He
passed her the lantern.

'My thanks.'

With a brusque nod, he spread a blanket across the
floor, rolled into his cloak and pointedly stretched out
full length with his back to her. He stared at a star the
lantern was casting on the hut wall. 'My lady, if I
might suggest…?'

She sighed. Rustling noises suggested she was
settling down for sleep.

'Keep your boots on this time, my lady—lest we are
disturbed.'

'Don't worry, I intend to.'

More rustling. The star on the wall grew faint and the
darkness thickened. Wulf sensed rather than felt her
body shift close to his. So, she did trust him. He became

aware of a softening sensation in the region of his heart and closed his mind against it. Any softening towards Erica of Whitecliffe would be disastrous, given his allegiances. His lord was planning to attack her would-be ally, and he had yet to learn how many rebels answered to her command.

'Wulf?'

A hinge creaked and before his eyes the star on the wall brightened and dimmed, brightened and dimmed; she was toying with the lantern shutter.

'Aye?'

'I know I did not seem so at first, but I am very glad you took me from the chapel. Will you be able to return me to my people?'

'If God wills it.'

'Thank you. Tomorrow, when I can see where we are, I will show you where we are lodged.'

Briefly, Wulf closed his eyes, shutting out the star on the wall. It was almost too easy. *Congratulations, Wulf, she trusts you. You are on the verge of achieving your ambition.* He would not think about the hollow feeling in his stomach. He curled his fingers into his palms.

'Wulf?'

'My lady?'

'It concerns me that Thane Guthlac still holds Ailric and Hereward. How likely is he to take his anger out on them?'

Very likely. 'I cannot say. But it was a choice of freeing either you or them, I could relieve only one of the guards. To have attempted more would have been to court failure. I am sorry I had to leave them behind.'

Clothing rustled. He sensed her turning towards him, and caught a whiff of sage from the soap he had lent her.

'Wulf, why did you do it? Why steal me from under Guthlac's nose?'

Wulf's stomach lurched. He opened his eyes and gazed blindly at the star. *Because I have the layout of Guthlac's hideout fixed in my head and I aim to discover the strength of your force. Because I am ambitious. I was not born to rank and position like you, ambition is all I have.* Yet even as that last thought came, he wondered if he were lying to himself.

A week ago Wulf had known exactly where he stood, he had known his place in the world. A week ago everything had been black and white; he had been led by his ambition. Simple. But since meeting Erica, no, *Lady*...hell. He could not fathom it, but she was Erica in his mind. And since meeting her, the ground was shifting under his feet, his priorities were no longer clear. Wulf was beginning to think the unthinkable— perhaps exceeding his orders in order to gain recognition was *not* what he should be doing.

God save him, of all the times to question his priorities, the very moment when preferment was within his grasp was exactly the wrong moment to start.

'Wulf? Did you get me out of there because you disapproved of the bloodfeud?'

'Something like that. Unnecessary bloodshed, endless fighting—it is nothing less than sinful.' That at least was the truth. Wulf did not hold with endless fighting whether it was between Saxon and Saxon, or Saxon and Norman. It impoverished everyone, whatever their rank in life. This was in part why he had attached himself to William De Warenne. His lord was one of the few Normans powerful and ruthless enough to bring peace to his portion of England. Ruthlessness did have its uses. 'Too much blood has been spilled.'

She squeezed his arm, the contact so unexpected that his heart jumped. 'You are a good man, Wulf Brader.'

The lantern shutter squeaked, the star dimmed, and Wulf stared unblinking and tight-jawed into the gloom. If she knew the truth…by her standards, he was about as far from good as it was possible to be. 'Go to sleep.' He had to clear his throat to continue. 'We take to the water at daybreak.'

The hand lifted from his arm.

Wulf lay listening to her movements, her sighs. He could count her every breath. She was not warm enough, he surmised, as she shuffled and fidgeted and pulled at the blankets.

At length, when the rhythm of her breathing told him she was asleep, he turned to face her. With the light turned low he could not see her clearly, but the warmth of her breath caressed his face, so she had not turned away. Heart pounding as it did before a fight, he reached for the lantern and teased open the shutter. Was that what this was then, a fight? And if so, who exactly was he fighting?

A star of light fell on her cheek. Another adorned her hair, her shoulder…

Her cloak had slipped. Gently, he pulled it up. Even here in the shelter, the cold was so sharp he could see his breath and hers, mingling together. She murmured in her sleep and Wulf snatched his hand back. But he continued, head pillowed on his arm, to watch her.

Lady Erica of Whitecliffe. Pure Saxon. A thane's daughter no less. Proud and aristocratic, but she *trusted* him, even knowing as she did of his illicit birth.

A shaft of longing shot through him. She was beautiful, no man could deny that, but it was not her beauty that attracted him most—no, it was her frank acceptance of his birth. It was something Wulf had never looked for in a lady with her blood-lines. He bit his lip. She might accept his humble background, she might even name him honourable because she thought him principled. But once she discovered his Norman allegiances…

He rested his fingers, just the tips, on the braid that was tumbling over her shoulder. Yes, it was soft—he had known it would be. So soft, shining in the lamplight and black as the night outside.

Inhaling, he drew the fragrance of sage soap deep into his lungs. It was mingled with another, more elusive scent which tugged at his senses. A hint of juniper. Of *her*. Again, he inhaled. And then, before he could check himself, he was inching nearer. Quietly, softly.

They were face to face. So close that Wulf could see the dark lashes lying on her cheeks; so close he could count the freckles on her nose; could plant the lightest of kisses—no! *No!* Erica of Whitecliffe was not for him, and never would be. He might consider himself responsible for her, but he must remember it was a temporary responsibility, it would soon be ended. Wulf could not become attached to anyone, not until he had succeeded in fulfilling his ambitions, and even then Lady Erica would remain as far above his touch as the stars that were hiding behind the clouds in the bleak East Anglian skies.

Wulf drew back, confused as to where his thoughts were leading him. She murmured in her sleep. And then she rolled and her limbs entangled with his, her head lolled onto his chest. His breath caught. He made a half-hearted attempt to ease away, but she gave a sleepy protest and pressed closer. They were both wound in their cloaks, but the full softness of her breasts was a forbidden joy, pressing into his side. The pleasure he felt was mingled with pain, and Wulf knew the first stirrings of a desire not only to have, but also to hold.

Her body drew his, irresistibly, as his seemed to draw hers. It sapped his will. Erica is seeking warmth, Wulf told himself. She is asleep and her body is drawn to mine for the warmth. He remembered that she had only recently broken a three-day fast, and it was a simple matter to convince himself that it would be cruel to awaken her and set her away from him.

And from there it was a small step, a very small step, to allowing himself to put his arm round her and draw her close. Better. Much better. A pain he had not known he had been carrying eased.

Turning his nose into her hair, he inhaled that tantalising scent. In this manner Wulf floated towards sleep, a small smile playing about his mouth while he ignored the message his head was giving him: *I am a Norman captain, she is sworn against me.*

In a shadowy corner of Wulf's mind, however, a less pleasant thought was biding its time. For the moment he was managing to ignore it, but soon that would be impossible. Erica of Whitecliffe would loathe him when she discovered his real purpose in the fens.

But this night at least, she thought him honourable— a true, loyal Saxon. So. For the moment he would make the most of her approval; he must simply ensure that, when she did discover the truth, he was long gone. Wulf did not want to see the hatred leap into her eyes when she realised that he was on a reconnaissance mission for William De Warenne, Lord of Lewes; he did not want to be around when she learned he was a Norman captain. But in the meantime…

Wulf stroked her hair; her ears were cold. He tugged up the hood of her cloak. In the meantime, he would do his best to keep her warm. A Saxon lady slept in his arms, a gently bred, beautiful woman. A week ago he would not have dreamed it possible. A sigh escaped him; they only had till dawn.

Chapter Nine

The birdcall roused him.

Daybreak. Erica had not moved from Wulf's embrace, but nestled against him fast asleep, her breathing even and unhurried. She felt warm and soft, the most womanly lady in the kingdom, the most comely. Wulf leaned his cheek against her hair and breathed in a complex tangle of scents: woodsmoke from the fire, the tang of sage and, beneath that juniper, the subtle, tantalising fragrance that belonged to her. Erica. Closing his eyes against a futile wave of longing, Wulf let his lips whisper over her cheek. It was beguilingly warm. He set his jaw and carefully turned his head away. A thane's daughter was not for a Norman captain.

The birdcall came again, deep and booming; it was getting nearer. A bittern? Wulf frowned, listening harder, yes, definitely a bittern. It was the signal he had been waiting for.

A greyish light was filtering around the leather door. Unfolding his cloak from about them, he lifted a beringed hand from where it had been resting on his chest and eased away, carefully placing her head on a folded section of blanket. She did not stir; she did not so much as murmur. It astounded him that she could sleep so unguardedly in his arms. She was far too trusting.

The bittern boomed again, closer yet. Wulf tore his gaze from the gentle curve of her cheek; he had better hurry. Lucien of Arques would be waiting to carry his report back to De Warenne's sergeant.

Creeping on his hands and knees to the entrance, praying she would not waken, Wulf pushed past the flap and headed for the fire-pit. The sky was clear, a perfect blue dome, and the sun remained low, hidden beneath the tree-line. It cast long thin shadows, like bars, across the frosty ground.

In the night the ice had taken over yet more of the waterway. If this cold spell lasted, in a couple of days' time, they would have to make skates to get about. Skating was rumoured to be a favoured method of transport in the fens during harsh winters. Before Wulf had come here he had dismissed the rumour as another fairy tale, but, having seen the watery nature of East Anglia for himself, he realised the idea might have merit.

At the fire-pit, there was ice in the bottom of the upturned cauldron and grey ash on the fire. There would be no hot water for Lady Erica that morning; the wood was damp and in daylight Wulf would not take the risk that the smoke might be seen. Their absence from the castle would certainly have been discovered and it was likely that Guthlac had men out searching for them.

He missed a step. Someone was sitting on a fallen tree trunk, but it was not Lucien; another lad sat there, hacking at a stick with his dagger. Wulf gripped his swordhilt. He recognised the boy from De Warenne's entourage, but he had had no dealings with him personally. Name of Gil, he thought. He dimly recalled him working in De Warenne's stables back in London. Gil had something of a reputation for playing tricks on his fellow grooms, which might explain why, at seventeen, he remained a stable-boy.

'Where's Lucien?' Wulf demanded, speaking in Norman French, for to his knowledge Gil could not speak English. His eyes quartered the perimeter of the clearing, ensuring no one else was about.

Gil got to his feet and stuck his dagger in his belt. 'Lucien is sick, Captain.'

'Sick?'

'Badly cured fish—he was puking his heart out all night.'

'I take it De Warenne's sergeant knows you came in his stead?'

The boy's eyes slid away. 'N...not exactly, sir. Lucien was afraid to tell him. "You go, Gil," Lucien said, "you must meet Captain FitzRobert in my place."' The boy shrugged. 'So here I am.'

'Your full name?'

'Blois, sir, Gilbert of Blois. I...I am sorry it is not whom you were expecting, but you may trust your message to me.'

'I hope so.' Wulf saw Gil's eyes flicker to his forehead, to the spot where Erica had near brained him with the chapel candlestick; he must have a bruise.

'You...you... Was there trouble, Captain?'

Ruefully, Wulf fingered his forehead; it was tender

and he could feel a small bump. 'Nothing to speak of. A minor encounter with a candlestick.'

'Captain?'

'Never mind.'

'Sir…' the boy stepped forwards, eyes shining '…you will trust me with your message, won't you?'

Recognising ambition in the eager eyes, Wulf knew a pang of fellow-feeling. 'On one condition…'

'Captain?'

'Next time be sure to tell Sergeant Bertram of the change of plan.'

'But he might not have let me come, and I want to—'

'Prove yourself? I know, lad, but you should still have told him, it should have been Bertram's decision, not yours.'

'I am sorry, Captain.' Unexpectedly the boy's eyes lit with a mischievous grin. 'Does De Warenne know you're with her?'

'Her?'

Gil jerked his head in the direction of the fisherman's hut. 'That woman. When I saw you with her, I thought I had best not disturb your slumber.'

Wulf frowned; the thought that the boy had looked in on him and Erica as they had lain sleeping was disconcerting.

'A native, is she?' Eyes gleaming, Gil set about using the whittled stick as a toothpick.

Yes, the boy's manner was clearly why he had been overlooked; it was also the reason why he would continue to be overlooked. Gilbert of Blois might be a hard worker, but his humour bordered on insolence. Yet Wulf's instincts told him that he was honest and might be replied upon.

'Is it true, Captain—' Gil tossed his toothpick aside '—that the women hereabouts have webbed feet?'

'Enough, Gilbert! That is a tale for young children, you should not be believing it.'

'I heard it from my lord Eugène of Médavy.'

It was Wulf's turn to grin. 'Quite so. As I said, a tale for children. Now, if you are prepared to be serious, I will give you my report, otherwise…'

The boy's face lost its smile. 'Captain FitzRobert, believe me, I am all attention. Sergeant Bertram is eager for your report.'

'I know it.' Briefly, Wulf described the rebels' hideout and its location. He made certain he pointed out the castle's most obvious weakness—that it was built entirely of wood. He described Guthlac, too, stressing that pride was his biggest flaw; he estimated the number of warriors Guthlac had at his disposal and, finally, he mentioned Erica's men, Ailric and Hereward, prisoners in Guthlac's lock-up.

'Prisoners, *Saxon* prisoners?' Gil's jaw dropped. 'The outlaw has imprisoned his own countrymen?'

'Aye.'

'How so?'

Thus it was that with a bitter taste in his mouth, Wulf found himself telling Gilbert of Blois about the blood-feud between Thane Guthlac Stigandson and Thane Eric of Whitecliffe.

Gil shook his head. 'It is most strange,' he said when Wulf had come to a close, 'to find Saxons at odds with one another like this.'

Wulf nodded; it *was* strange, to one unversed in Saxon ways. Even he, half-Saxon as he was, found it hard to comprehend. Tribal rivalries that flared up generation after generation—to a Norman they seemed primitive in the extreme.

'And that woman…' Gilbert nodded his head in the direction of the shelter '…she is involved?'

'She is Thane Eric's daughter.'

Gilbert's brow wrinkled. 'The heiress? And you rescued her? Then you and she—'

Wulf cut Gilbert off with a wave of his hand. 'It is not like that,' he heard himself say. 'Think, lad, her presence here means that Thane Guthlac is not the only Saxon figurehead taking refuge in the fens. Lady Erica has housecarls, too, men who once fought for her father. They come from near our lord's holdings in Lewes.' Wulf paused, aware of a reluctance to say more. Guilt ran its cold fingers down his spine. He felt as though he were committing some great betrayal, when in fact he was merely doing what he had set out to do when he had come to the fens—proving his loyalty to William De Warenne.

He had located Thane Guthlac and he intended to prove he was indispensable by locating Thane Eric's housecarls. He needed to explain that he wanted a couple more days to finish his investigation, but his tongue seemed to cleave to the roof of his mouth.

'The Lady Erica has more men—other than the ones held by Guthlac?'

Wulf forced the words past his teeth. 'I believe so. She is the reason I did not make the earlier meeting with Lucien.'

'He did wonder. When you didn't show up, Lucien thought you might have been killed, but Sergeant Bertram had faith in you. He told Lucien you knew what you were about and that you *would* make today's rendezvous.'

Wulf grunted. 'Lady Erica arrived at Guthlac's castle on the morning of the first meeting, so I had to make a quick change of plans.'

'And now?'

'I escort the lady back to her men so that I may assess their capabilities. Listen, Gil, this next part is most important. Tell Sergeant Bertram to get the archers to the butts as soon as possible. They are to practise zone-shooting in the Byzantine manner—he will know what I mean. In particular, they are to try for fifty and eighty yards. Ninety, if they can do it. They will need to practise until they can get the distance blindfold. And I mean that, blindfold.'

'Blindfold?'

'Yes. Oh, and they will be shooting fire-arrows, so make certain Bertram musters what is necessary. Now, repeat to me everything I have told you.'

Gil did so. 'Sergeant Bertram will be pleased with this report, Captain. Oh, and Lucien told me to be sure to tell you that De Warenne himself has arrived.'

Wulf's eyebrows rose. When Wulf had left Ely to join Guthlac, he had been aware that De Warenne had ordered the building of a temporary garrison there, and he knew that De Warenne wanted Guthlac dealt with, but he had received no hint that his lord would be joining them. 'De Warenne is in Ely?'

'He arrived yesterday with more infantrymen and archers—they are temporarily stationed at the garrison. Should you need to find it, the garrison is behind the tavern known as the Waterman.'

Thoughtfully, Wulf shook his head. 'I had not thought De Warenne himself would come farther north than London, but I am right glad he has brought more archers—we are going to need them.'

'The King has granted De Warenne lands in the north fens.'

That fitted, King William was no fool. A gift of lands to the north would ensure De Warenne's continuing interest in keeping the marshes clear of rebels. 'Do you return directly to Ely, Gil?'

'Aye.'

'Good. Since De Warenne has arrived, please tell Sergeant Bertram I will assess the strength of Lady Erica's force and report back to my lord directly. At the Ely garrison, you say?'

'Yes, Captain. The stockade has been thrown up at the top end of the high street.'

Wulf nodded his understanding. 'Be certain that either you or Lucien is waiting for me at the Waterman in, let us see, two days' time.'

'Yes, sir.'

'Where's your boat?'

Gilbert looked at a clump of willows. 'Other side of those bushes.' He turned to go. 'See you in two days' time then, Captain.'

Erica was crouching behind a log that was starry with hoarfrost, biting on her knuckles to prevent herself from crying out. She watched, dry-mouthed, as Wulf left the clearing with the Norman boy. She had not heard much, she had been too far away and her understanding of Norman French was poor, but she had heard enough.

Her mind was spinning. *FitzRobert? Wulf*

FitzRobert? FitzRobert was a Norman name! No. *No.* This was not happening. Not Wulf! Icy fingers clutched her heart, and she knew her ears had not deceived her. His name was Wulf FitzRobert, not Saewulf Brader as she had been told. Worse, had not that boy named him *Captain?*

Wulf had lied to her, he was Norman, a captain no less. She had awoken to find him nuzzling her cheek, but he was a Norman! Wulf was a spy, and it was most likely he had just told that boy—that *Norman* boy—how to find Guthlac's castle. Chewing on her knuckles, oblivious to the chill clawing at her knees, Erica drew a shaky breath. Wulf was not Guthlac's man then, but William's, King William's. A most unsettling feeling of loyalty towards Thane Guthlac rose within her.

Wulf's real name was FitzRobert—why was this so hard to stomach?—and he answered to a Norman lord, a man called De Warenne. The lord's name rang a bell, but Erica's thoughts were so disordered by what she had heard that she could not place it.

She stared after the warrior who, up until a few moments ago, she had been beginning to trust. Sweet Mother, more than that, she had been beginning to *like*. She had thought him noble to risk angering Guthlac when he spoke out to prevent her disparagement. And when he had dragged her from sanctuary and brought her here, she had thought he might have a liking for her that matched hers for him. She had thought—simpleton!—he had left Guthlac's castle earlier that afternoon to prepare the abandoned hut for her, for *her*. She had not minded when he had kissed her cheek this morning; worse, she had liked it, had been on the verge of a response when he had set her aside.

Erica swallowed; how wrong she had been. Clearly the hut was the base for his spying activities. He had dragged her from Guthlac's lair not for her own well-being, but for his own ends. She set her jaw. Wulf FitzRobert—*Captain* Wulf FitzRobert—was about to learn that he was not the only person capable of lying and cheating.

She glared at the willows behind which Wulf and the boy had vanished. He wanted to escort her to her people, did he? He wanted to learn their whereabouts, more like; he wanted to discover their strengths and weaknesses as he had discovered Guthlac's.

Her lips tightened. Betray her, would he? Well, Wulf FitzRobert, she thought grimly, I will take you back to my people, but your reception will not be exactly as you anticipate…

The sun was hauling itself over the tops of the trees even as she looked, but it was a pale winter sun that brought no warmth. Eyeing the icy margin at the water's edge, Erica shivered, and wondered how long it would be before the whole of East Anglia was one vast web of ice.

A rustling behind the willows alerted her to Wulf's return. Ducking down, she scrambled back to the hut. Her stomach churned. She must keep her wits about her; not by so much as the flicker of an eyelid would she reveal that she knew Wulf's game.

Affect ignorance, she told herself as she flung herself full length on the blanket and arranged her skirts so that it looked as though she had been sleeping. At the last moment she noticed the hem of her gown was dark with damp and her boots were caked with mud and melting ice. She twitched the blanket over them.

FitzRobert, not Brader. He had lied, Wulf had *lied*.

He was sworn to De Warenne. And then it hit her—
William de Warenne—of course! The name was familiar
because William de Warenne was the great Norman lord
who had been granted Lewes and the outlying lands
near her beloved Whitecliffe. The sea coast of Wessex
would never be the same again.

De Warenne was not a man to cross; rumour had it
that even fellow Normans named him ruthless. Erica's
temples throbbed. There was a time when both
her father and Guthlac had owed fealty to Harold
Godwineson for their holdings around Lewes, but in this
insane Norman re-working of the world, De Warenne
had become their overlord, De Warenne held lands that
had once been Earl Harold's.

Wulf crunched across frost-crisped grass.

Erica put a smile on her face. She would hide the
hatred in her heart, her anger at his lies. To think that
she had thought Guthlac perfidious, she had thought him
the one without honour. Set next to Captain Wulf
FitzRobert, her father's old enemy was a saint. Why,
Wulf FitzRobert wasn't even Saxon! Praying for
strength to deceive as she had been deceived, Erica
listened as his boots crushed the frozen grasses.

The flap lifted, daylight streamed in.

She yawned and made a show of sitting up, as he
hunkered down beside her. 'Why, Wulf!' she said,
keeping that smile pinned to her lips. 'Where have
you been?' Her lips felt stiff and the smile forced.
Could he tell?

'Readying the boat, my lady,' he said, and his returning smile made her heartbeat quicken, even though she
knew it was as lying as her own. 'We will leave as soon

as you are able. If this east wind persists, the waterways will not be passable for much longer.'

He had a dark bruise on his brow. How had that happened? It had not been visible last night, but then they had not had much light. Erica pursed her lips. She had a vague memory of flailing about with the candle-stick in the chapel. She would not mention it, his hurts were nothing to her, he was Norman. *And I am Saxon; there can never be anything but hatred between us.*

'My lady, we should be leaving soon.'

His English was perfect, spoken like a native, with no trace of an accent. There was no call to chastise herself for assuming him to be Saxon, but chastise herself she did. She forced another smile. *False, false, false,* her mind screamed, but her heart could not help but notice that he was looking at her mouth, and that for one brief moment he leaned towards her as though, as though...

Mouth dry, she edged back and hastily reached for the tie on her plait. 'Very well, but first, please tell me where you put your comb, I need to borrow it again.'

As Wulf passed her his comb, she made certain her fingers did not touch his. And that was not because she was afraid his touch would make her heart beat fast— no, it was not, it was because she had no wish to touch anyone to whom deceit came so easily.

'My thanks,' she murmured, even as she sent him another counterfeit smile.

You wait, Captain Wulf FitzRobert, when my men get hold of you, you will rue the day you set foot in the fens.

A wave of nausea swept over her, similar to the nausea she had felt at the castle each time Hrothgar had come close. It might be hunger, the result of three days' fasting in the chapel, it might be hate. Yes, the sooner they left this place, the sooner Erica could eat again and the sooner she could get away from Wulf FitzRobert. She was certain to feel better then.

The fens slid past the boat. Bulrushes made a spiky fringe along the edge of the land, like so many spears sticking up through the freezing water. The January sun hung low in the sky. The cold had deepened, and the wind sliced through both the fabric of Erica's cloak and the wool of the blanket that Wulf had given her. She held the edges tightly together and watched some alders slip by. Her stomach was hollow, the feeling of nausea remained.

From time to time, she watched him, covertly, through her lashes. He had discarded his cloak the better to row and his big, warrior's body seemed larger than ever. Strong. Unstoppable. Once or twice she caught his gaze on her. She surmised that her silence puzzled him, which was why, every now and then, she sent him a smile. She longed for this journey to be over. Though he deserved it, she hated having to deceive him, even in a matter as small as a smile.

Ahead, the water divided into two channels. It was a relief to recognise that they were almost at the cottage. 'Take the waterway on the left,' she said.

Nodding, Wulf gripped the oars. He rowed with regular, even strokes and his breath smoked the air between them, but he was not the least bit winded, he inhaled and exhaled steadily, timing each breath to match the dip and pull of the oars. Big though he was, he was not a man to waste his energy; every moment was economical and precise. He was a born warrior, comfortable in that strong body, and it would appear that he had honed it to perfection, had mastered it so it responded instantly to his every command. And, large though he might be—Erica sent him another quick look under her lashes—there was not an ounce of spare flesh to be seen.

'It is not far.' Erica hoped he could not hear the hollowness that had got into her voice. She chewed the inside of her cheek. She did not like what she was about to do, but could see no other way out.

'There!' She pointed and smiled what she hoped was a delighted smile. 'See that cottage, coming into sight around that curve?'

Wulf glanced over one broad shoulder, twisting at the waist. Really, he had a very narrow waist for so tall a man. His sword belt was plain like the rest of his dress, with a simple brass buckle that glinted in the feeble sunlight. His brown tunic was unadorned by even one stitch of embroidery that Erica could see; his undershirt seemed to be of a coarse cream linen. And as for his lack of arm-rings—her breath caught. Of course! It had struck her as odd that a man as strong as Wulf should have won no prizes from his lord, but since Wulf was not Saewulf Brader, but Captain Wulf FitzRobert, everything became clear. It was not the Norman way for a lord to reward his captain with golden arm-rings, Normans gave their men honours or land.

Briefly, Erica studied her finger-rings. Garnets and sapphires winked up at her. She turned the bracelets on her wrist—they were in fact her father's arm-rings, at least some of those that had not been lost at Hastings. The others she could not wear, they were too large, and after William the Bastard had seized King Harold's crown, Erica had been fearful of losing them. Siward had buried them in a box beneath the floor at Whitecliffe Hall. Were they still there? Or had that lord—*his* lord— she fought to keep the scowl off her face—had De Warenne found them?

The boat lurched and scraped on some stones in the shallows; they had reached the jetty by the cottage. Already.

Dry-mouthed and silent, she watched Wulf ship the oars and tie up with that swift efficiency of his. He sent her a smile. Was it her imagination or was there a slight tension about his mouth and his eyes? He vaulted lightly onto the jetty and offered her a hand to help her out.

One, two, Erica found herself counting. *It is my turn to play the wolf.* Her insides writhed. Smiling, she gripped his hand—warm, his fingers were so warm compared to hers—and stepped onto the jetty. Releasing him, she turned away and walked casually towards the cottage.

Three, four…it is the month of the wolves.

No one was in sight, no smoke curled through the thatch, no pigs rooted in the marsh, no hens scratched. The place looked abandoned.

Five, six…when push comes to shove we are all wolves…

He was behind her, walking close, taking long, easy strides. Confident. His hand would be resting on the hilt of his sword. He would be looking about him, and those bright blue eyes would be taking everything in, those spy's eyes…

There was still not a soul to be seen. Above the low-lying land, a straggle of geese flew in a perfect chevron across the blue sky. The cottage door was swinging on its hinges. Silence. There was not a breath to be heard, not a whisper. Throwing him one last smile—yes, that hand was at his swordhilt—Erica lifted her skirts and stepped over the threshold.

A shadow moved. Morcar. They were expected. *Good. Seven, eight…*

Another shadow shifted. Siward. Her men must have set a look-out somewhere on the waterway.

And then, as Wulf stepped over the threshold after her, another, smaller shadow—Cadfael—leaped for the door and slammed it shut.

Erica stopped counting and found her tongue. 'Take him!'

Morcar and Siward might have seen many winters, but they could still move.

Steel hissed as Wulf made to draw his sword.

No room. The thought flashed in on her, swift as lightning. *He has no room to fight.* And before another thought had time to form, she had stepped up to him and put her hand on his so that he could not finish drawing his sword.

For a moment, a breathless, burning moment, his large warrior's body was pressed to hers, chest to thigh. 'Lady, you hamper me,' he said, tightly, even as the shadowy shape that was Siward lifted a clay jug and brought it down with a crack on the back of his head.

Wulf crumpled at her feet amid a shower of pottery shards.

Chapter Ten

'I know,' Erica whispered, closing her eyes against the sight of that long body motionless at her feet. 'I know.' Sick to her core, she turned away.

'My lady!' Solveig flew out of the gloom at the back of the cottage, blond hair flying. 'Where have you been? We feared Thane Guthlac had killed you!'

'I am well, Solveig.'

'And Ailric and Hereward? Where are they? Did Guthlac…?'

'No, no, they are alive.' Erica drew in a steadying breath. 'But we had to leave them behind.'

Osred, another of her father's housecarls, stirred. 'Leave them behind? But…my lady…!'

Erica glanced down at her hands—they were trembling. Feeling oddly detached, she curled her nails into her palms. 'There is much to tell.'

Morcar coughed and nudged Wulf with his boot. 'Perhaps you might begin by telling us who this is? Is he one of Guthlac's?' He began kicking the broken pottery towards the wall.

Torn, Erica hesitated, but in her heart she knew she could not put off this moment. Slowly she shook her head. Snakes were writhing in her belly, snakes that made the bile rise in her throat. 'Not Guthlac's, but William De Warenne's. He's one of his captains.'

Morcar's eyes bulged. 'A *Norman*? Saint Michael save us. How come you are accompanied by a Norman, my lady?'

On the floor, Wulf stirred and his eyelids fluttered.

'Later, Morcar, later.' She waved her hand. 'For pity's sake, remove him, I can bear the sight of him no longer.'

Grunting, Morcar bent to grip Wulf under his armpits. Siward took his feet. With a heave they hoisted him to the doorway. Pausing on the threshold, Morcar lifted a grey-streaked brow. 'An execution, my lady?'

'*No!*' A wave of faintness swept over her.

Morcar's eyebrow twitched. 'But we may question him?'

'What?' The room tilted, and everything seemed a long way off, a *very* long way off. 'Question him?' Even her voice sounded distant. 'Yes, of course you may question him, but you are *not* to kill him.'

Siward muttered into his beard, a phrase which she would swear contained the words 'little accident'.

The cottage seemed to be swaying from side to side, Erica shook her head to clear it and put steel in her voice. 'No, Siward, there are to be no "little accidents". If it were not for this man, I would yet be in Guthlac's power. You are *not* to kill him.'

Wulf groaned. Morcar and Siward heaved and grunted and then, thankfully, that well-honed warrior's body was no longer in her sight. The door banged.

Solveig opened a shutter to let in the light and turned to look at her. She took her firmly by the hand. 'Come, my lady, you need to eat and rest, you are chalk white.'

Stumbling, sick to her stomach, Erica surrendered herself into the care of her maidservant and did her best to put thoughts of lying Norman bastards—even finely made ones with thick-lashed blue eyes—right out of her mind.

Wulf sat on earth that the frost had rendered hard as iron, with his legs stretched out in front of him. He had moved beyond pain, otherwise his arms would be killing him for they had been pulled to the point of dislocation before being dragged into the small of his back and bound.

Stripped to the waist, Wulf was tied to an ash tree and the rough bark was gouging holes in his shoulders and arms. He would be cold if he were not in that place beyond pain, for he had been kept under restraint by the tree for so long that his buttocks had lost all feeling. And that had to be a good thing, for when they had brought him out here it had been cold enough to freeze the marrow in his bones.

Lucky for him, then, that he was numb from head to toe. For a while there, while they had been beating him, he thought he might have lost consciousness. With difficulty, he focused on his toes, which were bare since one of her ageing housecarls had taken his boots. Blue toes. Blue from cold or blue from bruising? It was hard to tell much of anything, but in the fading light Wulf thought they looked like bruises. One side of his chest bore the clear imprint of Morcar's boot, the other Siward's. His cheek throbbed, as did his jaw; he was lucky not to have lost any teeth.

Lucky? Wulf shivered and frowned; the cold was getting to him again and his back felt twisted. Maybe he was coming round properly. Wulf didn't want that; he didn't want to feel the cold, the bruises…

Perhaps if he could sleep a while, he could forget the look on her face when she had ordered them to take him. Perhaps he could forget the pain, and the unremitting cold. Merciless it was, like her.

Closing his eyes, Wulf tried to cut out all consciousness of the wind. An east wind with the keenest of edges. Was this how it was to end, on the edge of a marsh in one of the most inhospitable parts of England? So much for his ambition. So much, Wulf thought bitterly, for compassion. For that was what had brought him here, compassion for a brave woman he had not liked to leave in Guthlac's care.

'I can bear the sight of him no longer.'

He took a deep breath and his ribs shrieked a protest. No, be honest, it was not simply compassion that had brought him to this pass, ambition, too, had played its part. He had discharged his duty as far as De Warenne was concerned; he had discovered where Guthlac was based; he had discovered his strength. For most men, Wulf acknowledged ruefully, that would be enough. He had fulfilled his commission and done it well.

But, no, he had to try and go one better. He had wanted to impress the new Lord of Lewes with his initiative. Hence the need to escort Lady Erica back here so he could acquaint himself with the size of her force.

Compassion, ambition and pride then, Wulf thought wearily, trying to blank out a renewed throbbing in his jaw and the pain in his ribs. He was covered in goose-bumps, and his lungs ached with every breath.

He glanced towards the cottage, but there was no sign of her. There was no sign of anyone save the boy, Cadfael, who they had left on guard.

'I am thirsty,' he said, voice a croak.

Cadfael hardly looked his way. 'No water, Siward said, no water, nothing.'

Wulf sighed and flinched. His ribs were practically creaking. A moorhen paddling about in the reeds at the edge of the fen seemed to fade as he tried, unsuccessfully, to look at it. 'No matter,' he said, with a grim attempt at humour. 'It would only be a waste, since I am like to be dead by morning.'

The boy squinted doubtfully at him through the last of the light. And then everything went dark.

'Night is upon us.' Erica glanced across the trestle at Solveig where they were preparing wild duck for the spit. There was barely enough meat, but she and Solveig had been doing their best to bulk out the meal. It was not work that a lady would usually undertake, but ladies who were outlaws soon learned to put their hands to most things. They had stuffed the birds with a mixture of oatmeal, onions and dried herbs, and had just finished trussing them. Erica set aside her skewer. 'I think it will be safe to light the fire if we keep the door closed.'

Nodding, Solveig rose and went to the hearth. Digging into the purse which hung from her girdle, she drew out her flint to strike a light. Like most women, Erica included, Solveig kept the means to make a fire upon her person. It was only sensible at the best of times, and here, out in the wilds, it was a necessity.

'Solveig, did we use the last of the honey?'

'No, my lady, there is a spoonful or two left.'

'Good, we'll use it to make a dressing for these birds.'

The men were out on the marshland somewhere, occupying themselves with tasks that Morcar had little hesitation in informing her were ill suited for housecarls: tasks such as netting more fowl, and fishing. Tasks that were, Erica thought, as she eased the last of the wildfowl onto the spit, nevertheless vital if their diminished household was to thrive. If ladies could cook, housecarls could certainly learn to fish.

She wondered how her other men were faring, the more able-bodied of the warriors who had gone deeper into the fens. Almost a hundred of them were awaiting her command either to emerge and join Guthlac, or to form a rebel alliance of their own. Would they be eating roast duck tonight? She liked to think so; they were survivors. As were they all, she hoped.

The door swung open and Cadfael hurtled into the room.

Solveig dropped the reed seed-head she was using as kindling. 'Cadfael, for pity's sake, were you born in a barn? Can't you see I am trying to get the fire going?'

'Sorry, Solveig.'

The door slammed. Cadfael approached the trestle. 'My lady?'

'Yes?'

'The Norman says he is thirsty.'

Erica set the spit down on a wooden platter. She had been trying not to think about Captain Wulf FitzRobert; the man evoked feelings that were too tangled to unravel. She was grateful that he had saved her from Hrothgar; she was grateful he had got her out of

Guthlac's clutches, but his motives for doing so had been far from pure.

Wulf must have freed her in order that she should lead him to her people; the entire time he had been planning to betray her. She misliked the thought and the fact that she had been coming to trust him only compounded matters. *A Norman*, she reminded herself, *a Norman*. What was she to do with him?

'Give him water, then,' she said. 'The jug is over there.'

Cadfael hesitated. 'Siward said not to give him anything, but the prisoner, he…he…'

'Yes?'

'He doesn't look too good. I would not have disturbed you, my lady, but he said he would probably not see the dawn. And I remember you telling Morcar and Siward he was not to be killed.'

Erica's heart sank, but she was puzzled. How long had it been since Wulf had drunk anything—since they had broken their fast at the fisherman's hut that morning? Certainly, he would be thirsty, and she could clearly recall how unpleasant that had been. But surely a sturdy warrior like Wulf could not be in so bad a state, not after a few hours? 'You think I should see him?'

'If you would.'

With a sigh, Erica rinsed her hands in the water bowl. 'Solveig, you will finish here?'

'Of course.'

Snatching her cloak and a wrap from the peg, Erica followed Cadfael outside, carefully shutting the door so Solveig could work on the fire.

Her feet crunched over grass bleached white with frost. The sky was darkening, save for an amber glow above the tree-line, which had a few stringy clouds straggling across it. The clouds turned even as Erica looked to violet and purple. The air was so cold her teeth ached, her nose tingled. She secured the cloak firmly at her neck and swathed her head with her hood and the wrap. Where was he?

There. She almost tripped. *Half-naked?* And, Lord, they had tied him to a tree.

Keeping her skirts clear of the frost, she hurried over. Wulf's head flopped to one side; he looked to be asleep. Sweet Heaven, several more bruises had appeared on his face, his lip was split and blood was streaked down his chin, dried blood. He was filthy and his arms—why, the tightness of his bonds must be cutting off his blood-flow…

'Wulf!' Falling to her knees at his side, she turned his face to hers, wincing as the last rays of the sun revealed the extent of his bruising. Those long eyelashes did not move. 'Wulf?' And his chest, even as the healer in her took note of the mottled marks—a boot—and there, another—even as she was wondering whether his ribs had been cracked, the woman in her could not help but notice his perfect male shape. Beautifully muscled arms, if they were not tied so awkwardly, that broad chest, sprinkled with dark hair, that flat stomach…his feet…*naked* feet? Holy Mary, even his feet were filthy and bruised beneath the mud and the scratches…

'Wulf?' He had yet to respond. Biting her lip, Erica gave his shoulder a careful shake. *'Wulf?'* His flesh was chill to the touch. Unfastening her wrap and cloak, she flung them over him. How long had he been left like this? Blue, the man was blue with cold, and the lack of response meant that he was unconscious, not sleeping.

A movement by the jetty caught her attention; Morcar and Siward were returning from the fens. Setting her teeth, she rocked back on her heels and gestured them over. 'Which of you did this?'

Two sets of eyes, both confused, peered at her through the twilight.

'Did what?' Morcar tossed a brace of fish onto the grass and put his hands on his hips.

'This.' Flicking back the cloak, Erica indicated the marks on Wulf's ribs, the dried blood on his chin.

'My lady?'

Pushing to her feet, she drew herself to her full height and looked Morcar in the eyes. 'You both did it.' Her voice rose. 'I told you not to hurt him!'

Morcar and Siward exchanged glances. Siward stirred first. '*Kill* him, my lady, you told us not to *kill* him.' He spread his hands. 'We have not killed him.'

'Would you have us coddle him, my lady? A Norman captain?'

'No, of course not, but—'

Morcar shrugged. 'You did say we might question him and that is what we have done.'

'You questioned him.'

'Yes, my lady.'

Erica clenched her fists; this was her fault. If she had not been at her wit's end when Wulf had brought her back to the cottage, she would have been more precise in her instructions. Wulf lay at the base of the tree, still as death. She should have thought—of course Morcar and Siward would be…vigorous…in their questioning. If Wulf refused to answer them, as he was bound to, being an honourable man—doubtless Wulf had sworn an oath to his lord in much the same way as a housecarl would bind himself to his thane. And if Wulf refused to answer them, they would resort to force.

'It is war,' she muttered. 'Bloody war. How I wish that it was ended.' Turning back to Wulf, she dropped back on her knees and lightly touched a bruised cheek.

'Yes, this is war.' Siward's hand was at her elbow, urging her up. 'And you should not be seeing this. Go back to the house, my lady.'

Erica jerked her arm free and refused to move. She was unable to prevent the scorn from colouring her voice. 'Not women's business, Siward?'

'Quite so, my lady.'

Erica glared. Siward and Morcar were her father's most loyal housecarls and for herself, she had never known a sharp word from either of them. Yet now…with their handiwork lying bloodied and broken at her feet…a memory stirred. In her mind she heard Thane Guthlac dismissing his wife, Lady Hilda, along with her ladies prior to making his announcement concerning her disparagement. Then, too, the women had been sent away.

War, she thought, bloodfeuds, they make monsters of us all: of the men for dismissing us, and of the women for allowing themselves to be dismissed. Erica frowned. She did not know how, but she would put a stop to this. It had to be wrong when good men, men like Morcar and Siward, were driven to beating an unarmed man— one who was—she shot Wulf another glance—trussed up as tightly as the wildfowl that she and Solveig had been preparing for their supper. God help us, she thought, there must be some way to stop this destruction of good men from continuing, there *must* be…

'No, Siward,' she said, pleased to hear the strength in her tone. 'I will not be dismissed.'

'But, my lady—'

'Enough!' She laid a careful palm on Wulf's chest. 'This man did save me from Guthlac.'

Morcar made an exasperated noise. 'That man—' his voice was dry as dust '—is a Norman captain. He would see us hang sooner than save us.'

Erica swallowed. It was true, Wulf was Norman. He had lied to her, he had pretended to have frequented Godwineson's hall in Southwark, and she did question his motives in bringing her back to her camp, but... She glanced at the bruised cheek, at the dark lashes that shielded those blue eyes. 'This I know, but there is no tampering with the fact that Guthlac would have had Hrothgar *rape* me, and this man prevented it—at some personal risk, given his true allegiances. It cannot have been easy for him among Guthlac's men—'

'You excuse him?'

'No, Morcar, I do not. But he did get me away from there.'

'My lady, the man is sent to spy on us!'

Erica clenched her fists and rose. 'He saved me from rape. In any case, you have disarmed him, he does not look to be much of a threat. Where is his tunic, and what of his cloak and boots?'

'Gave them to Hrolf.'

'Hrolf will have to give them back.' Erica looked pointedly at Wulf. 'Loose him.'

'My lady?'

'So help me, Morcar, you will untie this man from that

tree and bring him inside. And listen carefully—make sure you do not harm so much as another hair on his head.'

'I mislike this, my lady.'

It was a man's voice, Wulf decided, keeping his eyes shut, feigning unconsciousness. The voice sounded like Morcar, one of the brutes who had done his best to stove in his ribs with his boot. The one with the cough.

Wulf had recovered his senses some minutes ago, while rough hands had been heaving him into the warmth, depositing him by a fire. He had to have been carried inside the cottage; the flames were toasting him along his right-hand side. He could smell smoke and hear the crackle and spit of a fire largely made up with damp willow.

The rough hands left him and were replaced by other, softer hands that felt for the pulse on his wrist before sliding away to linger for a moment on his fingers. Realising it might be politic to continue feigning unconsciousness, Wulf kept his eyes closed. The gentle hands bared his chest and he heard the jingle of bracelets.

Lady Erica. Regret and longing shivered through him. He ignored them, as he had taught himself to do, long ago; there was no place for either here.

The faint tang of sage lingered in the air, of juniper. Yes, he was certain it was she. He heard water—a cloth being wrung out? Yes. He almost winced, but managed to control himself as a damp cloth feathered over his face. She was washing him.

Washing him? The bracelets clinked. Careful fingers probed his biceps; his shoulders; his chest. They hit a particularly tender spot and he sucked in a breath.

'I think he wakes.'

Yes, it was Erica. Not moving a muscle, Wulf allowed her to turn his face to one side, presumably to take stock of his hurts. Light fingers feathered across his cheekbone, and again, more painful than the bruises, longing twisted his insides. So gentle, she handled him so gently. Wulf could not remember the last time someone had… He caught himself, mid-thought. *Merde*, this would not do…

Someone, a man, cleared his throat. 'My lady, you must let me bind him again, he might do you an injury.'

He heard a soft sigh and the fingers lifted from his cheekbone. More water was being wrung out. Wulf caught the pungent smell of other herbs—a medicinal salve? And, behind that smell was another, one which brought saliva rushing into his mouth. Roast meat. Onions. Fresh bread. Lord. He fought the urge to swallow.

The careful fingers took his chin and a delicate stroking began. The medicinal smell intensified—she must be applying salve to his bruises. On its heels came the tempting aroma of roast duck. Wulf swallowed convulsively, it was that or choke on his saliva; he must be hungrier than he had thought.

'My lady?' It was the housecarl Morcar; his voice was closer than before and his tone was decidedly impatient.

'Hmm?'

'The Norman must be bound.'

'What?' Those careful fingers stroked over his cheekbones, fluttered over his mouth. Wulf repressed the ridiculous urge to kiss them, and held himself still.

'My lady, he must be bound.'

'Oh.' A sigh. 'Yes, Morcar, that is probably wise. But not so cruelly as before.'

And then the ungentle hands were back, taking his feet and arms and in moments ropes were gnawing his ankles, his wrists.

The gentle hands withdrew. Something warm—his cloak?—was draped over him. 'He sleeps,' Erica said, and a rustling of skirts told Wulf that she was getting up. He sensed her looking down at him.

'For the moment.' Siward's harsh voice cut in. 'Come, my lady, you must eat. You may as well enjoy what little there is while it is hot.'

'We shall have to move on again.' Her voice faded as she moved away. A bench scraped the floor; Wulf heard the clatter of knives and the thump of a serving dish as it landed on the trestle. 'I do not know exactly what he told his compatriot, but he may have told him about our band.'

So that was it, that was why she had thrown him to her men—Wulf had suspected something of the kind. He had had plenty of time to wonder, when they had been putting the boot in. Erica must have overheard him talking to Gil.

How much had she heard?

'We cannot remain here,' she was saying.

'Exactly my thoughts,' Morcar agreed. 'Ale, my lady?'

'Please. We leave in the morning.'

'And where do we go?'

Again Wulf felt the weight of her gaze upon him. 'We go where they least expect us.'

'Where's that?'

'Ely.'

'But the Normans are building a garrison at Ely!'

'Exactly.'

Someone, Morcar at a guess, laughed. 'Hiding in plain sight, eh? Yes, I like it.'

Conversation halted. There came the sounds of knives scraping platters and of ale being poured, of the pop and crackle of the fire. The smell of the duck was so good it had Wulf's stomach growling.

'What about our friend over there?'

'He comes with us,' she murmured.

'That's baggage I'd rather not take along, my lady, especially if Normans are trying to establish a base at Ely. He'll betray us if he can. Best finish him off here.'

A thud, as of a clay goblet being thumped down on the trestle. 'No, Siward, think!' Her voice was sharp. 'The Norman is our prisoner and as such he will be our surety, our guarantee of safety.'

The Norman. Well, that's what he was, half of him, at any rate. But Wulf did not have to like the way she said it. When he had got her out of Guthlac's clutches, he had begun to feel responsible for her and an unpalatable thought had gripped him. What if he had saved her from Hrothgar only to find she was destined for the same treatment elsewhere? He had caught himself wondering how to ensure that she never fell into uncaring hands. However, since she had placed him under guard, such worries had become irrelevant. The harshness in her tone was nothing to him, nothing.

Wulf continued to affect unconsciousness until the talk had moved on to practical matters. Then, when the girl Solveig was asking Erica whether they would be taking their cooking pots with them, he decided the time had come for him to waken.

He groaned and slowly opened his eyes, and the soldier in him peered past the fire, assessing the company in a moment. Erica of Whitecliffe's people.

There were not many, a dozen all told, huddled round the trestle. A couple of tallow candles lit the faces of a few tired old men, well past fighting age. Three young boys. Erica and the girl had their backs to the fire; neither was wearing a veil. Wulf could not see that any of them represented much of a threat to the Norman state.

She *must* have other men…housecarls who would respond if she made the call to arms. Wulf was becoming more certain by the hour that this was indeed the case. He was also beginning to question whether he had it in him to tell his lord about Lady Erica and her supporters. Time was when he would not have hesitated, but… Wulf clenched his jaw.

His duty was clear, but he did not want her harmed.

Neither she nor her people had heard him, so Wulf groaned again, more loudly. This time, Erica's head swung round and at once she left the trestle, skirts sweeping the beaten dirt floor. She had changed her gown for a blue one, which was much more serviceable than the one she had worn when attempting to treat with Guthlac. She had also removed most of her jewellery, but a bracelet or two caught the light as she came towards him. She still moved like a queen.

Drawing up a stool, she sat by him, a dark, glossy plait hanging over her shoulder. Her eyes glowed in the firelight. 'So, *Saewulf Brader*, you are awake.' Her voice was hard and she had no smile for him either. *Fool—how could she have, when she suspects you of betraying her?* 'Are you hungry?'

'My lady, you'll not give that swine our food?' Siward said.

She silenced Siward with a raised brow and turned back to Wulf. 'Hungry?'

Wulf cleared his throat. 'Thirsty, mostly.'

Erica gestured at the girl. 'Some ale, if you please, Solveig. And bring that platter of meat I had set aside.'

Green eyes watched as the girl set a cup to his lips and tipped ale into his mouth. She said nothing. What was there to say? And then Erica took the platter and the girl returned to her place at the table.

Wulf let Erica feed him, tearing pieces of duck from the bone and putting them between his lips with her fingers, babying him because he was bound. The meat was honey-sweet and fragrant with herbs. Like her, he said nothing, simply chewed and swallowed in silence while beside them the fire hissed and spat.

When he had finished, he nodded his thanks and let her drop a blanket over his cloak. Still he held his tongue.

He lay by the fire and watched as her household settled themselves for sleep. Erica was sharing a pallet with her maid. Wulf did not want to remember the night just past, when he had been free and she had slept trustfully in his arms. Instead, he set himself to wondering where Morcar had put his sword and how he might get it back.

Chapter Eleven

They had several rowing boats. After they had broken their fast, the entire household abandoned the cottage and used them to reach Ely—Eel Island.

Wulf's hands were still firmly bound behind him, and his companion in the boat, a spindle of a man named Osred, yanked Wulf's hood up so high he could hardly see out. In truth, this was a mercy that Wulf had not looked for because the hood kept the wind off his ears, though Wulf doubted that Osred had been motivated by compassion. The man wanted Wulf's face concealed, lest a Norman sympathiser recognise him.

Wulf took his place in a wintry dazzle of sun, thankful for the fur-lining to his cloak, for the cold went bone deep. Facing forwards as he was, and under Osred's gimlet eyes, Wulf had little chance to observe Lady Erica who, in a blue veil and cloak, occupied one of the boats behind them with her maid, Solveig.

Hrolf, the man with a limp who had initially taken his belongings, had been sent down a different channel. Why? Was Hrolf being dispatched with messages to other men? To the housecarls who Wulf suspected were awaiting the call to arms? Wulf twisted his head, keen to observe the man's direction. West—Hrolf was travelling west along a rapidly freezing waterway. Damn, there were no obvious landmarks, just a pair of swans and the usual border of leafless shrubs decorating the banks.

Hrolf had—with marked reluctance—returned Wulf's boots and most of his clothing, but the air was sharp and, despite his cloak, Wulf was hard pressed not to shiver. He had not had sight of his gloves, his money pouch or, more importantly, his sword. As Osred strained at the oars, it occurred to Wulf they would have done better to have given them to him. The exercise would have worked off some of the stiffness caused by his beating; it would have heated his blood. Osred was making heavy weather of it.

As was his habit, Wulf continued to take note of his surroundings, peering surreptitiously under the edge of his hood. The sky was bright and clear. To the west, in the direction Hrolf had taken, a hawk was hovering over a clump of alder whose branches were fat with frost, while, to the north, ahead, a larger island loomed. It was low-lying and flat like most of the islands in these marshes. Directly above it, the blue sky was scarred with trailing charcoal lines—the smoke from countless fires.

Ely.

Wulf's heart lifted. Would he catch sight of Gil or Lucien? It was possible. Osred's attention might waver for a moment and…he might be able to get a message to De Warenne. Flexing fingers that were so cold they had become thumbs, Wulf strained at his bonds, but they held fast as they had known they would. The housecarl

Morcar knew how to restrain a man. What Wulf needed was an implement of some kind, something sharp…

They approached the landing stages with their breath making clouds in the clear air and Wulf eyeing the oak palisade that marched around the island. It had been re-inforced in the past few days, the fresh stakes showed up paler than the old. Because land on the Isle of Ely was scarce, the docks were located *outside* the palisade and the jetties radiated out into the fen like the spokes of a wheel jutting out from the hub.

Today there was much traffic: a flotilla of rowing boats and coracles, a couple of ancient dugouts, as well as some larger vessels, the clinker-built dragon ships of the Northmen. These had curved prows in the shape of swans' necks and sea snakes. Their sails were furled. There was a sense of bustle, of urgency even, as though the people rushing to and fro along the jetties sensed that the water-ways were about to freeze, and that this might be the last time for some days that the ways would be navigable.

By the town gates, a brace of Norman guards, mail-coats a-gleam, were stationed at the head of the docks. Leaf-shaped shields were propped against the palisade; conical steel helmets bounced the sun back at him.

Seeing the direction of his gaze, Osred's eyes narrowed. Wulf caught a gut-tightening flash of steel as Osred jerked his shortsword. 'One word from you, and this will meet your liver.'

Wulf nodded his understanding.

As their boat gained the jetty, Osred flung a rope over a bollard and tied up. He gestured at Wulf to get out. With the boat lurching and with his hands fast behind him, Wulf struggled to keep his balance. Carefully, he hauled himself ashore, yesterday's bruises protesting at every move. Naturally, since his hands were concealed by his cloak, it was odds on that neither the people on the quays nor the guards at the gates would be aware that he was under restraint.

Erica's boat was next at the jetty. A blue veil fluttered, but he heard no jingle of bracelets. She had put off her queenly finery for this foray into Norman territory. And, naturally, she was not using her father's standard either; the white pennon with the blue sky and green sea was, in any case, lying at the bottom of her other boat, the one that had been left behind at Guthlac's stronghold.

Gaining the palisade, their party passed through the water gate and onto the cobbled market square. Several stalls were up, despite the cold. Fish, cured meat, leather, cheese, a metalworker....

Something sharp, that was what he needed.

Wulf's pulse quickened and he was eyeing a particularly fine dagger—*what the hell had they done with his sword?*—when a prick in the ribs brought his gaze back to Osred.

'No tricks, mind,' Osred said, urging him across the cobbles towards the high street.

Morcar and Lady Erica were following them, but the others were apparently remaining in the square. Siward, Cadfael and Solveig were huddled with the rest of her household by the wall of one of the abbey buildings. They must have agreed to meet up later, when Erica's business was concluded.

Osred's forehead was wrinkled with worry lines. 'My lady?'

'Mmm?' She was chewing on her lower lip, her eyes preoccupied. What was she about?

Something sharp, he must find something sharp.

'Are you sure you want *him*—' Osred gestured with his shortsword and Wulf received another sting in the ribs '—to come along?'

'He stays where I can see him.'

'He might signal to his friends.'

'Nevertheless, Osred, he comes with us. Make sure his hood stays up.'

Osred gave a grudging nod and twitched at Wulf's hood, obscuring almost all of Wulf's vision.

With the market square at their backs and the wooden abbey on their left, a narrow street lay ahead, running up a slight incline. Wulf knew where he was. According to Gil, the Norman garrison lay on the high ground at the top end of Ely's high street, and the tavern that Gil had spoken of, the Waterman, stood facing them at the junction. As they approached it, Wulf dragged his steps.

Out of the corner of his eye, Wulf saw smoke rising through the tavern's roof vents, an open door, the fireglow within. People were moving about inside. He heard laughter, he even heard a snatch of Norman French, but he was careful to keep his expression neutral as though he had heard nothing. He managed another sidelong glance, in the hope of seeing Gil or Lucien, but he could only make out dark shapes, shadowy figures silhouetted against the fire.

And then he noticed it, a square-edged nail protruding from one of the shutters. It was exactly what he needed. His heart thudded.

Another jab in his side. This, also, was exactly what

he needed. Letting out a yelp as though Osred had blooded him, Wulf stumbled, contriving to fall against the shutter. Desperately he scrabbled behind him to get his cloak out of the way. His wrist hit the nail. Sharp, smith-hammered edges dug into his skin. Good. *Exactly* what he needed. He gave a violent jerk with his arms so the rough edge of the nail would saw into the rope. Focusing all his strength into this small movement, he repeated the gesture. And again. He had loosened the nail, but the tension in the rope was altering…

'Get a move on.' The look in Osred's eyes was derisive, but Wulf did not care. 'I barely touched you.'

Wulf's fingers closed on the nail and he wrenched it free. Lady Erica and Morcar had taken the lead, they were walking on ahead past a blind man begging at the corner. She tossed the man a coin.

'Bless you, bless you!'

She strode on, Morcar pinned to her side. As Wulf quickened his pace to follow them, the rope began to part. In a moment he would be free, but he had to know what she was doing. Erica of Whitecliffe did not lack for courage, he'd give her that. What could be worth the risk of her, a known Saxon outlaw, being caught so near a Norman garrison? He could only think of one thing…

She continued for another hundred yards before stopping outside a workshop where she rapped on the door. Wulf's bonds loosened. He almost betrayed himself by dropping the nail. Gripping it firmly, he maintained his captive's stance with his hands firmly behind his back. He kept his head down and edged towards her, winning another sting from Osred, which he ignored.

Several bolts snapped back. When the door opened and Erica slipped inside, Wulf followed swiftly on Morcar's heels. The man was wheezing; the cold had clearly got to his lungs.

'Shut the door!' someone barked. Osred leaped to obey.

It was a gold merchant's, had to be, there were enough bolts on that door to keep out the Viking hordes. Against the walls lay strongbox after strongbox, each kept in place by thick iron bands buried in the stone floor. A quick assessment revealed that the shop walls had been also strengthened with heavy oak beams and extra planking. With the door and shutters closed, the interior was dim, lit by a couple of lanterns hanging from the ceiling. Imported, Wulf saw, noting the costly glass fittings, the clear glow of the flame.

The merchant stood behind a table covered in dark cloth, a bearded man at either elbow. In thick leather gambesons, with their belts bristling with arms, they looked burly enough to repel King William's entire personal guard. Wulf's eyebrows rose. This shop was more secure than the Saxon mint had been at Westminster.

Lady Erica fumbled in her skirts and brought out her bracelets—the arm-rings that had belonged to her father. She laid them reverently on the cloth where they gleamed softly in the lamplight.

Wulf saw her swallow as she regarded them. It was clear that she found the idea of selling Thane Eric's arm-rings abhorrent; some large, unknown purpose was forcing it upon her. Her reluctance to see them go was evident in the way her slender fingers lingered on one fashioned like a double-headed dragon. Jewelled eyes glowed red like the heart of a furnace.

What would it be like to feel those fingers moving on him in a like manner?

Frowning, Wulf sucked in a breath. He should be pondering on her purpose, not allowing her to distract him. But, Lord, she was such a distraction. And if she was doing what he suspected she was doing, someone ought to stop her. The woman needed looking after, she was yet again putting herself at risk. But for whom?

Her throat worked as her gaze met the merchant's. 'I am told you are a fair man.'

The gold merchant inclined his head.

'I would be grateful if you would let me know the value of these.'

The man's eyes sharpened. 'You selling?'

'If the price is right.'

The merchant ran his hands over the arm-rings, picked one up, held it to the light. Picked up another. Bit it. Stroked his beard. 'There is not much call for these nowadays.'

'But they are pure gold! Look, this inlay is garnet, and here, sapphire, and these…' eyes moist, she ran a delicate fingertip over the eyes of the dragon '…these are rubies.'

The gold merchant nodded, lips tightening, and Wulf knew that she was not going to get her price.

'Lady, you do not have to tell me my trade. Nowadays…' the man sucked air through his teeth '…such baubles are considered old-fashioned, some would say barbaric.'

Morcar's eyes kindled. 'Barbaric?'

The merchant took a hasty step back. 'So some would say. Normans, you see.' He lifted his shoulders and gave a regretful smile. 'They have the money and not many have the taste for them. It is as I said, lady, there are dozens of arm-rings going begging and no buyers.'

She lifted her chin. 'Still, they are pure gold, that has to have value.'

The merchant named a price, a price that even Wulf could see was a quarter of their worth.

She blinked. 'So little?' She took a deep breath and, gathering up the arm-rings, slid them into the pouch at her belt. 'My thanks, but I do not think I shall sell them today.'

Inclining her head, she waited for Osred to open the door before striding into the sunlit street. Her blue veil fluttered, her cloak swayed from her shoulders; she was walking towards the Norman garrison. Wulf's mind raced. Was she aware that every step was taking her closer to danger? She must be. What was she doing, hunting out another gold merchant? Someone ought to take her in hand before she walked into real trouble. What would happen to her if she were captured? Would Erica, like the other Saxon heiresses, be sold to the highest bidder? Would she be given to one of De Warenne's loyal knights? He frowned after the blue cloak. If he could get out of this with honour, he had been promised a reward… What would De Warenne's reaction be if he asked for Erica for himself? What would her reaction be? He shook his head. Madness. But…there was no harm in asking. He would take careful note of her reaction. He had not saved her from Hrothgar in order to plague her with his own unwanted lusts.

He watched her marching on up the street, straight into danger. If a Norman found her with so much gold on her person, she would be taken in for questioning, at best. The gold revealed her status, a Saxon noblewoman, and Saxon noblewomen had lost more than their menfolk at Hastings. Erica of Whitecliffe might not know it, but with the coming of the Conqueror, women had lost the right to dispose of either their lands or their person. Lady Erica had become subject to Norman law and her person belonged to the King, to dispose of as he willed.

And, at worst… Wulf did not like to think of the worst that might happen if she were caught, and they discovered that she was a rebel. If that happened, robbery or rape would be the least of it; she could be executed, no questions asked.

'My lady?'

At the junction of an alley, she turned and waited for him to catch up.

Wulf gritted his teeth; Osred was breathing down his neck and he had to remind himself that he would likely learn more if they thought he was yet under their control. 'Must your man stand so close?'

'Osred, some space, if you please.'

The man withdrew. Sweat was dewing his upper lip and the worry lines were becoming more pronounced. Osred was in a quake, he knew the recently built garrison was close, and, if he knew, then Erica must also know.

'My lady…' Wulf should not be thinking of her welfare, not when her men had beaten him half to death and she was likely planning some insurgency, but he could not seem to help himself. Yesterday, she had not wanted him executed, a point that pleased him more than it should. And in return for her compassion, Wulf could hardly stand by and watch her court execution.

'You should not be attempting to sell your father's arm-rings in Ely, it is not safe for you here.'

A dark brow arched, green eyes met his steadily. Coldly. 'Is it not?'

'There is a Norman garrison nearby, as I think you are aware.'

'Your point is…?'

'Your father's arm-rings betray you—your loyalties, your lineage. That gold merchant may well be an informer.'

'That, too, I know.'

Wulf felt as though he had walked onto boggy ground and could find no footing. He kept his voice low. 'Why run the risk?'

'Needs must—you would not understand. But I need more supplies. As you know, our ranks are somewhat depleted—'

'Ailric and Hereward,' he murmured, jaw dropping as it dawned on him what she might be about. She wanted to rescue her housecarls! And for that she needed money. Of all the idiotic, hare-brained notions! Loyal to a fault, Lady Erica hoped to mount an attack on Guthlac Stigandson's castle to rescue her men.

'Are you mad?' The words were out before he could stop them. 'Your chances of success are non-existent.'

That mouth, that beautiful, tempting mouth, tightened. 'I do not recall asking for your opinion, Captain FitzRobert. Nor do I recall telling you my plans. You are merely guessing.'

Dumbfounded, Wulf shook his head. What she was planning was nothing less than suicidal. If he were not pretending to be trussed up, he would shake some sense into her. She wanted to sell her father's arm-rings because if she had coins she could hire more men—unless…unless… Another possibility flashed in on him—unless Erica was in a position to call on the other rebels he suspected were hiding elsewhere in the fens… Hrolf—where *had* the man been sent?

If only he could dispense with this pretence and free his hands. Torn between wanting to kiss her—to *kiss* her?—and box her ears, Wulf met her glare for glare. Her eyes shone bright as jewels, her hood had fallen back and her nose was blue with cold. If his hands were free, he would pull her hood up and…

Her mouth was such a distraction. She wanted to rescue her men. Was it simply the bloodfeud, or was it insurrection? Hell.

'My household needs supplies.' She continued. 'We need—'

A harsh command cut into her words, as belatedly, Wulf became aware of the tramping of feet. *That mouth…*

'Hold! *Hold!*' A Norman sergeant, fully mailed and with his sword drawn, was bearing down on them. A dozen infantrymen, arms at the ready, were at his heels.

And now the tables were turned, his need for pretence was over. Jerking his hands free, Wulf flung his cloak out of the way. Erica's face emptied of colour and Wulf's gut clenched. *She is a rebel*, he reminded himself, *an outlaw.*

As the foot-soldiers fanned out around them, Morcar whipped out his sword and stepped in front of his lady. Osred was nearer. Wulf kicked out—thank God they had returned his boots—and Osred's shortsword clattered onto the cobbles.

With a choked cry, Osred darted down the alley. A second later he reappeared, backing into the street at swordpoint before two mailed troopers. Beneath his beard he was as pale as his lady. Spreading his hands in surrender, he was shepherded towards the sergeant. 'Saints have mercy,' he muttered.

They were surrounded. Towards the back of the troop, Wulf saw a grinning face, one he knew. 'Gil!' The boy's grin widened.

'Captain FitzRobert.' The sergeant tipped back his helmet; it was De Warenne's sergeant, Bertram.

'Sergeant, good to see you,' Wulf said, in Norman French. His wrists throbbed. With a glance at Morcar, Wulf shook his head and switched back to English. 'Put up your sword, man. It would be folly to fight, you are hopelessly outmanned.' Morcar glanced at Erica, whose face remained impassive, and Wulf made his voice stern. 'And you imperil your lady.'

Slowly, Morcar lowered his sword.

Wulf jerked his head at Sergeant Bertram and, a heartbeat later, the troopers had both housecarls under restraint.

And Lady Erica? Biting those pretty, distracting lips. Lord, that woman, she was wilful, brave to the point of foolishness…

Sergeant Bertram's eyes had fastened on her pouch, the one into which she had slipped her father's arm-rings. A large hand reached out. 'What's this, then?'

Quickly, Wulf took her arm and drew her, unresisting but with her head averted, out of reach of that hand. 'Leave the lady alone.' Glancing at the back of her head, he drew her firmly up the street in the direction of the garrison. 'Please do accompany me, my lady.'

A man-at-arms was approaching, rope in hand. Wulf dismissed him with a frown. 'I repeat, leave the lady alone, I have her.'

He was rewarded with a brief, black look before she jerked her head away. Her lips were thin and her cheeks were white as snow, but two small spots of colour flared in her cheeks. Then her veil fell forward and her expression was lost to sight. Sergeant Bertram kept pace with them while the troopers escorting Morcar and Osred brought up the rear, boots drumming on the cobbles.

Wulf pitched his voice low, for her ears alone. 'Erica, my lady, please listen. When we reach the garrison, you must follow my lead.'

The veil shifted fractionally in the chill air; it was not much, but it told Wulf she was listening.

'If you value your life, my lady, follow my lead.' He did not know why it should be, but desperation was clawing at Wulf, wreaking havoc with his insides. William De Warenne dealt fairly with those he trusted, but his reputation with his enemies was harsh and uncompromising. Wulf did not like the thought of the Lord of Lewes deciding that Erica of Whitecliffe was his foe. 'My lord can be ruthless with those he considers his enemy.'

'I care not.' Her response was quiet, but chillingly firm.

Tightening his hold, Wulf ignored the curious stares he was receiving from the sergeant, who was no doubt wondering why he was muttering in Saxon to the outlaw whose men had taken him prisoner. He inched his head closer and caught the fresh tang of herbs. 'It is not only your safety that is at issue, my lady. What of Solveig…that boy, Cadfael…what of the others waiting faithfully for you back in the market square? If Guthlac

Stigandson would happily have seen a fellow Saxon, a thane's daughter, harmed, then what chance will your maid have in a garrison of Norman soldiers?'

The veil trembled. 'You are a worm, you are beneath contempt.'

'No, my lady, I am warning you, for your own sake and that of your people. Think.' Their gazes locked and ruefully Wulf indicated the bruising on his face, the smudges her men's bindings had made on his wrists. 'I am De Warenne's man, and, like any good lord, he seeks to protect those who swear fealty to him. He will see these, he will draw his own conclusions and he will act accordingly.' Her eyes were like ice, green ice. 'My lady, you are a rebel as far as De Warenne is concerned, an outlaw.'

She jerked at her arm, but Wulf held firm and pressed on relentlessly; he had to, for her sake. 'You know the law as well as I. Anyone who is declared an outlaw is said to bear the wolf's head. You and any one of your people, even Solveig and young Cadfael, could be so judged. And once that has happened, they may be put to death with impunity. No questions need even be asked. No one would be punished for killing them.'

'You hypocrites, that's Saxon law, not Norman!'

Wulf shrugged. 'It will make no odds as far as my lord is concerned. De Warenne has come to these fens to clear them of rebels—'

'We fight for what is rightfully ours!'

The wooden watchtower was looming up ahead; Wulf had little time to get his point across. 'No, my lady, your father and his companions lost everything at Hastings. It was an honourable battle—'

'*Honourable!*'

'And by refusing to accept Norman rule,' Wulf pressed on relentlessly, 'you and your people have become outlaws and will be dealt with as such. When we march through that portcullis, you have one hope. You *must* trust me and follow my lead.'

Her nostrils flared and they passed through the portcullis. Wulf was unable to judge whether she was prepared to do as he suggested. Trust was fragile at the best of times and the claw that was ripping at his innards was telling him that she had lost her trust of him and would not follow his lead. For the first time in years, he sent up a swift prayer—he prayed that he was wrong.

Erica's thoughts were in chaos. She had scarcely heard a word that Wulf—that *Captain FitzRobert*—had said to her; the only thing she could hear was the blood pounding in her ears.

They had bound Morcar and Osred and were making them walk behind her, that much she did know. Her own hands remained free. Wulf's grip on her arm had not slackened and this, Erica was ashamed to discover, relieved as much as angered her. Nor had he permitted that other Norman, that sergeant, to paw over her father's arm-rings.

Vaguely, she noticed that the garrison stockade was in good repair, wood, but solid, very solid. The teeth on the portcullis were filed to sharp points. How easy, she wondered, would it be to fire it?

Erica wanted to notice everything, but her mind would not obey. When she walked into the yard, her whole body jerked. The place swarmed with soldiers in chainmail, with archers. Aliens. Invaders. *Normans*, like the man at her side. How had she ever thought him Saxon?

Dogs barked; men shouted; steel clanged; and the acrid smell of burnt horn wrinkled Erica's nostrils—a horse was being shod nearby. Several archery butts were being stacked in a cart. Preparations were underway, it seemed. For what? Her heart jumped about in her breast.

Around the yard there were a number of wooden buildings, another of stone, and there, yes, that must be the stable. Horses were being groomed in the winter sunlight. They were huge beasts with chests that were broader than the chests of the oxen that used to plough the peasants' strips by the river in Lewes. Destriers, they called them, warhorses. Terrifyingly huge. Bits jingled, harnesses flashed. And—her breath caught—soldiers, more mailed foot-soldiers. At sea in the midst of so many Normans, Erica shot a look at Wulf…no, at Captain FitzRobert, and struggled to keep the loathing from her face.

'This way, my lady.' He directed her towards the largest of the wooden buildings. It had a double doorway, oak, that was flung wide like a giant mouth. It had huge iron hinges and two sentries guarding the entrance. Erica did not want to go in and she clenched her fists as a chilling thought came to her. Once inside, she would never leave, this hall was a monster, a Norman war monster, and it was about to devour her.

Boot on the threshold, Wulf paused to signal at the troopers who had Morcar and Osred under escort. He gave a swift command in Norman French. With a salute, the troopers bore her men towards the stone building.

Unnerving as it was to hear Wulf speaking French

with such fluency, Erica managed, briefly, to marshal her thoughts. 'Where are they going?' Uncurling her fingers, she clutched at his arm. 'What did you tell those soldiers to do to them?'

A broad hand came to rest on hers. In another world, in another time, she might have interpreted the gesture as comforting. 'Do not fear, they will be safe.'

She craned her neck as Morcar and Osred disappeared through a shadowy archway. 'But…but…'

'I repeat, they are safe, they are merely under restraint. They will be fed. They will not be beaten.'

Her cheeks stung and she avoided his gaze. 'I…I did not want you beaten. I did not realise what Morcar and Siward intended, I…' Her voice trailed off. Wulf would never believe her. She was his prisoner and he would think she hoped to soften him. With a sigh, she stiffened her spine and raised her gaze to her hand on the sleeve of his brown homespun, at his broader one covering it. 'What now?'

He gazed at her for a long moment, and ran a finger down her cheek. His touch was light as a feather, but it burned, how it burned. And something in his eyes, in the way he looked into hers, made her breath stop for a moment. Then to her surprise, Wulf released her and stepped back. 'Your part is simple, you must follow my lead. My lord De Warenne is holding council inside.'

With a bow, he offered her his arm and guided her through the wide oak door.

Chapter Twelve

William De Warenne, Lord of Lewes, the Norman who had been granted vast tracts of King Harold's lands in southern England, was holding court at the head of a wide, rough-hewn table. Erica did not need to have him pointed out to her—De Warenne was every inch the overlord. Ensconced in the central seat between two of his knights, wearing a natural air of command, he looked to be in his early forties. No peacock, his grizzled hair was cropped in the simplest of Norman styles; he was clean-shaven and wearing a stained leather gambeson that had seen hard service.

A couple of troopers were wrestling. Stripped to the waist, their backs gleamed with sweat as they grunted and heaved and scuffed up the rushes. A large crowd was noisily exchanging wagers on the outcome. In a flurry of flailing limbs, the wrestlers rolled and came to an abrupt stop at Wulf's and Erica's feet. The entire hall fell silent.

Erica's stomach tightened as every eye seemed to fix on her. It felt as though these men could tell just by looking that she was Saxon, and a rebel. Did they loathe her as much as she loathed them? It took every ounce of her willpower *not* to shift closer to Wulf.

Wulf frowned. 'Edward, Giles, the hall is no place for fighting, get you into the yard.'

'Yes, Captain.'

'Sorry, sir.'

As Wulf shouldered his way through the dispersing men, De Warenne glanced across. 'FitzRobert, good to see you—a day early, too! And you look…reasonably hale.' As Wulf bowed, his gaze flickered over the bruises on Wulf's face. 'When Gil came running and said he had spotted you under restraint in the market square, I could scarcely credit it.'

De Warenne's accent was alien to Erica, but, since she had some understanding of Norman French, she caught the main gist of his speech.

'It is good to see you, too, my lord.'

Wulf had answered in the same tongue and it was discomposing to hear him speak it with such fluency. *FitzRobert, Captain Wulf FitzRobert.* Erica swallowed down a lump in her throat. She had been stunned to hear that name by the fisherman's hut, but to hear his facility with the language of her enemy… Wulf had been so convincing as a Saxon. She had liked him. Saints, her cheek even felt hot where he had touched it some moments ago…

De Warenne dismissed the knights around his council table. 'My thanks for your reports, we shall finish this later.'

'Aye, my lord.' The knights withdrew, spurs clinking.

'Wine, Captain?'

'Please.'

'Help yourself. And your…companion?' Courteously, De Warenne inclined his head at Erica. 'Would this lady take some wine also?'

'My lady?' Again Wulf's hand was warm on hers, and for an instant his thumb curled round to caress her palm. The pain of betrayal twisted her heart. Did Wulf have to appear so…so solicitous, so caring towards her? She pushed aside her hurt, briskly reminding herself of the need for calm, of the need to remain clear-headed. For the moment it might be wise to keep her knowledge of the French tongue, rudimentary as it was, to herself.

'I…I beg your pardon?'

'Would you care for wine?' Wulf asked, in English. Both his voice and the expression in his eyes were patient.

'Y…yes, please.'

A clay goblet was pressed into her hand. The wine was warm and smelt faintly of cinnamon and cloves, spices so exotic that Erica had not smelt them since she had led her people from Lewes. Slowly, she raised her eyes, forcing herself to look directly at De Warenne. I was fleeing *you*, she thought, struggling to keep her emotions out of her face. Her breath caught and her brows snapped together. Oddly, this Norman lord put her in mind of her father. A shiver ran down her spine.

'My thanks,' she managed, in English.

Nodding briefly, the Lord of Lewes returned his attention to Wulf. 'The report you sent via Gilbert was most timely, FitzRobert. I have been able to incorporate your intelligence into my immediate plans. Guthlac's tenure in that so-called castle of his will be short-lived.'

Understanding enough, Erica stiffened. What did De

Warenne mean? Were the Normans about to lay siege to
Thane Guthlac, was that the cause of the hustle in the
yard? Erica had no reason to love either Guthlac or any of
his housecarls, but what about Ailric and Hereward? She
wanted them out of their prison. If De Warenne's army was
to storm the castle *before* she could help them...how
would Normans treat Guthlac's Saxon prisoners?

Wulf's expression was unreadable, as hers must be.
Feigning a complete lack of understanding of the conversation, Erica made a play of looking about her.

The garrison hall put her in mind of Guthlac's, save
that this one was larger and longer. There was the same
smell of recently sawn timbers, and here, too, the smoke
winding out from the fire had not had time to blacken the
walls. It was a room for soldiers, with few concessions
in the way of adornment. There were no tapestries, no
wall hangings, just an unremarkable yellow curtain at the
back of the hall, dyed, Erica reckoned, with an everyday
dye made from birch leaves. Rows of hooks ran the length
of the walls, hooks upon which these foreign soldiers had
hung a menacing array of arms: swords, battleaxes and
lances; bows and quivers; swordbelts; shields...

The knights that De Warenne had dismissed had drifted
to a trestle and were engaging in conversation with yet
more knights. Soldiers were lounging on benches; others
warmed themselves by the fire. Sitting with these, an
archer was busily setting arrowheads on shafts with a glue
and twine. Judging by the heap of arrows at his side, the
archer had been at work for some time. Dear Heaven,
Erica thought, if the fens are *already* overrun with
Normans, how am I to rescue Ailric and Hereward?

'Gilbert assumed you ran into trouble after he took

your report,' De Warenne was saying, gesturing at Wulf's bruises. 'You found more rebels? Another nest of outlaws?'

Wulf ran his hand through his hair. 'I thought so at first, my lord.'

Scarcely daring to breathe, Erica affected a deep interest in a wolfhound scratching at its fleas at De Warenne's feet. Did Wulf suspect that she had sent Hrolf to find her father's warband? He must do.

'You were mistaken?' De Warenne's eyes were on her; she felt them as a brand. Her heart sank. Her people were lost, if Wulf let fall that she had more men at her disposal—her people were lost. Fighting to keep her expression relaxed and untroubled, she felt the tension wind inside her. She wanted to pick up her skirts and run, but that would not help. One of these men would be on her in an instant…

'Indeed, my lord.' Wulf's voice was calm and unhurried; it even had a smile in it. 'I found I misread some of what was happening in Thane Guthlac's hall.'

Cup cradled in his hands, De Warenne propped his hip on the edge of the trestle. 'How so?'

'The Lady Erica was…held there, and at first I could not determine her purpose among Guthlac's men.'

'You took her for a rebel and outlaw also?'

Wulf smiled in her direction and, though his smile was relaxed, Erica sensed an urgent message behind it, he was not as relaxed as he appeared. Like her, he was moved by an emotion he was striving to conceal. 'Yes,' Wulf said. 'However, closer observation revealed my lady as a woman under duress, a woman desperate to save her…household.'

De Warenne's brows snapped together. 'Household? Captain, who is this woman? Describe her circumstances…how many housecarls can she call upon?'

'I did not see many, it is a small household. A couple of ageing men accompany her, one might have been a warrior, but he is well past his prime, as to the other…' Wulf shook his head. 'My lord, you may judge for yourself, they are here under lock and key.'

'I'll look in on them later. What was the lady doing in Guthlac's company?'

Erica gripped the wine cup as though her life depended on it. It was not lost on her that, despite being asked to reveal her full identity, Wulf had not yet done so. Beneath his calm demeanour, there was definitely a nervousness that she could not pin down. It was true that De Warenne was a great lord, a man of enormous power, and talking to De Warenne would intimidate most people, but there was more to it than that, she was sure. Wulf did not appear to be in the least bit intimidated, at least not by his lord, but something was definitely worrying him.

'There was much talk of a bloodfeud between her family and Guthlac Stigandson's,' Wulf said.

'Bloodfeud?'

'Aye, and since she was under some duress at the castle, I did not consider her a risk.'

De Warenne snorted. 'FitzRobert, she is a Saxon, and as such I would always consider her a risk. Good Lord, man, look what they have done to your face! Gilbert said you were largely unmarked when you met him at the rendezvous. Did someone in this…*small* household of hers do that to you?'

Wulf shrugged and shot Erica another unfathomable look; she wished she understood it. 'Ah, that, it was merely a slight misunderstanding. They thought I meant them ill. But I had…other ideas.'

De Warenne's brows snapped together. 'You are not saying there is something between you?'

Reminding herself to continue feigning ignorance of their tongue, Erica gave Wulf what she hoped was a passable smile and bent over her wine cup. Wulf made no answer, but, glancing under her lashes at him, Erica watched with astonishment as his cheeks darkened.

De Warenne let out a bark of laughter. 'A lover's tiff, was it? Some tiff.' Sharp eyes narrowed. 'Who *is* this woman, FitzRobert—what is her name in full?'

Those warm fingers wrapped round hers and Wulf drew her up to De Warenne. 'My lord, this is the Lady Erica of Whitecliffe. And I would ask—'

De Warenne's eyes went to their linked hands and the furrows in his brow deepened. 'Captain FitzRobert, I do not recall giving you permission to do your courting among those in the Saxon aristocracy.'

'My lord, I have not done so, but—'

'Erica of Whitecliffe, you say? And her sire?' De Warenne's voice was cold.

'Thane Eric.'

'Lost at Hastings?'

'As I understand it, my lord. He was a South Saxon. His hall is, if it still stands, at Whitecliffe near your holding in Lewes.'

Pushing away from the table, De Warenne took her by the chin and turned her face this way and that, *examining me as though to draw out my last secret*, Erica thought. With a jolt, she recalled that Thane Guthlac had examined her in like fashion. Then, too, Wulf had stood at her side, but he seemed to be hiding more tension today than he had then, which was odd.

'The Lady Erica's father served Harold Godwineson,' Wulf added.

While De Warenne scrutinised her features, Wulf tightened his hold on her hand. There it was again, that hint of tension in him, like a tightly strung bow. Yet his manner seemed confident; she must be mistaken.

Abruptly, De Warenne released her. 'So I had heard. His lands have been placed in my gift.'

Wulf cleared his throat and the pressure on Erica's hand increased. He began speaking so rapidly that his words were lost on her. 'My lord, please know that I do not have any expectations with regard to her land, but I do have something to ask you…'

'FitzRobert?'

Wulf squared his shoulders. 'When you gave me this commission, you spoke of a reward. I would like to lay claim to it.'

De Warenne frowned. 'Now? In the middle of a campaign?'

'Yes, my lord. I know my timing is poor, but this is the reward I would claim. I do not ask for a knighthood, or lands, or coin. My lord, I would be most grateful if you would give me permission to marry this woman.'

Erica forgot to breathe, for those last words she had understood—Wulf was asking if he could *marry* her? Was he serious? At least his request had stopped De Warenne from asking probing questions about her men.

But Wulf could not be serious. His face remained impenetrable, his fingers firmly wrapped around hers.

De Warenne made a dismissive sound. 'A *thane's* daughter? You ask me for the hand of a *thane's* daughter, Captain?' Sharp eyes skimmed Erica's person before resting for an instant on the pouch that hung heavy at her waist. He must guess it contained a portion of her father's gold-hoard. 'This extraordinarily beautiful and *rich* thane's daughter?'

'Yes, my lord, but I would stress that it is only Lady Erica's hand that I am asking for, not her land or her baubles.'

'Just the woman, eh?'

'Just so.'

'You have discussed this with her? She is in agreement?'

Erica wanted to speak, but she bit her tongue, gagged by the chill in De Warenne's voice and the instinct that had warned her to affect ignorance of Norman French.

'My lady…Erica.' Wulf switched to English. His stance as he looked down at her was that of a conqueror, but he was not all arrogance, there remained an almost imperceptible hesitancy about him.

Erica forced a smile, or the ghost of one. Marry him, marry Captain Wulf FitzRobert? Her mind whirled. Who *was* Wulf FitzRobert? The man was an enigma. He was kind, he had saved her from Hrothgar, but he was also a liar who from the first had not been straight with her. He was a warrior, young and strong and as handsome as any she had met; he was a Norman…

The Norman in question murmured, 'And please do not react…badly at my next words.' Blue eyes caught hers. He had such clever eyes; he could make them appear earnest at will, apparently. It was very convincing. There were light flecks in them and they shaded almost to green near the pupil. 'Not only is your life at issue, but please to think about your people, of those we left but an hour since…'

Swallowing, Erica nodded. Solveig, Cadfael…Wulf knew their whereabouts, he knew their faces—must she agree to marry him in order to save them? Was he threatening to turn them over to De Warenne if she did not?

He took a deep breath. 'I am asking my lord for permission to wed you.'

'You want me to m…marry you?' She let her mouth fall open, as though she had only at that moment understood him. Beside them, De Warenne shoved his thumbs in his belt. His expression was dour and Erica was under no illusions, Wulf's request had displeased him. Did De Warenne speak English? Erica had no way of knowing.

'Yes, I am asking you to marry me. Erica…my lady, please smile at my lord, accept my proposal.'

Her throat was so dry she could not get the words out at first. 'F…for the sake of my people? You will do your best for them?'

A small crease appeared between his eyebrows. 'Of course, but know that I am asking above all for your sake. Marry me and I will do my best to see to your people's safety. *All* your people.' Wulf shifted, and for a few moments was a shield between her and his lord. Erica found herself staring at the dark rim defining his eyes as he lowered his voice. 'My lady, I want to help you, but this is a long shot, a very long shot. De Warenne is not inclined to agree because of my birth.'

'You are not a fit mate for a thane's daughter,' she said, speaking the words that he expected to hear, not the ones that she believed.

Wulf's mouth thinned. 'Quite so. But given that you have fallen into the care of Normans, your person may be disposed of as my lord wishes. He could give you to anyone, but he owes me some recompense for my services and, believe me, it would go better for you and for your people if you accepted me. I am working for peace. Besides…' he lowered his voice further, and his lips twisted '…you were already given to me by Guthlac, so you know I would not hurt you.'

Erica thought quickly. Wulf had not drawn his lord's attention back to her father's arm-rings, but doubtless one of them would relieve her of the pouch, should she accept him. According to Norman law, that would be their right. And despite Wulf's fine words, that would be why he had asked for her hand. He wanted her for herself? He wanted to save her people? Was it likely? 'And what of the others—will you hurt them?'

'Others, my lady?'

She lifted her chin, angry at her careless wording. It seemed to have brought that tension in him back to the surface, as if Wulf did indeed suspect that more of her father's warband had survived Hastings. 'I mean Ailric and Hereward, naturally. What else might I mean?'

His nostrils flared. 'Agree to marry me, my lady, and I swear I will do my utmost to see to their safety.'

Erica had no course but to believe him. Trembling, she reached for the bruised and stubble-darkened face and, rising on her toes, pressed a brief kiss to his cheek.

'I agree, Captain FitzRobert. If your lord permits it, I will marry you.'

Triumph flared in the clever blue eyes and when he about-faced and grinned at his lord, it struck her that she must have imagined that brief hesitancy of manner. At this moment there was little of the supplicant about him—a tall, well-muscled young warrior stood boldly before one of Normandy's most powerful lords. Wulf himself did not have a noble bone in his body, but he faced his *seigneur* with a straight back and a proud set to his head.

Wulf's nobility lay in his heart. Where had that thought come from? She could not be certain of it. Doubt fought with hope; she could only pray it was true. If it were not true, she had just made the biggest mistake of her life.

'Yes, my lord, Lady Erica is in agreement.'

Originally, when Wulf had accepted his commission in the fens, he had hoped to be knighted as a reward for his services. He had surprised himself with this request. It was not a sensible request, particularly as his commission was not yet completed, but he found himself holding Erica of Whitecliffe's hand in the garrison hall at Ely and waiting with bated breath for his lord's reply. What demon had prompted him to risk not only his lord's anger, but also the wreckage of years of gruelling work and careful planning? There must be more of the Saxon in him than he realised; he really did not want to see her people die. Neither did he want to see her handed over to someone else, particularly after her humiliations in Guthlac's hall.

'First things first, FitzRobert.' De Warenne gave him

a brief and abstracted smile. 'Be assured I have noted your request to marry the Lady Erica. As to my answer, there is much to be resolved before a *suitable* husband may be found her.'

'But, my lord—'

De Warenne made a dismissive gesture. '*Enough!* I have been patient. You have served me well, Captain, but you overreach yourself. The question of Lady Erica's marriage will wait until we have strengthened our position in the fens. Tomorrow our winter campaign begins in earnest. We engage with Guthlac Stigandson. Fix your mind on that, if you please, you will be needed.'

Wulf dipped his head. 'Of course, my lord.'

Thoughtfully, De Warenne ran his gaze over Erica. 'Comely, isn't she? Quite a prize, in fact.'

'My lord?'

De Warenne ran his hand round the back of his neck. 'When we have done with Stigandson, I want you to see that she reaches the King's Court at Winchester. It is vital she reaches there chastely and safely. And note this, FitzRobert, I am trusting you to fulfil this commission as earnestly as you have always fulfilled your other commissions.'

'Yes, my lord.'

'The question of Lady Erica's marriage will be settled in Winchester.'

Wulf blinked. 'By the King, my lord? Is not her father's land in *your* gift?'

De Warenne shot him a sharp look. 'I thought you were not interested in the lady's land, Captain?'

'I would take the lady alone, if it pleases you.'

'It does *not* please me.'

It was a frank and outright rejection—had he really expected otherwise? Wulf gripped Erica's hand, astounded by the wave of disappointment that crashed over him. *She was not to be his, she could be taken away and handed over to a stranger, she was not to be his.* He clenched his teeth to hold back a barrage of objections that would do him no service. Realising he was frowning, he forced his face into neutrality. He had only offered for the woman in order to distract De Warenne from questioning the motives behind that morning's visit to Ely. He should not be feeling like this.

But, Lord, how the regrets were piling up, a confused, messy heap of them. There was the regret that he was, as Erica herself had been swift to point out, not a fit mate for a thane's daughter. Any marriage between them would be unequal. This was doubtless De Warenne's chief objection. There was the regret that, in order to save her and her supporters from an uncertain fate, he had been prepared to risk his knightly ambition and damn himself as a lovesick fool in his lord's eyes. There was the worry that perhaps his desire to save her had not been entirely led by chivalry. He shot her a swift, sidelong glance—she was chewing her lip, that too-kissable lower lip, that *distracting* lower lip. A stab of yearning streaked through him. Worst of all, he wanted her. *Merde.*

He lifted her fingers to his lips, eyes seeking hers. 'I will not abandon you,' he muttered in English. 'After the battle I am to escort you to the Winchester Court.'

Even as he sought to reassure her, Wulf was kicking himself for asking for her hand. When he had come to the fens the last thing he had wanted to do was to saddle himself with a wife, however beautiful. He had come to win honours—perhaps a knighthood, perhaps some land. But a wife…too soon, it was too soon for him. When he had established himself, then perhaps he might look for a wife. But by then it would be too late for him to look towards Erica of Whitecliffe.

He shook his head, but he could not clear it of the image of Erica standing alone and defiant in Guthlac's hall, facing the cruelty of her countrymen in order to secure a decent future for her father's household. He had not been able to stand by then, he had had to help her, in memory of his sister, Marie.

So, he had succeeded in getting Erica away from Guthlac, but for what? Here in Ely she was at the mercy of his lord, who could and would marry her where he willed. It was no easier to stomach the thought of her being forced to marry a stranger than it had been to stomach her being 'slighted' by Hrothgar. It was galling, the effect Erica of Whitecliffe had on him. She made him do things that put a lifetime's planning in jeopardy…

An expectant silence told Wulf that his lord had spoken and was looking to him for an answer. 'I…I am sorry, my lord, what was that?'

'Your sword, Captain, you seem to have mislaid it. I may not have granted your request to marry, but I can supply you with a decent sword. I was asking you if you would care to choose another.'

'I…I…' Wulf pulled himself together. 'My thanks, I would indeed.'

'Come, then.' De Warenne jerked his head towards the yellow screen at the back of the hall. 'I have one that is perfect for a man of your height and weight.'

'And Lady Erica?'

'Morgan will keep an eye on her. *Morgan!*'

One of the sentries stuck his head through the door. 'My lord?'

'See to it this woman doesn't wander off, will you? And guard her well, she is not to come to harm.'

'Yes, my lord.'

Erica's temples began to throb—she was to be abandoned in a Norman barrack-hall? She stood frozen as Wulf lightly touched the back of her hand. She couldn't seem to tear her eyes from him and his touch sparked off a painful twist inside of her. He would forget about her; he was, after all, a man, and once he got talking tactics with his lord…

'I will return,' Wulf said, even as he followed De Warenne to the yellow curtain. 'We are to attack tomorrow, my lord?'

Curtain rings clattered and the two men vanished from sight, but De Warenne's reply floated back to her. 'Aye, tomorrow. I hear you have great plans for the archers?'

'Aye, my lord. In London I met a man but lately back from Italy, he had made a study of the tactics used by Byzantine archers.'

'Zone-shooting, yes, I have heard of it. But…a night attack, FitzRobert, are you certain?' Their voices were fading, but Erica caught the incredulity in De Warenne's tone.

'I think it will work. But tell me, my lord, will you attempt negotiation first?'

Erica strained to hear De Warenne's reply, but at that moment the group of wrestlers, the wrestling over presumably, burst back into the hall. Effacing herself as well as she might, a Saxon in the heart of enemy territory, Erica found a stool by the fire and wished she were invisible.

Time dragged while Wulf was in conference with his lord. The archer's heap of arrows grew and, at close quarters, his gluepot stank. The trestles were put up, supper was served and eaten, and then the trestles were removed once more. The guard, Morgan, did not forget his orders; he brought her a platter of unidentifiable salted meats, but Erica's appetite was weak. She huddled by the fire, oblivious of its warmth, desperate that no one should address her. She was, however, unable to ignore the curious glances that were shot in her direction when the soldiers began rolling out their mattresses and bedding.

Though Erica's body was still, her thoughts ran in many directions.

Where was Wulf? Had he forgotten about her? He had promised to return, but when would that be? De Warenne obviously had need of him. And De Warenne had commanded Wulf to escort her to Winchester, if she had understood him aright. Winchester, the old Saxon capital, where this Christmas past a *Norman* king had held his court. Winchester, where a husband would be found for her, a *Norman* husband, one she would loathe with every fibre of her being. The smell of the glue was making her feel quite ill.

Wulf, where are you? Do you expect me to sleep in this place?

'My lady?' Wulf's voice broke into her thoughts as though she had conjured him. The tension fell away. He was striding towards her in a clean grey tunic as simple in design as his brown one had been. His chausses were black, with blue cross-gartering, and he had a bundle under one arm and a sword strapped to his side. This sword was of another order altogether than his old one, the one she had let Hrolf keep. Metal gleamed on the hilt and scabbard where silver banding bound the leather in a criss-cross pattern. His lord might not have granted his request to marry her, but he had certainly favoured Wulf in the giving of this sword. Its quality was such that even her father would have been proud to own it.

Wulf reached for her hand and curled his fingers round hers. She had returned the pressure before she thought to check herself. He had shaved, and with his cheeks clear of stubble she had the impression she was looking at a stranger. A handsome stranger with bruises on his face. He gave her a courtly bow and her cheeks burned as they had done when he had touched her. She felt…shy.

'I have found us accommodation, but there will be no feather bed, I am afraid.' Wulf led her past the watching eyes and out into a barrack-yard where torch-light gleamed on frost and their breath turned to white clouds in an instant. His smile was rueful. 'But it is at least reasonably private and you ought to know by now that I cannot provide you with feather beds.'

He was leading her to the stables, Erica realised, lifting her skirts to hurry across the cobbles. She ought to be insulted. Her old self, Lady Erica of Whitecliffe, daughter of Thane Eric, probably would have been insulted, but she had felt bereft in the barrack-hall, and she was pleased—no, she was honest enough to admit she was more than pleased to see him. She glanced down at their interlinked hands. When he had pushed through that yellow curtain and taken her hand so firmly, so *openly*, it had been as though he had been declaring that she was his. She frowned. Wulf's allegiance was to a Norman lord, one who had denied his suit; she ought to feel insulted by so public and defiant a declaration, but she only felt relief that he had returned for her. How could that be? Of course, she herself had had first-hand knowledge that Wulf would not hurt her. And while his lord had denied him his suit, De Warenne clearly thought Wulf honourable enough to be entrusted with her safety while they travelled to Winchester.

They entered the stable and, taking a lantern from a hook by the door, Wulf pointed to a ladder. 'Up you go.'

Erica raised a brow. 'A hayloft?'

He grinned. 'I did warn you. It's the best I can do, if you want privacy.'

A stable hand was making his bed in one of the stalls. Looking pointedly at him, Erica raised a brow. 'You call this privacy?'

His grin broadened. 'More than would be afforded in the barrack-hall, I can assure you.'

Cheeks growing hotter by the second, Erica flung her veil over her shoulder and set her foot on the bottom rung. She had no desire to sleep amid a troop of Norman soldiers.

A warm hand settled on her waist. 'Can you manage?'

'Yes, thank you.' The hayloft was pitch dark. At the top, she scrambled to one side while her eyes adjusted.

Wulf muttered to the stable lad below and followed her up, lantern in hand. The light showed a steeply sloping roof with beams mere inches above his head. Several bales of hay were stacked in the gable end.

Wulf hung the lantern on a nail and tossed down his bundle. Blankets. Erica's heart began to beat in thick, heavy strokes. Straw rustled. Blankets, bales of hay…slowly Erica's gaze went from the hay to the man, as it occurred to her to wonder whether Wulf had bothered to find 'private' accommodation for the night because he had changed his mind about not touching her.

No, no. De Warenne had commanded that Wulf keep her chaste. Could he be trusted? Almost, she wished that he could not. What if he planned on taking what he had not taken when Guthlac had given her to him? In a stable. He was a man, after all, a strong, healthy, young warrior and strong, healthy, young warriors were—she could well recall Ailric's tavern wenches—not entirely reliable. Erica shivered. Thank Heaven Wulf could not read her thoughts. For he *was* reliable, but her thoughts, it seemed, were not. They were wanton thoughts that did not belong in the head of a thane's daughter. They must be dismissed, immediately.

Chapter Thirteen

'Here, my lady.' When Wulf took her hand, Erica almost jumped out of her skin, but he merely led her farther to one side, away from the trapdoor. He booted it shut with a thud and released her. 'That's better, don't want you to fall through in your sleep.'

Sleep? He thought she could sleep in the heart of a Norman garrison? He thought she could sleep when his lord had ordered that she be sent to Winchester to marry one of these…invaders?

He had a dagger out, the blade winked in the lamplight. Another new weapon; William De Warenne had been generous. Wulf sliced through the twine that held a bale together and set about strewing straw on the floor, making a bed. *Their* bed? The blood drummed in her ears. He would not dare. He had not touched her in Guthlac's castle, so why should he now when his lord had ordered him to take her safely to Winchester? Where she must marry someone fitting. *Fitting?* Saint Swithun, save her.

'There you are, my lady.'

'Th…thank you.' Mind awhirl, Erica sank onto the straw.

Where was he intending to sleep, with her? And there it was again, *another* unladylike thought—where were they coming from? When Wulf produced another blanket and used it to make up a second bed a few feet from hers, her breath released on a sigh. Kicking off her boots, she loosened her girdle and removed the blue veil. Her hands were trembling. Taking slow, deep breaths, she made herself fold the veil neatly and set it to one side. She was easing the tightness of her braid when Wulf, ensconced on his own makeshift pallet, paused in his preparations and glanced across. There was an arrested expression in his eyes.

'Wh…what?'

The dark head shook, his lips curved. 'Nothing, my lady, I was merely struck by your beauty. I thought I would grow accustomed to it, but it seems that time has yet to come.'

Truly? He thinks I am beautiful? It is more likely he seeks to flatter because he wants…he wants…

Wulf leaned forwards, eyes gleaming in the lamplight. He was so close she could feel his breath on her cheek, warm and fragrant with good Frankish wine. His gaze dropped briefly to her lips and back to her eyes. Erica might lack experience in matters of the flesh, but there was no mistaking that look. His hooded, dreamy eyes warned her that Wulf did not simply covet her gold, her former lands. Her stomach tightened and it was not an unpleasant sensation, it was more in the way of…anticipation? She bit her lip. Surely not?

Callused fingertips reached for her cheek, touching

her in a light caress before falling away. Erica couldn't breathe. Her mouth was dry and it was definitely not from fear—the shocking part of it was that she was attracted to Captain FitzRobert. And worse, this was not the simple attraction of one friend for another, for they were enemies, this was the more complex attraction a woman felt when a man…when *her* man…no, no, *no*! Wulf might have asked his lord if he could take her in marriage, but that was because he coveted her land and her riches. He did not love her. He was simply a young man, and like other young men he had hot blood when it came to the pleasures of the flesh…

With more of an effort than she liked, Erica wrenched her gaze from his. How could she? He was Norman, *Norman*—her father would never forgive her. She had to fight this attraction, it had come from the devil. Wulf might ask for her hand in marriage, but she would never marry him. De Warenne would not permit it.

'Goodnight,' came the soft murmur, and that light touch was back at her temple, turning her face to his.

Again she saw that swift downward glance to her mouth; she noted also a dark slash of colour on his cheeks—clean-shaven cheeks, cheeks that she longed to touch, to test their texture. Purely on grounds of curiosity, naturally.

Erica had not touched many men and certainly not in *that* way. Noblewomen were not encouraged to do so, their purity must be unimpeachable, which was why Guthlac had chosen to have her disparaged. It was a particularly terrible fate for a high-born woman to lose her innocence, especially one who was unmarried.

As a child Erica had bounced on her father's knee and

pulled his beard; she had touched Ailric that once when he had tempted her into kissing him behind the stable. Ailric's beard had been soft and silky, the touching had been minimal and the kiss a disappointment, he stank of the tavern. But Wulf—if she were to touch his face…why, the thought alone heated her blood…what would that lean cheek feel like?

And if Wulf were to *kiss* her?

Wulf leaned in, slid his fingers round to the back of her neck, and then they *were* kissing. Or rather, Erica thought wildly, as warm lips covered hers and the clean male scent of him surrounded her, he was kissing her. His kiss was subtle, surprising, a gentle but relentless assault on her senses.

She did not move, not to draw him close nor, to her shame, to repulse him. She sat stunned on her pallet while Wulf FitzRobert's fingers slid back and forth, caressing her cheek, her ear. Her cheek and ear burned. His touch had that effect on her, it seemed. Hot. Kissing Wulf made her hot. He melted her bones. And then his fingers were at the nape of her neck, holding her firmly in place as though he feared she might attempt to break free and he did not wish her to. But why should she? Escape was the last thing on her mind. It was no disappointment, kissing Wulf.

She forgot to breathe. As Wulf's tongue touched hers, a sinful heat wound through her and her thoughts were confused with something that Erica very much feared was lust. There was a peculiar swooping sensation in her belly, she ached to press herself against him, to reach blindly for those broad shoulders. Her eyelids fluttered shut. Almost she could wish that De Warenne had agreed to their union, almost she could wish…the devil, she thought, these un-ladylike feelings have come from the devil…

'Erica.' His voice was hoarse. He drew back and pressed a kiss on her nose. 'We must be chaste, but I will fight for you, my lady, I will not give you up.'

Breathless, she opened her eyes. He was still very close, too close for a Norman captain she would never marry, and his eyes were no longer blue, they were black. They were watching her with that careful attention she had noticed in him. Spy's eyes. Someone fitting? It could not be him, it could not. An illegitimate Norman captain? Such a match would never be countenanced, even by Normans.

'Wulf…' She swallowed. She had no idea what she had been about to say.

He smiled, so befuddling her that it was some seconds before she noticed his fingers were in her hair, finishing the job of loosening her braid.

'No, *no*.' Her voice was appallingly weak, unconvincing, even to her ears. The man had bewitched her.

'One more kiss, *ma belle*?'

His mouth, clear-cut and tempting, seemed to draw her, it made her want to drift back towards him, to lean against that strong chest.

His lips curved. She clenched her fingers into fists to prevent herself from reaching out, but when he brought his head closer she placed her palm on the centre of his chest.

'No.' Her face was on fire. 'I…I cannot.'

'*Ma belle*, I am only asking for a kiss.'

That repeated endearment, that *French* endearment, brought her to her senses. 'N…no, no more.'

Another smile. Careful fingers were drawing circles

on the nape of her neck. Her skin burned. More burning, everywhere he touched. Again he caressed her ear and still it burned.

'Are you trying to seduce me?'

A dark brow lifted. 'Would I succeed?'

She looked away, shaking her head, but he brought it back to him. He was determined when he wanted to be.

'All I am asking for is another kiss, a simple kiss that would not damage your purity. I have sworn to keep you chaste and that I will do. Neither am I so great a fool as to assume that Erica of Whitecliffe would welcome a Norman and a bastard into her bed, or…' he paused, the light fading from his eyes '…into her body.'

There it was again, that wealth of bitterness and hurt in his tone. Erica did not like to hear it. She did not like it either when he sighed and his hand fell away. He backed onto the bed he had made for himself and busied himself unwinding his leg-bindings, rolling them into a neat coil and setting them carefully under the eaves. Something about the gesture caught her attention, but she could not say why that was. Her heart ached.

'Wulf?'

'Mmm?'

'I…I thank you for your care of me.' She almost blurted out the truth—that part of her longed for another kiss. She wanted to be able to tell him that she would have married him, if his lord had agreed. A sigh escaped her for that, of course, was the last thing that she could do. 'Wulf?'

'Aye?'

'I have been wondering—how is it that you speak English with such fluency?' By the fisherman's shelter,

Erica had been so shocked to learn that Wulf was Norman that her mind had frozen. But it was dawning on her that for him to speak English like a native, he must in part be Saxon…

'My mother.' He indicated the coils he had made of his leg-bindings. 'My mother was Saxon, we lived in London where she made braid for leg-bindings. Hence my name.'

She blinked, murmuring, 'Brader, I see. So your Saxon name is a true name.'

'Yes, but I have a Norman name, too. I am known as FitzRobert to my lord.'

'Yes, but you are half-*Saxon*.' Erica gazed at him, wondering what it must be like—his conscience must be troubled by divided loyalties. 'Does your mother live in London?'

The dark head shook. 'She died when I was in my eighth year.'

'And did you really meet King Harold?' she asked, wondering if there was any truth in what he had told her in the rebel castle. It could not all have been lies, else Thane Guthlac would not have recruited him as part of his warband.

'Aye, as I said, in Southwark. He was Earl Harold then.'

Wulf's leg-bindings were blue, Erica had noticed them at Guthlac's castle because they made a vivid contrast with the rest of his attire, which was plain and unadorned. His Saxon mother must have made them; for Wulf to have hung on to them over the years, he must have loved her. 'Your mother made those,' she said, touched, struggling to imagine Wulf as a small boy who had lost his mother. 'And after her death?'

'My father came for me, he took me back to Honfleur to live with his *legitimate* family.'

That slight stress on the word 'legitimate' hinted at the difficulties Wulf must have encountered when he was thrust upon his father's wife. Had the woman welcomed him into her household, or had she hated him, a permanent, living reminder of her husband's liaison with a Saxon mistress? Wulf's stepmother would have had to possess an unusual strength of character not to have taken her jealousy out on him. 'Honfleur?'

Wulf's mouth twisted. 'A Norman port. My father is a wine merchant.'

'But you are part-Saxon.' Erica's heart was lighter. She frowned. Why did this please her? It should not please her; Wulf remained half-Norman, and he answered to a Norman overlord.

'Aye.' Wulf must have sensed her ambivalence, for his mouth came up at one corner and he leaned towards her. 'Does someone who is half-Saxon merit that second kiss?'

'Certainly not!'

He shrugged and reached for the lantern shutter. The light dimmed and he rolled into his cloak amid a rustle of straw.

Thoughtfully, Erica settled herself. So, Wulf FitzRobert was also Wulf Brader. He had been born in England, but his father had taken him to live in Normandy. What must life have been like for a small Saxon boy, being taken away to a foreign land? What had it felt like for him in Guthlac's hall, torn by old loyalties and by new? It could not have been easy. 'Wulf?'

His voice floated back through the cold semidarkness. 'I cannot talk all night. Go to sleep, my lady, there is much to be done in the morning.'

Erica woke with a start at the first cockcrow, blinking into a grey light. The lamp on the hook had burned out, and daylight was leaking through cracks in the thatch and the planks at the gable end. It took a moment for her to remember where she was, namely in the stable loft of the Norman garrison at Ely.

Wulf lay on his back a sword-length away, with one hand flung over his eyes. Still sleeping. Swallowing, Erica drew her head back to look at him. Against all the odds, she had had another good night's rest at his side. It would seem that the only time she slept properly in East Anglia was when this man was close.

Biting her lip, she studied the hand—his right—that covered his eyes and hid the worst of his bruises. It was relaxed, the fingers curled slightly, and the strengthening light fell on the calluses on his palm. They were the calluses of a warrior, a Norman. Wulf might be part-Saxon, but he was sworn to De Warenne, sworn to uphold the claims of the Norman King against his Saxon countrymen. Regret was a sharp pain in her belly.

She estimated him to be in his early twenties, but he had the self-containment of a more seasoned man. His sense of honour was strong, as strong as that big body. She now realised that the nervousness she had felt at the thought of sleeping with him again had been excitement, not fear. Wulf would never dishonour her. Her gaze lingered on his wide shoulders, it travelled up and down his long length—Wulf would never use his strength against her, as Hrothgar would have done. No, here lay a man—the one man—who, if he were wholly Saxon, might have tempted her into wanting marriage, for reasons that had nothing to do with politics…

No, no, *no*. That road was not to be walked upon. Wulf was—or he would have been—her father's enemy. He had lied to her. Despite this, she felt no hatred towards him, Wulf could never fill her with hate or fear. Her teeth continued to nibble at her lower lip. He was so very large and solid, she liked that about him. Was it that which made him appear dependable? And warm, he was warm, too. A smile escaped her. Wulf's size and warmth had in no small measure contributed to the soundness of her sleep.

But these days his loyalties lay with Normans. Sighing, Erica rolled on her back and stared at a split in the rafters. It was a riddle, the attraction she felt for this man. But certainly in the months since fleeing White-cliffe Hall, she had only had three decent nights' sleep and every one of them had been spent in his company.

She had trusted him in Guthlac's castle, when he had saved her from Hrothgar; she had trusted him after he had spirited her away from the castle in the marshes. But on both those occasions she had thought him Saxon. This morning she knew his true colours, she knew he was capable of lying to her and yet—another sidelong glance and she was staring at the line of his nose, at the curve of those finely cut lips, at the overnight growth of beard on his bruised cheeks—and yet…enemy or not, some part of her, some deep instinctive part, trusted him.

Wulf shifted and sighed. His hand moved and she found herself meeting that intense blue gaze.

'Good morning.' He reached out to trail a long finger

down her cheek. Heat blossomed within her. 'Cockcrow already?'

'Yes.' Saints, the man even affected her voice, it was croaky as a frog's.

Yawning, Wulf sat up and set about beating the straw from his tunic. 'Hell, I'm tired, I could sleep past noon.'

She had to clear her throat to speak. 'I know that feeling.' Whatever was the matter with her voice? She hoped she had not caught a chill.

Clambering to his feet, Wulf offered her his hand and pulled her up. 'Lady, my duty is to my lord this morning, I would ask you to remain here.'

She lifted her chin. 'In the stable? Is it my prison, then?'

'Prison? Of course not. But…' Retaining her hand, he stepped closer and tugged her to him. When he slid his hands round her waist, Erica found herself holding her breath and angling her lips a little, only a very little, to enable him to… But he simply pressed a swift, irritatingly chaste kiss to her forehead and set her firmly away. 'My lady, will you promise to do as I ask?'

Swallowing down her disappointment, she had wanted that second kiss last night, that *lover's* kiss, as she wanted one this morning. No, she would not allow herself to be disappointed, she was a woman of high birth, and she did not permit herself to give in to feelings sent from the devil, however tempting they were. It was most confusing. Briskly, she shook the dust from her skirts.

'My lady? I need that promise, you must remain here until I return.'

Her hand went out, took his forearm, she could feel the muscle and sinew through his tunic. 'Saewulf—'

'Wulf, remember?'

'Wulf.' He was so tall, his shoulders so wide. And why did she have no breath, was it because she was about to lie? She could *not* remain here, her duty would not permit her. 'I…I promise.'

'I am prepared to fight for you.'

She stared. 'Yes, you said that last night, but…'

He dragged his fingers through his hair, trying to order it. 'In the hall, you did consent to marry me.'

'But your lord refused, and besides…'

'You do not wish to marry me.' His voice was flat. 'You only agreed to save your people.'

Erica said nothing. His blue eyes held hers, his expression so determined that she could not doubt that he wanted to marry her. De Warenne might not have blessed their union, but Wulf FitzRobert wanted to marry her. How he thought he would achieve this in the face of his lord's opposition was a mystery, but…

Erica averted her gaze and stared at a bale of hay. If they were married she would have to…they would have to…this handsome young warrior would have the right to…oh, Heavens. Somehow what she had once coolly contemplated in connection with Ailric seemed another matter entirely with Wulf. There had been no heat that time when Ailric had kissed her, no burning trail where his fingers had touched her, no swooping sensation deep in her core. Ailric would *never* take her breath away. She had even, for the sake of a truce between her people and Guthlac's, been prepared to sacrifice herself to Hrothgar, a man she could never like should she live to be a thousand. But Wulf—the way his eyes seemed to reach into her heart, the way he stole her breath. The thought of permitting him to run those large hands over her naked skin…

Sweet Lord, whatever had possessed her to agree to marry this man? Of course, De Warenne had refused his request and in reality Wulf would not disobey his lord, but what if De Warenne had agreed? In truth, Erica could never have married Wulf. It came to her that the reason she could not marry him had nothing to do with Wulf's Norman blood—no, Erica could not marry Wulf FitzRobert because he made her *feel*.

When Ailric had returned from the tavern with the reek of perfume clinging to his tunic, she had felt nothing save mild exasperation. But if Wulf were to visit the tavern girls? Her gut clenched—she had to admit the thought was upsetting. But why should the thought of Wulf behaving like Ailric upset her? She had only known him a few days. To be sure he had saved her from ravishment, but he had also conspired with her father's enemies against her people, he was a liar and a deceiver.

Nevertheless, he came across as entirely honourable and his lord had complete faith in him as both a tactician and as a man. She swallowed down a sigh. And she had accepted him as wholly Saxon—it seemed her judgement was not reliable where Wulf FitzRobert was concerned.

'So, my lady…' Wulf shook his cloak out with a snap '…remember your promise to remain in the compound?'

'I…I'm sorry?'

He wound the cloak round his shoulders. 'For your safety. Your person will be quite safe here. And should you want for anything, the lad below, the one sleeping in the empty stall, will try to help you. His name is Gil. He has little English, but I have told him it is time he learnt.' He sent her a crooked grin and her heart lurched. 'He thinks I will be knighted and he has a fancy to be a squire. Given my birth, it is unlikely that he is right, but I have told him I would tolerate no squire who could not speak English.'

Erica tipped her head to one side. 'That is your chief ambition, is it not, to be knighted?'

A dark brow arched upward. 'Let us say that it is an ambition I have held for many years, but I am beginning to see I shall never attain it.' He reached for the ring in the trapdoor. 'My lord denied me the reward I really wanted.'

Wulf meant her, she knew he did, but Erica did not believe he wanted her personally. First and foremost, Wulf wanted advancement. And the carnal attraction that had flared between them? That took second place behind his ambitions. As for love—*love*? She was a fool if she thought to find love here. It was only women, she thought, who longed for love; men were warmed by their ambitions. Politics was everything for a man. Ailric had wanted her because she was the daughter of a thane, and Wulf was most likely the same.

'Ask Gil should you want for anything,' he was saying. 'You will have to be patient with his lack of English, but he is a good lad. And, Erica…?'

'Yes?'

Wulf lowered himself through the aperture. 'It would be safer for you if you bear in mind your promise not to leave the garrison.'

Erica watched his dark head disappear as he went down the ladder. It would be safer for her to stay in the garrison? Her foot tapped. Wulf thought her safer among Normans than among her own kind?

His voice reached her, slightly muffled. 'If I do not see you this evening, I will see you in the morning. Gil will fetch light for you, food and water, whatever you need. He will guard your sleep. Farewell, my lady.'

Erica remained motionless while his quick footsteps faded. A horse snuffled, a cock crowed. He was going into battle against her countrymen, a battle in which men would be maimed and killed, yet he spoke as though he were merely going out for a stroll. She did not want him hurt, she did not want *anyone* hurt. Briefly, she closed her eyes. God willing, Wulf would return safely to the garrison, but when he did, she would be long gone.

'I cannot marry you,' she whispered, 'any more than I can accompany you to Winchester as De Warenne commands. I will not submit to being handed over to a Norman master.'

Erica's chest ached. Wulf FitzRobert might owe his allegiance to a Norman lord, but he was a good man and he seemed to hold a peculiar fascination for her. Was this fascination strong enough to make her forget her duty?

Her father's words rang through her brain. *Cut your losses*, his voice said. *Rarely can we have everything we want, so it is vital to learn when to cut your losses. You will not go far wrong if you remember your duty.*

In that instant, Erica knew what she must do. Her father was not just a warrior, her father had been a wise leader, too. She had her people to think about—that must take precedence over a promise extracted by a man who was taking part in the campaign against Thane Guthlac.

Erica lingered long enough to give Wulf time to clear the yard. Much as her heart ached, much as she might regret breaking her promise to him, she had to cut him out of her life.

And what of Ailric and Hereward, languishing in Guthlac's lock-up?

She gritted her teeth. More losses she would have to cut? Yes, much as it grieved her, she would have to abandon Ailric and Hereward to their fate. They were but two lives and she had a couple of hundred to consider. There was not only her household, but the rest of her father's warband—the housecarls who had gone deeper into the fens—they must take precedence over Ailric and Hereward. Not to mention their wives and children…

Erica's duty was clear, to get a message to the warband, and the sooner the better, preferably while Wulf and his lord were occupied with Thane Guthlac. No one would have time to take note of her, and Wulf—noble fool—apparently considered her bound by her promise to remain in the garrison.

How hard would it be to give the boy Gil the slip? Biting a finger, she listened to the movements below. There were men speaking Norman French. She heard a cough and a splutter of laughter, she heard troops tramping across cobbles, she heard horses…

Her breath feathered out like mist in the January air. Odd that she had only at this moment noticed the cold. Shivering, she fastened her cloak and attached the pouch containing her father's arm-rings to her belt. It was odd, too, that Wulf had not relieved her of this. Norman law was made for men and surely that meant that her father's gold belonged to De Warenne? Wulf would have been within his rights to have taken it for him; in his rush to arms he must have forgotten.

Opening the pouch and drawing out a couple of bracelets, she slipped them on. She hesitated before drawing out another, and then that, too, she put on. Brow creasing, she retied the drawstring. De Warenne could not have meant her to keep these; Normans were known to be an avaricious breed. And while her knowledge of Norman ways was small, she had heard that their women were not allowed to hold property in their own right. Everything, down to the smallest thimble that 'belonged' to a Norman woman, in truth belonged to the woman's father, and once the woman was married, to her husband.

A cold lump formed in Erica's belly. This was, naturally, why Wulf had asked to marry her; he had seen her father's hoard, he knew her status. As she turned the bracelets on her wrist, her thoughts ran their course. The arm-rings must have slipped Wulf's mind, eclipsed by concerns over the forthcoming battle.

More fool he, because this morning Erica had a use for her father's gold.

Chapter Fourteen

Moving to the trapdoor, Erica peered down. Straw was scattered over the cobbled floor; a horse snickered; hoofs clopped. Better that Wulf had tied her, for she must not consider herself bound by her promise to stay here, any more than she was bound to accompany him to the King's Court at Winchester. It mattered not that she had been thinking the unthinkable, that she could have some liking for the man. She must be realistic. Wulf might be part-Saxon, but he had not hesitated to work against Thane Guthlac. She stared blindly at the stepladder. Had he found it easy to mislead the rebels? Had his conscience bothered him at all? No matter. Wulf's allegiances had led him to lie to her, she could not trust him.

And as for her acceptance of his offer of marriage—that, like the promise she had just made him, had been made while she had been under duress. With unspoken threats hanging over Morcar and Osred, and the further threat that Wulf might reveal to De Warenne that others of her household were loitering in Market Square, Erica would have promised to marry King William himself. She had thought to buy time to win freedom for her people— a noble aim. None the less, guilt twisted within her—she, Lady Erica of Whitecliffe, was about to break her word.

No, she was not. She was cutting her losses exactly as her father would have wished. A promise extracted under duress was not a true promise; it did not have to be honoured. Erica's first duty was to her people; many lives depended on her.

Stiffening her shoulders, she transferred her skirts to one hand and reached for the ladder. *I shall not see Wulf again*, she said in her mind as she climbed down rung by rung. *And I do not care that he will think badly of me.* If she repeated it often enough, it would acquire the ring of truth. *I do not care.*

Back on *terra firma*, she moved quietly past the stalls. The boy that Wulf had mentioned was not awake as she had imagined; instead he lay asleep, curled into a ball in the stall nearest the door. Thank the Lord. Giving Gil no more than a glance, she crept past him and paused on the threshold.

It was not yet full day. The sky overhead was clear, but a greyish pall hung over the yard. An army of mailed foot-soldiers filled the garrison courtyard, troop after troop after troop. Blinking at the sight, Erica's heart thudded and for a moment she was unable to move. Forcing her mind past her panic, she looked beyond the soldiers.

The building next to the hall had gouts of smoke billowing from the roof vents. It must be the bake-house; even across the yard the smell of fresh-baked bread was strong enough to make her mouth water. A girl emerged with a tray of loaves and laughingly dodged past an archer with an outstretched hand. When she bore it into the hall, there was one loaf less on her tray.

The sun had edged up over the top of the garrison palisade; it was glancing off the chainmail of men tramping out through the gate. Heavy boots pounded the cobbles, arms clattered. No sooner had the troop passed under the portcullis than another marched in.

Was the entire Norman army stationed in Ely?

The soldiers' breath wreathed about them like smoke, and in Erica's mind the returning troop was transfigured into a metallic dragon, a fire-breathing dragon with a footfall louder than the pounding of Thor's hammer in Valhalla. It was enough to make one fear that the old gods walked again.

Erica leaned against the stable doorpost and shrank into her cloak, trying to watch without being watched. The returning troop broke ranks, and before her eyes the fearsome dragon disintegrated. A foot-soldier removed his helmet, revealing a tousle-haired lad with a face that could have made him the twin of Cadfael; another leaned his spear against the wall of the hall and gestured for a comrade to help him out of his chain shirt. Several headed straight for a water-trough, water sparkled as they splashed it over their faces; others eased their shoulder muscles and made a bee-line for the bake-house. Tired men, men who were aching and hungry, human beings like herself.

Feeling in some way wrong-footed by her observations, Erica turned her father's bracelets on her wrist and sucked in a breath. It ought to be a comfort to learn that many of these Normans were little more than boys, boys like Cadfael. They would not hurt her, especially since she had been placed under the protection of Captain FitzRobert. Boldly, she stepped into the yard.

Pewter-coloured clouds were drifting in from the east, but there was a distinct yellow cast to the sky. Snow? Holding her breath, half-expecting to be challenged, Erica walked steadily towards the building she had marked as the bake-house.

First, she needed supplies.

Second, she would speak with Morcar and Osred.

Once more the guilt rose within her—*he will think badly of you*—it had a bitter taste. Head down, trying not to meet any of the soldiers' eyes, she continued across the yard.

How would Wulf react when he found her gone—would he shrug those broad shoulders and forget her? Would he be angry—would he see her defection as an affront to his pride? Would he try to find her? Not that she cared, she was cutting her losses.

The bake-house door was open and, as Erica approached, a couple of archers in stained leather gambesons emerged. They were cramming steaming hunks of bread into their mouths, moaning in appreciation. It was hard not to smile, but she managed it. The archers fell silent. One gulped down his bread and, wiping his mouth on his leather wrist-guard, gave her a sheepish grin. The other, still chewing, gave her an ironic bow and waved her inside.

Pulse jumping, Erica squeezed past. It was like walking into a warm wall. The baker was pulling a batch of loaves from a brick oven; when he turned her way, her jaw dropped. Saxon—the baker's long hair and beard were styled in the Saxon manner.

His eyes ran her up and down, as he in his turn made his judgement of her. 'Lady?' His face was crimson. Sweat streamed down his face and into his beard, it darkened the neck of his tunic.

Wondering what he thought of her, feeling a blush rise to her cheeks that was in no way connected to the heat in the bake-house, Erica lifted her chin. 'I…I need a couple of loaves, if you please.'

'And who might you be?'

There was no reason to lie. 'Erica of Whitecliffe.'

The baker's gaze sharpened. 'You're the Saxon lady who came in yesterday.'

'I…yes.'

'With Captain FitzRobert.'

'Yes.' Her cheeks burned and she braced herself for a lewd comment about passing the night in the stables with De Warenne's captain, but none was forthcoming. The name FitzRobert carried with it a measure of respect, apparently.

'Help yourself.' Mopping his forehead, he indicated a batch of loaves cooling on a trestle. Erica took two and wrapped them carefully in a piece of sacking. They were deliciously warm.

Feeling the baker's interested gaze boring into her back, Erica mumbled her thanks and hurried out.

Next, for Morcar and Osred. She had a feeling that this would not be quite so simple…

Reaching the prison building, Erica dropped the loaves to one side by the door and approached the guard. She went cold as she looked at him. No boy this, she realised, staring past the metal noseguard of his helmet at eyes that were grey and hard as flints.

'Please, sir,' she said, making deliberate show of playing with one of her father's arm-rings. Pulling it on and off, staring at it to make quite clear to the man what might be his, should he agree to let her past him. On, off, on, off, dangling it in front of him. Remembering to keep up her pretence of understanding no French whatsoever, she made certain to speak in English. 'Please, sir, I should like to speak with the prisoners that were brought in yesterday evening.'

On, off. On, off. The arm-ring gleamed softly in the morning light as she wriggled it between her finger and thumb. The man spoke English, at least enough to realise what she was doing, for the flint-coloured eyes moved from hers to the arm-ring and back again. And while the merchant had not offered her much yesterday, the arm-ring had to be worth a fortune to a common man like him. Normans might not value arm-rings for their artistic worth, but they must have *some* value in mercenary terms…

The guard's helmet hid most of his expression, but his lips tightened. 'No, my lady.' He shook his head. 'You may not pass.'

'Please, sir.'

'No!'

It would be futile to argue, Erica heard it in his tone. A man of stone, the Second Coming would arrive before this one would relent. Like Wulf, he was set on his course. She swallowed down a sigh; there must only be two such men in the entire Norman race, and naturally she had to run up against them both. But for Morcar and Osred's sake, she must try once more. Mentioning Wulf's name had worked like a charm on the baker, perhaps it would here…

'Please, sir, I beg you. Captain FitzRobert—'

But this time Wulf's name was no charm; the flinty eyes stared through her, he didn't even deign to reply.

Erica's shoulders drooped, though his response was hardly surprising. With a grimace she jammed her father's bracelet back over her fist, scooped up the loaves and started walking back to the stables. The guard's eyes bored into her shoulder-blades every step of the way.

At the stable door, she glanced back. The man had been drawn into conversation with a fellow trooper, praise the Saints. Her whole body quivered.

It was time.

With a swift, furtive glance around the compound, Erica took a couple of side-steps, and walked towards the open portcullis and the street beyond. *Be bold*, she told herself, hugging the loaves to her breast, *be bold. No need for guilt. Wulf has no right to hold you to him, not when you gave him your word merely to win time. Think of Solveig and Cadfael, think of Hrolf and the others who need you...*

Boldly, she smiled at the guards by the portcullis and sauntered past them into the street. No one attempted to stay her. Immediately she turned left, towards the quays. Ears open, every muscle tensed for the cry that would be her signal to pick up her skirts and fly, she took one casual step, then another. Another.

At a smithy the furnace was glowing like the devil's eye, and the blacksmith was going at it hammer and tongs. Erica passed by without incident. Next came a butcher's stall. A couple of geese hung from the awning, plucked ready for the pot, nearby a black pig was tied to a post, scratching its ear with its hind leg. That, too, she passed without outcry.

Boldly. Boldly. She skirted some horse-dung, slipped on a patch of ice and almost fell.

Ahead, the street was opening out into the market proper; beyond it lay the town palisade and the quays. Freedom! The January air hung heavily in her lungs, her chest felt tight. Erica could hardly breathe, braced as she was for the shout that would tell her that her involvement with Captain Wulf FitzRobert was not after all at an end.

The sky was looking wintrier, a snowstorm was surely brewing and she had much to do before it broke. A wave of weariness swept over her. If only she were not alone. It was most dispiriting, but for the first time since fleeing Lewes, Erica found herself contemplating certain defeat.

There were *so many* Normans—had she set herself an impossible task? She could not back down from it though, not when the others were relying on her. She sighed. Although she had but lately left a garrison that was bursting at the seams with Normans, and although the people of Eel Island were pushing past her—boatmen, hawkers, townsfolk—she had never felt so alone.

Be bold, you are Thane Eric's daughter, your duty cannot be shirked. The fight must *go on.*

Even if you have lost the taste for it? a demon asked.

Even then.

Erica increased her pace, walking swiftly past a woman pulling hot chestnuts from a brazier, past a man selling wine from a steaming cauldron…

Finally she was standing outside the city boundaries on the Ely dockside, gazing about her, hoping against hope that she would see one or other of her household. Yesterday, she had given them instructions that if she did not return, they were to go deeper into the fens to meet up with her father's warband. Of course she hoped they had obeyed her, but one of them might have waited…

There was a flurry at the water gate that led from the market square onto the docks. A shout. Slowly the gate pushed open and mailed figures came swarming through. Troopers were streaming onto every quay and wharf, long lines of them, like so many silver snakes. There were archers in leather jerkins, their quivers spiky with arrows. Orders rang through the air, jetties groaned. And then, as Erica's gaze ran over a cluster of boatmen, her attention was snared by a particularly tall figure, a tall, broad-shouldered man wearing a brown tunic and a cloak the colour of—Wulf?

But, no, it could not be Wulf, Wulf had already set out on his mission for his lord, he would be in chain-mail. Another Norman captain was directing a troop towards one of the barges—but he did not have Wulf's height. Yet another was hurrying along a group of archers—this one was too burly. And another… Lord, what *was* she doing, searching for Wulf FitzRobert when she ought to be looking for Cadfael or Solveig?

Hoisting her skirts clear of a mess of eel heads and fishguts on the planking, Erica picked her way down one of the emptier wharves.

A Saxon ferryman in one of the smaller rowing boats smiled her way. The beard protruding from his voluminous hood was black and bushy, his eyes were sharp. 'You need a boat, my lady?'

'Perhaps.' Erica fingered an arm-ring.

The boatman stroked his beard. 'Look no further than Alfred.' He tapped the side of his boat with an oar. 'Finest oak, soundly built. Where do you go, the London road?'

Erica twirled the arm-ring. 'Later, perhaps. But first, I have another destination in mind. I am bound for an inn called the Willow. Do you know it?'

Alfred went very still. 'The one past Wicken Fen, in the west?'

'I believe so, but I have not been there myself.'

'The Willow's not much of a place for an unaccompanied young…lady.' Alfred tugged at his beard and lowered his voice. 'Full of rebels and outlaws.'

Erica's chin lifted. 'Nevertheless, I need to get there. Will you take me?' She turned her father's bracelet on her wrist.

'I'll drop you off, but I'll not be staying, the place gives me the creeps. And if one of those—' Alfred jerked his head at the foot-soldiers climbing aboard one of the barges '—discovers I've been there, my ferrying days will be over.' He made a slashing gesture across his throat. 'You understand?'

Erica swallowed. 'Perfectly. I don't expect you to stay, simply ferry me to the Willow and this arm-ring will be yours.'

Alfred dipped his head in agreement and offered her his hand.

Erica hesitated; she was ill-prepared for this journey. She needed a dagger, she needed more food. But more Norman soldiers were snaking through the water gate, she dared not. Better she reached the Willow hungry than risk recapture.

'My lady?'

Ice was forming at the margin of the jetty. No time, there was no time, in any case.

'I...I, yes, Alfred, my thanks.'

While Erica settled herself in the boat, Alfred relayed his destination to the ferryman next to him. It was common practice to let your peers know your whereabouts whenever possible and only sensible in these uncertain times. When she looked across, Alfred was paler than he had been a moment before.

'Alfred? Our agreement holds?'

'Yes, my lady, but the job is more risky than I had thought and, what is more, Bran here reckons that snow is on the way. I shall be wanting more than one bracelet, my price is two.'

'*Two!*'

'Aye.'

She gritted her teeth and glared at the other ferryman, who would not meet her eyes. Alfred had her over a barrel and he knew it. 'Very well, Alfred, Two gold armrings.' Pulling one off, she held it out. 'One now and one when we reach the Willow.'

Grunting assent, Alfred pushed her father's arm-ring over his fist and reached for his oars.

With her blue veil and cloak wrapped closely about her, Erica watched the quays and wharves of Ely diminish as they headed out into the waterway. So focused was she on looking out for a tall, particularly broad-shouldered Norman with dark hair that she failed to notice the slight figure of the groom, Gil, as he pelted up to the quayside. Chest heaving, the boy's eyes followed her boat as it nosed out towards the western reaches.

* * *

Alfred's nose was red, hers was sure to be the same. Rearranging the folds of her cloak around her feet, wishing for the marten furs that had been left behind in Whitecliffe, Erica wriggled her toes. If only she had had time to stop for more supplies. Frost was nipping her ears and fingertips; she longed for a thicker cloak and her lost gloves.

Alfred was not wearing gloves either; his hands were bound with lengths of fabric, like bandages, dirty bandages. But the cold did not appear to affect him; the boatman was rowing steadily with an even stroke like Wulf's that spoke of years on the water.

Last night Wulf had told her that he had been brought up near the river in Southwark. Blue eyes swam into her mind, dark as they had been after their kiss. She touched her mouth. If she tried, she could almost feel the echo of his lips on hers. No, *no*, she must not think of him; their friendship, such as it was, was impossible.

Alfred was jumpy. While he rowed his head was never still, it craned this way and that as he scoured the frosty margins of the waterways. He was always on the look-out and it was most unnerving. They came to a fork where one of the channels was much wider than the other. Their boat angled into the narrow channel and the wider waterway was soon lost to sight behind a screen of twiggy willows and alders.

The sun did not reach them here, it was dark and shadowy and the trees seemed to stretch towards them, spiky black arms, lightly rimed with white. Goose-bumps feathered over her skin. The bottom of the boat scraped against an obstruction, Alfred was steering the boat towards the bank. They came to a standstill with a bump and he shipped the oars.

Erica frowned. 'Alfred?'

A hand was slapped over Erica's mouth. 'Hush,' he breathed, rolling his eyes at the island screening them from the broader channel. 'Listen.'

Suppressing a grimace, for Alfred's bindings smelt distinctly of garlic, Erica peeled his hand from her mouth and nodded. A lump of ice formed in her belly. Had they been followed?

Alfred reached for a branch to hold the boat in place. A minute passed. A coot called. Another minute. The wind was brushing through the willows, but Erica could hear nothing else. Tossing back her hood, she tipped her head to one side and then she caught it, a soft clunk, faint but distinct. The unmistakeable clunk and squeak of a pair of oars being pulled in their rowlocks.

'Who?' she mouthed, heart all but stopping. 'Normans?' *Wulf must not find her here, Wulf must not find her here.*

Alfred put his finger to his lips.

A splash, a mutter. A hissed command and then more silence. Only the wind stroking the willows and the honking of geese flying overhead in long straggling lines.

There was no sun in this murky backwater, nothing but shadows and wind. So little light. The sky was filled with clouds, and then she saw it, the first tiny flake. *Snow!* As more snowflakes landed on her lap, Erica made as if to speak, but Alfred's unsavoury hand clamped over her mouth.

She jerked free and scowled, mouthing, 'What?'

'It is Normans,' he muttered, pointing. 'Look, whatever they were planning in Ely, it's going to happen nearby.'

Out in the main channel on the other side of those trees, shapes were drifting slowly by, boat after boat and barge after barge, laden with silent soldiers. Several barrels were stacked on one and arrow shafts were sticking out of crates in another. Subtle and quiet as ghosts, they slid by, barely visible through the bushes. De Warenne's barges.

They waited in Alfred's little wherry, turning into blocks of ice as snow clouds darkened the sky and the whole of King William's invasion fleet, or so it seemed, glided past on the other side of the island.

At length, Alfred stirred. 'That's it,' he said, blowing out a breath. 'They didn't see us.'

'Saint Swithun be praised.' Erica rubbed her hands together to get the blood going; her fingers wouldn't work. More snowflakes were floating down; those that landed on the island were settling, but those that fell into the black waters vanished in an instant.

Alfred peered intently through the undergrowth. His hands were bunched into fists, Erica could see the pale gleam of his bones. She bit her lip, struck with a sudden fear. Would he abandon her here? Or worse? She fiddled with her father's other arm-rings. His eyes followed the gesture. Saints.

Reaching for his oars, Alfred pushed them away from the bank, rowing into the centre of the narrow waterway. Nose redder than ever, he was hunched in his cloak against the snow, and whenever she tried to catch his gaze, he looked the other way. Oh, Lord.

Had Wulf been on one of those barges? Wulf's reconnaissance meant that he could lead De Warenne straight to the rebel base. Wulf also knew the location of the cottage that Erica and her household had been using, but since he had been with them when they had abandoned it, he would not lead his lord there. No, Wulf would be in the vanguard of those barges, leading them to Guthlac.

Skin crawling, she closed her eyes. Ailric and Hereward! What would happen to them, caught in the middle of a battle, neither on one side nor the other? Would they be given arms and a chance to fight, or would they be slaughtered out of hand?

Cut your losses, you cannot have everything.

A wave of nausea rose within her. *No, Father*, no. *I cannot do this! Not Ailric and Hereward!*

It was one thing to heed her father's precepts in theory, but in reality… Erica felt sick, sick to her marrow because the hideous truth was that she could do nothing for Ailric and Hereward, who were as good as dead. Even if she managed to reach the Willow and link up with others in her father's warband, it would be too late for Ailric and Hereward.

Cut your losses, daughter, cut your losses.

'Alfred, do you know Guthlac Stigandson?'

Behind his beard, Alfred's cheeks went the colour of the chalk cliffs near her home at Lewes. 'I know of him.'

'Is his castle nearby?'

Alfred's eyes shifted. 'I'll not be taking you there, my lady…' he threw a wary glance over his shoulder '…not with them in the offing.'

'We're close though, aren't we?' Even as the words left Erica's lips she knew the answer. They *were* close— something about the shape of the alders on the land to their left was familiar. Her mouth went dry. Yes, she knew this place, Wulf had brought her here when he had snatched her from the chapel. A little way past those trees, a little farther inland, there was a fisherman's smokehouse and a crude hurdle shelter....

'The castle *is* nearby!'

Alfred was watching her as though she had sprouted several heads. His face went hard. 'I'll not take you there, not today. Not if you offer me every bauble in your possession.' Pulling strongly on one oar, he turned the boat to face the smokehouse and edged a dagger from his belt.

Erica stared, heart in her throat. She had no dagger of her own, nothing with which to defend herself. The boat lurched over the shallows.

'Out.' Alfred gestured with the dagger. 'Out you get.' Branches of an overhanging willow snagged in her veil as they came to rest by the bank. 'Go on, get out. I don't know what game you are playing, my lady, and I don't want to know, I have a daughter and I plan on seeing her grow up. I won't take you any farther. Out.'

Erica blinked through a flurry of snowflakes. 'But you can't!' Already the snow on the island had filled in the hollows, turning all to white. It was a desolate and inhospitable spot, particularly since Wulf…since she was alone.

The dagger jerked and she flinched back. 'Alfred, *no*. You can't leave me here!'

'Your game's too dangerous. I am but an ordinary man with a wife and child to think about.' The dagger flashed in the last of the light. 'Get on with you.'

'No, *no*.' Erica did not want, she *really* did not want to be left alone here, she would surely freeze to death. 'Alfred, take me to the Willow. *Please*.'

'Out. There's a shelter nearby, make the most of it. Think yourself lucky I don't slit your throat and make off with the rest of your father's valuables.'

Instinctively, Erica's hand went to her pouch. 'You…you knew my father?'

Alfred shook his head and his hood fell back. Snow-flakes were catching in his beard. 'Not personally, my lady, but I know enough to guess that he was a thane. Loyal to Harold, was he? Died at Hastings, did he?'

Alfred's tone confused her; it was bitter and scathing, and she could not fathom it. Alfred was Saxon. And these past few years, since William the Bastard had come to England, Erica had held her father's memory close to her heart. Thane Eric's loyalty to King Harold was something to be proud of, his bravery was unquestionable, and yet Alfred…why did he sound so scathing, so cynical? *I am but an ordinary man*, he had said.

Questions were bubbling up in her mind, but before Erica was able to open her mouth, a last sharp movement of Alfred's dagger stilled her tongue. 'Out.'

Gripping the side of the boat with one hand, clutching the bread in its sacking with the other, Erica clambered out of the boat.

Chapter Fifteen

Dusk, a thick and silent dusk that was full of snow, Wulf thought, shaking his hood and blinking the stuff from his eyes. He was stationed in one of the barges that De Warenne had commandeered as a troop carrier. The barge was lying in wait near Guthlac's hideout, behind the cover given by a shrubby spit of land on the eastern edge of the lake.

Absently, he brushed more snow from his cloak. This had to be the most difficult military exercise of his career. They were to attack a defended castle, across water—he had told De Warenne that a decoy was essential. This is where the archers came in.

For all that the archers had been practising zone-shooting as he had ordered, it remained a chancy business. In the failing light, they would need every ounce of their skill. Visibility was almost non-existent; to all intents and purposes, they would at the beginning be shooting blind.

While Wulf waited for the bowmen to position themselves, he kept his gaze trained in the direction of the rebel hideout. Two circles glowed in the snow-filled dark. Since he had arrived, there had been no traffic across the lake, no sound from within the palisade. The whole fen was as quiet as the grave.

He grimaced. Perhaps Stigandson was learning circumspection—the blazing torches had vanished. Had he somehow got word of the attack? Only the faintest flicker of light showed in the vicinity of the portcullis. Another glimmer was visible higher up, where Wulf would place the hall door on the mound walkway.

The barge swung sideways, nudged by another. Like his, it was full of shadows, but for an instant a lantern in its prow threw out a beam of light. Someone swore softly and the light was quickly extinguished, but not before Wulf glimpsed the bowmen.

Good, here was his decoy, or part of it. The archers were there to distract those in the castle with fire-arrows and provide cover for the infantry while they forged their way to the jetty. Following his suggestion, more archers had been deployed in the west, on the other side of the island.

A ramp thudded onto the spit of land, and a barrel was levered out—the pitch for the arrows. They weren't about to fire the pitch on board, not if they could avoid it. It rumbled as it rolled down the ramp, like distant thunder. One of the bowmen was minding a coal-filled brazier; he would keep it shielded until the last possible moment.

The snow was settling. Impatiently, Wulf flicked more from his shoulders. He was wearing his sheepskin gloves, but he didn't like fighting in gloves; he would remove them when the attack was sounded.

Snow. He squinted skywards. More snow, hell. As far

as chainmail was concerned, snow was as bad a curse
as rain. He only had one mailshirt—Gil, who insisted
on playing the part of his squire, had better have done
a good job with oiling it, he couldn't afford to let it rust.
And, sheepskin gloves or no, the cold was gnawing his
fingers off; he flexed them to keep them moving. At
least Erica was safely ensconced in the garrison, she
would not be covered in snow, freezing to death.

Another boat, a small rowing boat that had no place
here, knocked the side of the barge as it squeezed in
between the troopship and the archers.

'Captain? *Captain!*'

'Gil?' The bottom dropped out of Wulf's stomach.
Gil, *here*? Gil was meant to be watching Erica.

A pinprick of light flickered. Wulf signalled to the
boy to speak quietly. The snow would muffle sound;
hopefully, it would keep the Saxons in their motte
ignorant of any threat until the last moment, but he did
not want to push his luck. Surprise was a large element
of their attack and it had to be successful, De Warenne's
continued good favour depended upon it.

'What in hell are you doing here?' Wulf hissed,
leaning out to steady the boy's boat.

'I…I am sorry, Captain, but I knew you would want
to know. The lady…'

'Yes?'

'Sh…she got out of the garrison and I think she has
run away.'

'Run away?' Wulf's heart turned to ice.

'Yes, sir. Leastwise I think so.' Swallowing hard, Gil
ploughed on. 'I kept an eye on her like you said. After
you had gone, she wandered around the compound, got

some bread, tried to see her men. And then she…she just walked out.'

'*Merde.* Couldn't you stop her?'

'No, sir. By the time I realised what she was up to, I couldn't do anything without causing a scene and there were so many of her countrymen about and…' Gil's throat convulsed '…I thought it best not to lose her.'

'Quite right, go on.' Wulf kept his voice low, pleased his voice was calm. Inside his mind was in turmoil. She had broken her promise, she had run away. He flung a glance at the snow-filled night. Where would she go, what would she do? *Hell.* He could throttle Gil for letting her get away. Erica was not safe. *Erica…*

Gil's eyes were fastened on his, large with anxiety. 'I…I'm sorry, sir.'

Wulf shook his head. He would not chastise the boy; he himself was probably more to blame. He had hoped Erica could trust him, but why should she?

Circumstances had conspired against him. He had broken into her sanctuary and forced drink down her throat; he had picked her up like a sack of wheat and thrown her over his shoulder; he was fighting for the Norman cause…the list went on. It had been naïve to believe that she would keep her word to him. Truly, she was her father's daughter, Thane Eric's standards were hers. He frowned. The standards Erica of Whitecliffe followed might be flawed, but they were the ones she had grown up with.

Of course! That was why she had been able to walk up to Guthlac and offer herself as a sacrifice. Her father had followed ancient laws, tribal laws. Wulf might think them barbaric, but they were familiar to her; likely she was blind to the injustice of them.

And as for himself, circumstances had forced finesse out of him and he had not given Erica any reason to suppose that he or De Warenne would treat her any better. She probably thought Wulf was as barbaric as Guthlac. He had hoped to prove otherwise. He sighed. 'Gil, the fault does not lie at your door, Lady Erica has a will of her own.'

'Yes, sir.'

'Did she leave Ely?'

'Yes, she hired a small wherry. I knew you'd not want to lose her, so I…I took this boat and followed her.'

'Good lad. And…?'

'*FitzRobert!*' De Warenne's voice came over his shoulder.

Biting down a curse, Wulf tore his attention from his would-be squire. He almost laughed aloud. He would never be knighted after this débâcle, *never*. To lose the lady he was meant to be escorting to Winchester…hell. 'My lord?'

'Give the order to ready the fire arrows.'

'Yes, my lord.' Swallowing down a curse at the ill timing, Wulf swung back to Gil. 'Bang on that barge three times.'

Gil picked up his oar and did as he was asked. A second later the splintering of wood announced that the head archer was breaking open the pitch. A spark flickered. And then flames were rippling over the surface of the pitch, flames that were visible to Wulf, but were screened from the sight of Guthlac's look-out.

On the spit of land, several dozen spikes shifted,

black against the golden glow of the fire, as the archers strung their bows. The acrid smell of warming pitch floated out over the barges and towards the lake.

Wulf tore off his gloves and thrust them into his belt. He must fight, but within him a battle was *already* raging.

Erica! Every nerve and sinew in his body was screaming at him to jump into Gil's boat and snatch the oars. He wanted to scour East Anglia until he found her. The thought of her out there alone and in the dark—his heart was beating a wild tattoo, one which had nothing to do with the forthcoming battle and everything to do with a certain Saxon noblewoman.

But he could do nothing, not when the attack on Guthlac's castle was finally at hand. He had been charged with seeing this fen purged of rebels and he would fulfil his commission. His entire life he had been waiting to prove himself and the moment was at hand. Wulf ought to feel triumph, but his head was pounding and his temples throbbed…*merde.*

'Gil?'

'Captain?'

'Get out of the line of fire, we shall finish this conversation later.' Without waiting to see that Gil had obeyed him, pulled in two by the need to ensure that Erica was safe, Wulf turned to his chief oarsman. 'The men are ready?'

'Yes, Captain.'

'Wait until the archers in the west have loosed their first volley, then row like hell for that jetty.'

'Aye, sir.'

Wulf watched as a cauldron of flaming pitch was swung into position. Much as he wanted to chase after

Erica, he had work to do here. Once the cauldron was safely on its tripod, he reached for a lantern and flung back the shutter. 'Ready the bowmen!'

'Aye, Captain!'

'Shoot the moment you can track the arrows from across the lake. Etienne, you command the archers.'

'Captain.'

And then the dark sky above the castle was alive with streaking lights—flights of arrows shot by the archers across the lake. Battle was joined.

Wulf's barge juddered. 'Shields up!'

Roman fashion, his men clicked their shields together over their heads as protection against missiles. On the land behind them, scores of fire arrows were flickering over faces that shone with melting snow-flakes. The bowmen's eyes gleamed grim with intent.

Etienne held up his arm. 'Ready, aim...*fire!*'

As the second volley of Norman arrows arched through the night, a cry went up from across the lake. A horn sounded.

Wulf's barge pushed away from the bank and his oarsmen leaned into their oars. As they slid towards the rebel stronghold, the black fenwater burned with re-flected fire-arrows, hundreds of gilded ripples, like writhing water snakes.

Erica! Where the hell was she?

The hours dragged when one was freezing.

Erica was curled up in the fisherman's shelter, teeth chattering. The hem of her skirts had been damp when she had crawled in, most likely it still was, but her legs were dead to her and she could no longer tell. It was pitch black. The starry lantern was at her side, but she had been unable to light it.

Its soft glow would have banished the night to outside the hut, but her fingers had been thumbs, she had dropped the flint and it had bounced away. She couldn't find it in the dark. And it was dark, so very dark in here. Erica had always disliked the dark, but tonight the cold was by far the worst danger. Exhausted, chilled to her marrow, she huddled in a ball and imagined the glow of the lantern, the heat of a real fire. A fire would warm her, it would untie limbs that were hamstrung by cold, it would help her sleep.

What had happened at the castle, what had happened to Wulf? No, *no*, why was this so hard to remember? Wulf was banished from her mind. But Ailric and Hereward had not been banished, what had happened to them?

A twig snapped outside the shelter, breaking into her thoughts. A fox? Her eyes went wide as a shiver shot down her spine. A *wolf*? Saints, no! But this was the month of the wolves, the time when hunger made them lose their fear of men and drove them towards human habitation. Did wolves haunt this watery part of England? She had no idea. Scrabbling frantically in the dark, her frostbitten fingers closed on something—a stick? She gripped it as though her life depended on it.

Black. Everything was so black. *Lord, save me.* She strained her ears.

A footfall came, very soft. Her breath stopped. She swallowed down an extraordinary desire to laugh. She, kill a wolf? With a little stick? If a wolf was prowling about outside, she would probably drop the stick and die of fright.

Something made a crunching noise and her mind filled with images of strong jaws closing on bone. Grasping the stick as best she might, she held it in front like a dagger and stared at the entrance.

Silence.

The leather flap was swept aside and a blast of freezing air hit her in the face. Something came in, but she could see nothing. Breathing, she could hear breathing.

'Erica?'

The stick fell from her grasp and a mad laugh escaped her. 'Wulf? *Wulf!*'

Clothes rustled as he came towards her, and then hard hands clamped down on shoulders. He shook her, shook her so hard that her teeth rattled, but she did not care.

'You *fool!*' His voice was curt and he was breathing heavily as though he had been running. His fingers dug into her flesh like hooks and he smelt…no, he *stank* of smoke. He shook her again and her hood fell back. 'Faithless woman, you swore you would stay at the garrison, you swore you would come to Winchester with me.'

Wulf! Elation filled her and she gave another wild laugh.

Another shake. 'It is not safe for you alone. Don't you realise there is more evil in England than the hatred of a bloodfeud or your hatred of Normans? Not a few months since, Earl Oswulf was slain by robbers.'

'Earl Oswulf? Of Bernicia?'

'The same. You fool, you…' Wulf's grip shifted and a callused hand found her face, rough fingers touched her cheek, her temple and her forehead before sliding down to her neck. At her shiver his voice shed its anger. 'Lord, you stupid woman, you're frozen. Here.' He released her for an instant and a heavy weight settled on her shoulders.

Fur, his fur cloak. Erica hugged it to her, bemused by the strong reaction his arrival had caused in her. Overwhelming relief. Her fears, of the dark, of wild animals, were gone the instant she heard his voice. Even the cold seemed a small thing beside the large, the very important thing—*Wulf had come to find her*. He had been concerned for her.

When she had left the garrison that morning, her first thoughts had been for the warriors awaiting her guidance in the fens. It had occurred to her that Wulf would be angry when he discovered her absence—but concerned?

'You disobeyed me,' he said, voice muffled.

Her heart sank. No, not concern, pride. His pride had been injured. She shook her head. Concern, how wondrous would that have been? Wulf might be half-Norman, and he might be illegitimate, but he was a man. And men, even half-breed Norman bastards, had pride. She would best remember that. This man was first and foremost a warrior and she would be a fool indeed were she to search for any softness in him.

With his thick fur cloak round her shoulders, she listened to the sounds he was making. He was picking up the lantern, striking a spark from his flint. Once, twice. Sparks flew. One caught in the tinder and gathered strength. And soon yellow stars were splashed on the hurdles over their heads, and on each other.

He set the lantern on the floor. His face was covered in dark grime, he was filthy. Noticing her flint in a corner, he picked it up and held it out. 'Yours?'

'Yes, thank you.' She slipped it into her pouch and,

frowning, reached for his cheek. 'Soot? Wulf, you're covered in soot!' That reek of smoke was far more than the usual smell of a household fire, and her mouth went dry as the realisation went home. 'The castle, it is burnt?'

He nodded.

'To the ground?'

Another nod.

'And…Thane Guthlac?'

'Refused to surrender.'

Erica bit her lip, she had expected as much. Guthlac Stigandson would die before he surrendered, that was his way. 'And wh…what of Ailric and Hereward? Did…did you see them?'

A hand covered hers, it was dirt black and the knuckles were scraped and bloody, but she drew comfort from it none the less. 'They are unhurt. Since they were imprisoned, they were not involved in the fighting. I made certain they were granted safe custody.'

Some of the tension left her, but worry remained, skirting the edges of her mind. 'Your lord, I had not heard that he was merciful. Will he…will he…?'

'I repeat, Ailric and Hereward are well. They were not bearing arms and they have been given another chance. De Warenne has asked them to consider giving their allegiance to him.'

'My father's men, swear fealty to a Norman?'

'It might be in their best interests.'

'I doubt it.' Questions were forming in her mind; Erica opened her mouth to give them voice, but his dark head shook.

He scrubbed at his face and gave a jaw-cracking yawn. 'Enough, I am beyond weary. We both need sleep, and since it is so cold that only madmen are abroad, we shall not be disturbed.'

'And Normans hold this corner of the fens,' she said, unable to keep the bitterness from her tone.

'They do indeed and that, my sweet Saxon, means that you and I are safe in here.' He tugged off his boots, pushed them to one side and raised a brow at her. 'Do you keep your boots on?'

He reached for her ankle and scowled. 'Lord, Erica, do you lack all sense? Your skirts are soaked.'

'I know, the ferry…there was water in the bottom. I did not realise until it was too—Wulf! What are you doing?'

He had his knife out and, before Erica could blink, had sliced a good foot off the hem. 'There's a sharp frost,' he said. 'We cannot have a fire in here, and you simply must not sleep in wet skirts.'

Mouth open, more astonished than angry, she watched as he tossed the damp fabric towards the entrance. 'But…but… this is the only gown I have with me and you've ruined it!'

The broad shoulders lifted. '*Tant pis.* Too bad. I won't have you catch your death. I promised my lord I would escort you safely to Winchester.' He took her chin and for an instant his eyes flickered to her mouth. 'We will have to share my cloak.'

Silently, she nodded and opened his cloak. He pulled her to the ground and arranged both their cloaks over them, drawing her body into his beneath them. 'Sleep now,' he said, gruffly. 'Sleep.'

The words froze on Erica's tongue. Wulf smelt of soot and smoke and sweat and even, faintly, of blood. The smells of battle, disturbing smells. His growing beard scratched her forehead. But he smelt of Wulf, too, and that was not disturbing, it was…reassuring. Inhaling, Erica focused on his scent, on Wulf. Safe. She blinked at a yellow star on the side of the shelter.

'You are hot as a furnace,' she muttered, as her muscles relaxed into his warmth. 'I am glad you came to find me.'

'Are you, my lady?' A large hand adjusted the cloak, cocooning them in his heat.

'How did you know where to look?'

'Gil.'

The stable boy, of course—he must have followed her. Before sleep claimed her, Erica imagined the gentle press of lips on her forehead. Her thoughts drifted.

The call of a coot rattled through the dawn air. Wulf stirred and reluctantly opened his eyes. Erica lay in his arms, body soft and relaxed as she slept. In the weak light filtering around the door flap, he could just make out her features.

His fingertips traced a gentle line over her shoulder before tangling in a dark skein of hair. Her hand lay on his waist. Gingerly linking his fingers with hers, he lifted it, noting the differences between her hand and his. His fingers were bigger-boned, sturdier, the nails cut straight across, and they were filthy and bruised. Hers were fine-boned, clean and unblemished. She wore two gold rings, one plain and the other bearing some sort of device. As he lifted her hand closer to examine it, her bracelets jingled. Catching his breath, he gently replaced her hand against his chest. He didn't want to wake her.

True, he wanted to get her out of the fens with all

speed, but her life as an outlaw had taken her to the end of her tether. In truth, she was so worn out that she had slept like a log every night they had been together; her exhaustion made her forget to hate him.

He looked at her dark lashes, at the smooth lines of her cheek, at the bow of her lips. In his arms. Unconsciously he tightened his hold. When Erica was asleep she forgot her mistrust of men. Of him.

Small wonder she mistrusted men when the politics of her people were such that she felt obliged to offer herself as a sacrifice, and when a fellow Saxon like Hrothgar had been prepared—even eager—to rape her. That damn bloodfeud had much to answer for. Her housecarl Ailric had been the only one to speak out against it. His mouth edged up. Ailric was a man of good sense, even though he had been outnumbered in Guthlac's hall.

Outside the creaky call of a coot regained his attention and his gaze wandered to the entrance, to the light outside. He sighed. He had to get her away from here. God knew he had no wish to see her married to some great Norman lord, but better that than she be forced to eke out her days in this watery world. As an outlaw. A rebel. On the run, and surely prey to more exhaustion than she could bear.

His commander was on campaign in East Anglia, charged by King William to clear the fens of rebels. And while De Warenne had taken a liking to Erica when he had met her at the garrison, that would soon change if he learned she had tried to escape being taken to Winchester. Worse, if De Warenne were to catch so much as a whisper of what Wulf suspected—that Erica was set on urging a band of housecarls to open rebellion—there would be no saving her. And as for the knighthood that he was aiming for—that would be consigned to the devil.

Another cry from the coot had Wulf unwinding himself from his cloak. Yes, De Warenne had the bit between his teeth with regard to Saxon outlaws. He might have acted leniently with regard to Ailric and Hereward, but that had been in the wake of a victory against Thane Guthlac. Wulf would not care to put him to the test again. He glanced at Erica. If matters were to be resolved to his satisfaction in *every* regard, he had much to do.

He dragged on his boots and laced them. Leaving the shelter, he headed for the abandoned smokehouse, scrubbing at his face to chase away the sleep. Lord, look at the grime on his fingers. His face was doubtless equally filthy.

He had no intention of watching Erica marry someone else, but even that would be preferable to seeing her rot in these icy marshes or fall prey to the Lord of Lewes in one of his angry, retaliatory moods. His lord would give her only one chance. For both their sakes, Wulf had to get her to Winchester with all speed. He didn't know what she had hoped to achieve when she had left the garrison yesterday, but, whatever it was, he had to put a stop to it.

His boots crunched through last night's snowfall and he had gone a few yards before he took proper stock of his surroundings. The world was a dazzle of white. Frowning, he broke his step. Snow and ice everywhere. Branches were weighed down with it. Ducks were skittering about on iced-over fen-water. The smokehouse was covered in ice crystals, and icicles hung sharp as daggers from one of the rotting beams.

Ice. *Mon Dieu*, the waterways were frozen. The sky was an unblemished blue and the air was glacial. It chilled his teeth.

Striding to the fire-pit, Wulf found the bundle of wood he had secreted under an oilcloth some days earlier; it was dry enough and he had no fears about who might see smoke this morning. He set about building a fire. There would be no thaw today…which meant they must either wait for the thaw or skate to the London road, because by hook or by crook he must get Erica out of these fens.

Hadn't there been a rubbish pit nearby? Full of discarded animal bones, as he recalled. Yes, he was certain. Once the fire had taken hold, Wulf rose, dusted frost from his knees and went in search of the midden. No, he had no wish to see Erica marry someone else, but he must get her to Winchester before she had a chance to do something his lord would see as treason.

Wulf recalled the snatched conference he had had with De Warenne just after the battle. 'The King has summoned me to Winchester Castle in a sen'night. See to it that you collect the Lady Erica and bring her safely there. With all speed, FitzRobert, we can't have stray Saxon noblewomen providing a focus for more rebellion.'

'Yes, my lord.'

And then De Warenne had looked Wulf directly in the eyes. 'And mind I trust you to bring her chastely as well as safely, Captain.'

'My lord?'

'Lady Erica will suffer no disrespect at Norman hands, you understand?'

'Perfectly, my lord,' Wulf had replied, sick to his stomach at the thought of someone else taking her to his bed. 'Chastely and safely.'

Chapter Sixteen

When Erica opened her eyes, the lantern was out and it was broad day. No Wulf.

She pushed his cloak aside and reached for her boots, brow puckering when she saw the state of her skirts, ragged at the bottom where Wulf had sliced off the wet hem. Where was he?

Moments later she was outside with the welcome weight of his fur-lined cloak back on her shoulders. Saints, it was a bitter morning. Bright and—Erica sniffed—woodsmoke! He had lit the fire.

Wulf was sitting on a log by the fire-pit in his other cloak, carving a stick bleached white with age.

'Good morning, Erica—my lady.'

'Good morning.' He had washed the soot from his face and had managed to shave, for those high-boned cheeks were clear of stubble in the fashion that he favoured, the Norman one. Half-Norman, she reminded herself, he is only half-Norman. His bruises were fading. Wulf was, she realised with something of a wrench, a handsome man. Her smile fell away; in truth, he was far too handsome for her peace of mind.

'There is hot water for you, my lady.'

'My thanks.' He had found one of the loaves she had brought from the garrison and had set it next to the hearth to warm. She shot him a glance. A consideration she would not have looked for in him. No. Mentally she rebuked herself, warming the bread was *exactly* the sort of thing Wulf would do.

A pang of guilt made itself felt. He intended escorting her to Winchester, but she could not let him, not when she had to find the Willow and get a message to the housecarls. Straight-backed, she picked her way across the snow-covered ground. Using what was left of the fullness of her skirt as a pot cloth, she reached for the cauldron. Considerate or not, she had to escape him. The warband must be warned that Thane Guthlac had been vanquished by Wulf's lord.

'My lady?' Wulf broke into the train of her thoughts.

Good Lord, he was handing her cloths with which to wash, Erica realised, bemused, as she took one and dropped it into the water. Hot water, wash cloths—this man was rare indeed. 'Yes?'

His expression darkened. 'I know you hired a boat, Gil told me. But I am curious as to why the ferryman left you here.'

She lifted her chin. 'Yes, I did hire a boat to take me… I wanted it to…to help me get away.'

'The thought of going to Winchester was so repugnant?'

'I…I, no. That is, yes, yes, it was.'

He stared at her, eyes bluer than they had a right to

be, intense and compelling. She jerked her head away. 'I have no wish to marry a stranger. Also…' she hesitated '…I have responsibilities…elsewhere.' A brow went up and again she could not hold his gaze. 'Wulf, do not press me, I cannot say.'

He sighed. 'Perhaps you could try trusting me? It is possible I might help.'

She sent him a haughty look that hid the longing his words had awoken. If only she could. Lord knew she wanted to. But her loyalties were inextricably tangled up with the loyalties of her father's housecarls while Wulf's were to his Norman *seigneur*. She might want trust to spring to life between them, but that was impossible. 'Help me? I think not.' She frowned. 'What are you doing with that stick?'

He held it aloft, a stick that she now recognised was no stick, but the thigh-bone of a pig. Three similar bones were stuck into his belt. 'This, my lady, is what will help us reach the London road.'

She looked blankly at it. 'I beg your pardon?'

'This, my lady, is a skate.' His dark head jerked towards the mooring and Erica saw that the waterways were blocked with ice.

'Oh, no.' She bit her lip. How could she not have noticed? It was Wulf's fault, her wits became addled whenever he was close. He came a step closer. *'No,'* she repeated. 'I've never skated in my life.'

'Neither have I, but that is not going to prevent us. When you have broken your fast, we are going to skate to the London road.'

'I can't!'

'You can and you will.'

His gaze was fixed on her mouth and Erica had to fight a sudden need to cool her cheeks with the back of her hands.

'For I…' Wulf cleared his throat. 'You will not trust me and I have learned that I may not trust you either. But you must leave these fens. I have sworn to take you directly to Winchester.' He turned away, muttering, and Erica thought she caught the words 'chastely and safely,' but she could not swear to it.

Soon they were out on the ice, not very far out, admittedly, holding hands as they skated in one of the narrower channels. Wulf had tied the hand-made skates to their boots with his spare cross-gartering and, after half an hour's practice and a fall or two, Erica made a discovery.

'I can do it! I can skate!' Erica found herself laughing freely for the first time in years. She grinned at Wulf, tugged her hand free and even managed a mocking little curtsy without overbalancing. 'I like this! And I thank you, sir, for altering my gown. It would be far more tricky in a long skirt.'

Wulf skated doggedly after her, his breath pluming in the air and Erica came to a halt, observing him. Wulf could skate, too, but he was not taking to it as easily as she. He wobbled, steadied himself, and came on again. There was something awkward about Wulf's gait on the ice; perhaps here his strength worked against him. The ice creaked. He was so large. She fiddled with her bracelets as she watched and glanced towards the main waterway. The ice was thick here in the backwater, but it would be thinner on the main channel where the water flow was more powerful.

She narrowed her eyes, measuring the distance. If she could reach that far, and if she skated like a demon, she might be able to give him the slip…

'Enough,' Wulf said. 'We have proved this is a viable means of transport. Wait here while I fetch my pack.'

Nodding, Erica came to a complete stop. *Now. It's now or never.* A cold knife twisted inside her as he reached the bank near the fire-pit where he had left his pack. As he reached for it, it occurred to her that Wulf's fur-lined cloak was something of a handicap. It weighed too much; it would slow her down. Unfastening the clasp, she slung it over an overhanging branch.

Now!

She turned and began skating for the central waterway with her blue cloak streaming out behind her. Beneath her skates, the ice hissed. Her heart pounded. No shout yet, Wulf had not noticed.

Faster, faster, she must go faster. Ahead, a swan was waddling across the frozen waterway, ungainly on the ice where Erica was not as she flew towards it. A goose honked from a nearby islet.

'Erica, *no!*'

A fist clenched in her stomach. Hardening her heart against the anguish in his tone—she must be imagining it—she pelted on.

'Erica!'

She wasted seconds glancing over her shoulder and almost fell. He had flung his pack aside and was skating after her, powerful thighs pumping.

'Erica!'

He was fast for so large a man, too fast. Resolutely, Erica turned her back on him and raced on. If she could only make that main channel where the water flow was stronger. The ice must be thinner there, and Wulf would be forced to stop.

In the back of her mind the memory of an ancient saying was surfacing, she had first heard it when coming to the fens. Here in East Anglia, ice was not entirely un-welcome. True, ice made fishing hard, if not impossible, but the natives did say that travelling became easier. Now she understood what they meant. Not everyone could afford a boat, but *anyone* could fashion a pair of skates as Wulf had done…

Breathless, she sucked in a lungful of cold air and skated on. That saying—if only she could call it to mind…

'Erica, wait! *Erica!*'

He sounded desperate, you really would think that he cared. But Captain Wulf FitzRobert did not care, not for her. He cared about his duty to his lord. He had promised to escort her to Winchester and therein lay his desperation, he did not want to fail in his duty to William De Warenne.

She sped into the main channel. A swift glance upstream and down—no one in sight either way—just Wulf behind her with those strong thighs working as he came after her.

Below her, the ice creaked. Dark ice, black below. Weeds? Fish? There was no time to see. What *was* that saying? She racked her brains. The ice gave a tiny cracking sound, prompting her memory. Ah, yes, she had it—*ice: if she cracks, she bears; if she bends, she breaks*. The ice crackled beneath her, so it would bear her weight. She skated on.

'*Erica!*'

She looked back and wished she had not. Wulf was hurtling across the ice and out into the central waterway, chips of ice flying from his skates, heedless of his own safety.

'Erica!'

He shot out onto the wider expanse of ice and the ice at her feet creaked. 'If she cracks, she bears,' she muttered, skating furiously. She had to get away, she must get that message to Hrolf and the men, telling them that they were on their own, that it was no good looking to make an alliance with Guthlac. Guthlac, like her father, was dead. Perhaps now, she thought, as she tried for more speed, chest aching with the effort, perhaps it was time for her housecarls to consider making their peace with the Normans. When they had taken up the call to arms, they had left families behind at Whitecliffe—women and children who needed husbands and fathers…

The ferryman's face flashed into her mind. Alfred was an ordinary man, he had sympathy for her cause, and like her he was Saxon. But Alfred was practical. He had not liked to thrust her from his ferry and abandon her—why else had he made a point of mentioning the shelter? But practical Saxon Alfred had his family. Exactly as Hrolf and her housecarls did. Was it time to let them make their own decisions?

Even if it meant them abandoning her father's cause?

Yes, even then. *Cut your losses, daughter.*

Another glance over her shoulder. Wulf had gained the widest point where the ice was not properly formed. The surface was bowing, he was too heavy for it. *If she bends, she breaks.* Heart in her mouth, Erica willed him to notice, but his attention was on her. He kept coming.

'No, Wulf, get back!'

Without thought, she turned and began skating like a fury, back the way she had come. Instinct drove her. She hugged the banks, where the water would be shallower, and prayed Wulf would do the same.

'Get to the side! *Wulf!*'

The ice sagged under him. *If she bends, she breaks.*

Erica dug in her skates and came to an abrupt halt, frantically gesturing. 'Get to the bank! It's giving way!' She was gripped with a grim vision of that perfect warrior's body still and cold and white at the bottom of the fen. She must lure him to the bank, so that if the ice did give way he would be in the shallows. 'Wulf!'

He turned, was charging at her. He was five yards out… four…three…

She skittered about on the edge of the ice. Two…one…

And then he was upon her, grabbing her arms as he fell. The ice splintered.

He bore her down with him and they landed in the shallows, half in, half out of the water. Gasping with cold, winded by Wulf, it was a moment before Erica had any breath. The fen-water was freezing, but her feet had yet to feel it.

'You, you…' She struggled for breath.

The bank was hard as rock beneath her. Large hands gripped her by the shoulders, and his big body kept her pinned in place. Chest heaving, he made no attempt to move, but blue eyes glared down at her, glittering with fury.

'You fool, Erica, you might have killed yourself!' His eyes fixed on her mouth, a hand shifted to her chin, and his mouth came down on hers.

Angry. Hard. Not chaste at all. Pressing against her

so strongly, she might be bruised when he had done. He tilted his head, altering the angle, and nipped her bottom lip. In a daze, because although this was not a gentle kiss, Erica was not afraid and she could not fathom it, she put her hands on his shoulders and opened her mouth.

His tongue slid between her lips and he groaned. Instantly the kiss changed. His mouth gentled, was no longer punishing. No more bruising, but soft tiny kisses, little nibbles of her lips that encouraged her to touch her tongue to his. Another groan.

'Erica.'

'You fool, Wulf,' she murmured, 'you might have killed *yourself*.'

More kisses, he was showering them over her cheeks, tracing a line to her ear. He nipped it. His breath was hot and flurried in her ear.

Sliding a hand round his head, testing the texture of his short Norman hair with her fingertips, Erica was taken by a most unladylike urge. She wanted to bite his neck... Saints, she *had* bitten his neck!

He pulled back, panting, and they gazed at each other, chests heaving. His mouth came up at the side and he shook his head. 'Lord, chastely and safely indeed, what a commission.'

'Wulf?' She had shocked him, that bite must have shocked him. Ladies did *not* bite. Embarrassed, she tore her gaze from his and fixed it on the silvery-white branches of a nearby alder.

He brought her head back; he was smiling and dropped another kiss on her mouth. She noticed that his tunic sleeve was scorched from the firing of the castle. 'Lord, Erica, the things you make me do.'

She studied him. Wulf did not seem shocked; in fact, his eyes were on her mouth, they were no longer cold and that sudden stillness on his face told her that he wanted *another* kiss. He gave himself a slight shake, and smiled that lopsided smile and she realised that her hand was cradling his head, as though she, too, wanted another kiss and was just waiting for the right moment when she would draw his head back down and—

She snatched her hand away.

He grinned and rolled off her, grimacing at their wet feet. 'I should have tied you up, we're drenched. A couple of water rats.' He lost his smile. 'You were running away. Again.'

'Yes.'

'But you stopped, turned back. Why?'

'Because the ice in the middle was about to give way and I…I could not let you fall through.'

He gazed at her, a line between his brows and said nothing.

'Wulf, it's deep there, you might have *drowned.*'

He gave her an unexpected smile and his face transfigured. So handsome. Erica's chest seized up and it was not because Wulf had winded her, it was because she wanted to slide her fingers back in his hair and draw him to her. She wanted…no, no, she must remember, she was a lady, a *lady*.

'You, sweet Saxon, are coming with me to Winchester, but first we had better find dry clothing. There's a tavern not far from here, they will have something.'

A tavern? Would this be the Willow? Erica wondered, hoping he could not read her thoughts. But Wulf must have gleaned something from her expression, because he shot her a sharp look, asking, 'Will you betray me?'

'What?'

'At the inn. It will be full of fen-folk—will you give me away?'

She lifted her nose, despising herself for her weakness, but knowing that she could not betray him. She had hated it when Morcar and Siward had beaten him, neither had she been able to countenance the thought of him falling through the ice. But she was not about to admit as much, not to his face.

Those blue eyes stared at her, those wide shoulders lifted. 'We shall have to see, won't we?'

It took them over an hour to reach the inn. An hour in which the sky turned dismal and dropped more snow onto the fens. They skated most of the way, hugging the banks with Wulf holding her hand. He insisted she wore his gloves, but even through the sheepskin his grip was like a vice.

He has learned two lessons, Erica realised, one, to keep firm hold of her, and two, not to venture far from the margins. If the ice broke again, they would not drown.

Her lungs ached, partly from the exercise and partly from the piercing cold. And though Wulf drove her without mercy, her feet were numb, she could not keep going much longer. What would he do if she keeled over? A faint smile lifted the edges of her mouth. Would he sling her over his shoulders again? The man was as strong as an ox. A flurry of snow slapped her in the face and her cheeks stung. So, there was life in her yet.

The landscape passed in a haze of white, of bone-aching cold. Leaden skies and a biting wind. Even her eyeballs ached. She fixed her gaze on the pack slung across Wulf's shoulders. She had no pack herself, but his fur-lined cloak was a dead weight on her back and she could carry it no farther. She was on the point of shrugging it off when he turned his head.

'We're almost there. Look!' He pointed.

Erica peered through the snow. A pall of grey smoke hung over a long wooden building. The tavern! By the door, a flock of geese had congregated to peck at scraps. Boats were drawn up at the moorings, frozen in place. As they skated past the jetty to the bank, Erica glanced surreptitiously at the image on the signboard. A white swan. Her heart sank; her message to the housecarls would be very much delayed.

The White Swan was filled with fen-folk caught out by the weather, but once they had removed their skates, Wulf commanded a place by the fire.

'My lady is in need of warm dry clothing and a hot meal,' Wulf said, digging in his pouch for money. Would Erica betray him as a Norman captain? He could not be sure. She looked to be in no fit state to stand, never mind think of betrayal. He nudged her closer to the fire. Her hair was bedraggled, her teeth were chattering, but somehow she stood tall in her blue cloak and that wreckage of a gown, while the snow melted at her feet. As was her wont, she maintained her dignity.

Some few minutes later, Erica had been escorted behind a curtain by the innkeeper's wife and had re-emerged clothed in simple homespun and with her hair braided into two tidy plaits, which hung over her shoulders. She wore no veil—the innkeeper's wife probably did not have a spare one. The gown was a muddy green in colour and the wool was assuredly coarser than she was used to wearing, but she made no complaint that Wulf heard. She looked warmer and at least the gown would be dry.

With a smile, the innkeeper's wife waved them to a table where they could sit with their backs to the fire. She served them steaming bowls of pea-and-bacon broth with chunks of wholewheat bread generously slathered with butter. They were given creamy cheese and wrinkled apples and mugs of ale.

Since the space by the fire had been booked for the night, Wulf bribed the innkeeper to let him have the box-bed. There was only one and it was set into one of the gable ends. It had thick curtains to keep out the drafts.

Erica's eyes brightened when she saw it. 'It is like my bed at Whitecliffe,' she said, sending him the first genuine smile since they had come to the inn.

In truth, the box-bed was a simple affair; with a mattress set on the floor in what was little more than a stall. It was short and narrow and was scarcely big enough for a child, let alone a tall woman like Erica. Wulf doubted that it was filled with down as her bed in Whitecliffe must surely have been but, small though the bed was, it did not prevent an unholy image flashing into Wulf's mind, of her limbs tangling with his in just such a bed, a longer one, of course, with a much wider mattress…

'Rest, my lady.' Swallowing hard, Wulf gestured her inside.

She ducked in and crawled onto the bed without as much as a murmur; there wasn't enough height for her to stand. The curtains closed. Wulf dragged up a stool and sat as near as he could.

A moment later the curtain opened and he caught the faint scent of meadowsweet from the mattress mingled with juniper. She was kneeling on the bed, twirling her bracelets. 'Wulf?'

'My lady?'

'Wh…where do you sleep?' she asked, heightened colour on her cheeks.

He grinned and pointed to the floor in front of the box-bed. 'Close to hand, lest you should need me.'

Her lips twitched, it was the merest suggestion of a smile, but it warmed his heart. She leaned towards him, keeping her voice low. 'Lest I should try to escape again, you mean?'

Mon Dieu, her mouth, when she smiled like that— he had the devil's own job keeping his hands to himself. *Chastely and safely*, he reminded himself. But then un- luckily for his good intentions, Wulf noticed that *her* eyes were on his mouth and he found himself leaning towards her. She did not back away; indeed, it seemed to him she was lifting her mouth to his, begging for a kiss. Her eyes, they were so dark…

He dipped his head and their lips met. Soft as this- tledown. His fingers curled round the back of her neck as one of her hands came to rest in the centre of his chest.

One kiss, a chaste one, little more than a peck.

Another, and Wulf's teeth caught at her lower lip.

And then, even more unfortunately for Wulf's good in- tentions, she gave a sensual murmur that had his belly clenching. *Pull back, Wulf, pull back.* Gentle fingers were tracing a meandering path up and over his cheekbones.

His face burned. She touched him so gently. And now, he held down a groan, now she was playing with his hair.

Chastely be damned. Drawing in a lungful of air, for he could scarcely breathe, he set his arm about her waist and pulled her properly against him.

Her lips parted. His tongue was dancing with hers and she…she was definitely not helping. He heard another of those breathy little murmurs. Her body was pushing against his chest, she was clinging to his shoulders and in a moment she would have him off this stool…for the feel of her breasts, soft and full through the wool of his tunic, was melting his bones.

His manhood throbbed, and though Wulf should be remembering his promise to De Warenne, he held her to him, he pressed himself against her, wringing another of those bone-melting moans out of her and…

Lord, he wanted nothing more than to tear that gown from her back and fall with her into the softness of that mattress and…

At the fire, someone barked out a laugh. A woman tittered. Flushing, Wulf sucked in air and pulled back. Dimly he heard someone mutter an obscenity.

Erica's cheeks were pink and one of her plaits was no longer sleek in its braid. Wulf had no recollection of disordering it. Her eyes were soft, glowing in the firelight. In short, she looked like a girl who had been soundly kissed.

'We must not do this.' Wulf shoved his hand through his hair. It felt as untidy as hers. Lord.

'No, no, of course not.' She frowned.

She was trying to look disapproving. It made him want to kiss her again.

'It is not chaste,' he said.

'Or ladylike.' Her frown deepened.

Struggling with an urge to kiss the frown from her face, Wulf withdrew his hand from her waist and eased back. Thank God the length of his tunic hid the fact that he was very much aroused.

Her eyes flickered downwards for an instant. Cheeks aglow, she was struggling for composure. She had to know, the witch, how much he desired her. 'You said that before, I think. Chastity is important to you?'

Wulf gritted his teeth and kept his voice low. 'As you well know, my lord—' he could not mention De Warenne's name out loud in this place '—my lord charged me with bringing you chastely to Winchester, chastely and with due respect.'

A brow twitched and green eyes gleamed with light reflected from the fire. She was such a trial.

Chapter Seventeen

Just five days later, Erica found herself approaching Winchester on horseback. In an age when most people travelled on foot, it had been a whirlwind journey. No sooner had morning broken at the inn than Gil had appeared; Wulf must have arranged for him to meet them after the razing of Guthlac's castle.

Wulf's purse had been deep enough to buy not only the green gown and some gloves from the innkeeper's wife, but also to hire horses and a few other essentials.

'The London road,' Wulf had told her. 'We can reach it easily from here.'

And so had begun their journey. Wulf rode at her side and Gil brought up the rear. It was hard riding, especially for a woman not fully recovered from her fast and the rigours—not that Erica would admit this to herself—of a life on the run. She rode astride, simply because it was easier.

London passed in a haze of exhaustion. Busy streets, and the cobbled ones were slippery with ice. Icicles fringed the horse troughs; there were frozen pails in the stables. Blue fingers. Red noses.

They rested at night in the common room of an inn and Erica had been too weary to notice its name. She found herself flanked on her right hand by Wulf and on her left by Gil. By rights she should sleep among women, but having Wulf and Gil close to hand did not feel like an impropriety. How could it? She felt far safer with Wulf and Gil than she would with complete strangers, even if they were women. And in any case, Erica suspected that, were she to complain, she might find herself quartered in King William's garrison at Westminster.

Erica rose when shaken awake and hauled herself up, ready for another never-ending day in the saddle. Somewhere in London they paused for Wulf to exchange one of the hired horses for his own, a gelding called Melody. It was a sweet name for such a big-boned animal. Melody had a thick black winter coat, and Erica soon discovered he was a gentle creature, with none of the aggressive tendencies she associated with Norman warhorses.

She had stared when she had seen him, allowing him to snuffle gently in her ear, his breath the only warmth in the stable.

'What a beautiful horse,' she had exclaimed. 'And how delicate his manners.'

Wulf threw Melody's saddle on his back, and lifted a dark brow. 'You are surprised I have a beautiful horse?'

She had shrugged. 'It was just that I expected something more…'

'Warlike?'

'Exactly.'

Wulf yanked Melody's girth. 'Melody is not a

destrier, my lady. Trained destriers are far too rare a commodity for an ordinary captain.'

She had laid a hand on his arm. 'Perhaps your lord will give you a warhorse.'

Wulf shook her off and Erica wrapped her arms about her middle. Since they had left the fens Wulf's manner towards her had been cold; it was as though he was deliberately keeping himself at arm's length. He glanced at her, gaze so impersonal you would never believe they had slept in each other's arms, and kissed.

'It is not likely.' He patted Melody's neck. 'In any case, I am grown accustomed to Melody.'

And so it continued day after interminable day: rising at dawn, climbing into the saddle, riding through a dazzling white landscape on roads that were barely passable, past trees with branches that were furry with frost. But they rode on doggedly, forcing Erica to conclude that Wulf had tired of her company and was eager to be rid of her.

She guessed that he was leaning more and more towards the Norman half of his heritage. It would make sense, particularly since the whole of England seemed to be firmly under the thumb of William of Normandy. It had already occurred to her that it could not have been easy for Wulf in Guthlac's hall, he must have felt torn. Yet feeling torn had not prevented him from delivering his report to William De Warenne. There was a definite streak of ruthlessness in Captain Wulf FitzRobert.

As they neared Winchester, the town that had once been the central seat of power for the Saxon kings, Wulf sent Erica a sidelong glance. Her cloak flowed about her like a blue sea but he could not see her face for the fall of her hood. Her hardihood astonished him. Wulf had yet to hear one word of complaint fall from her lips. He wondered at the demon that had goaded him into driving their relentless pace, but he could not help himself.

Their kiss at the White Swan had set him on this course. He had realised then that he must distance himself from her, at least until he was more certain of his ground. She was simply too beautiful, too much of a temptation. A distraction. He stole another glance at her profile, which was all he could see of her, that perfect profile. But, in truth, Wulf did not have to look at the woman in order to ache for her; blindfold, he knew her features. That wide brow, clear and unlined, those dark eyelashes that set off eyes as green and bright as any he had seen. Mercifully, today her hair was out of sight beneath her veil and hood.

Momentarily, Wulf closed his eyes. One plait today—this morning he had watched her braid it. One plait, soft, dark and glossy and thick as his wrist. He knew its scent—that hint of juniper; he knew its texture—like silk.

Setting his jaw, Wulf glared in front of him. The time was not ripe. His heart contracted. Slowly ahead of them, a grey wall rose out of the snow, a wall that had been built by Romans in another age. Winchester City.

'Look, Wulf!' A gloved hand pointed, her face turned to his. 'Winchester?'

'Aye, nearly there.'

Her cheeks lost colour and she bit her lip. Wulf had no difficulty reading her. She did not want to reach Winchester. She longed to communicate with her men, back in the fens. If only she would trust him…

'Wulf?'

He grunted.

'Will…will De Warenne be there?'

'He will join us in a few days.'

'And what of your king?'

Your king, Wulf noted, *your* king.

'I do not know. Erica…' As the city walls loomed, Wulf reached for her reins and looped them round the pommel of his saddle. 'Erica, I am sorry…' His voice trailed off and for a moment he lost himself in her eyes. What could he say? That he was sorry he had been ill tempered, that he had no choice but to keep his distance, it was that or ravish the woman and break his oath to his lord. He could not let her in on his plans, which might not, in any case, succeed.

'Wulf?'

He shook his head; the tension that had been building during this journey was reaching unbearable levels. This was torture. 'Winchester,' he managed, stupidly, 'we have arrived.'

To have to escort her to the heart of Wessex, to have to stand by while she was wedded to a stranger… When Wulf had left East Anglia he had realised that this was one commission he might not fulfil. He smiled grimly. Today he was in no doubt.

He could not do it; he would break ranks rather than lose her. Erica liked him. He took comfort from the fact that out there on the ice in that freezing East Anglian bog, she had turned back and let him recapture her rather than see him fall through the ice. And her kisses, innocent kisses, which none the less betrayed her liking for him. He would not lose her. Naturally, he would do his best to win her with De Warenne's blessing, but if necessary he would marry her without it.

'Erica?'

That clear brow wrinkled. 'Wulf, are you well? You look very…strange.'

Wulf focused on the city gates and urged Melody into a trot. Clearing his throat, he directed the horses towards the guards standing sentry at the gates. 'I am quite well, my lady, I thank you.'

The Winchester garrison stables had once been the Saxon palace. When King William's men had first taken the town, they had seized the building for their headquarters, but now a stone castle was being built at the top of the hill and the Saxon mead-hall had been given over to the horses. Such was conquest.

They rode past the cathedral and up to the stable yard. In the winter sunlight, Erica's features were drawn. She was chewing the finger of one glove, a hunted, desperate look in her eyes. Glancing about him, Wulf knew the reason. A squadron of Norman knights and their squires were dismounting in the old palace courtyard, the air was full of the jingle of bits and the clatter of hoofs. At their backs, a troop of soldiers in chainmail were using the cathedral close as their drill yard; their presence in this ancient Saxon stronghold must be hateful to Saxon eyes. To top it all, Norman French was coming at them from every direction.

'Wulf FitzRobert!'

Recognising the voice as one he knew well, Wulf flung a distracted smile in the knight's direction. It was the garrison commander. 'Sir Richard.' He pulled

Erica's horse closer and their knees bumped. It was probably a weakness in him, but it was not one he could ignore, and while he might not confide in her yet, he wanted to reassure her. 'Erica? My lady?'

She removed the glove from her mouth. 'Where are you taking me?' Her voice was little more than a whisper.

If she would but trust me, he thought, hating to see that pinched look on her face. The castle loured over the entire town and Wulf gestured up the hill towards it.

The work of Frankish masons brought by King William across the Narrow Sea, one of the round towers had recently been completed. Unfinished though it was, the castle already looked impenetrable. It was a magnificent replacement for the wooden motte and bailey that had been flung up in the early days of Norman rule. The new towers were a visual reminder that King William's authority was here to stay.

Frosted scaffolding criss-crossed the unfinished walls, but today the snow-covered walkways were empty of workmen. The weather made it too dangerous to work on high slippery timbers, and anyway, the mortar would crack rather than set.

Erica swallowed. 'You take me into that.'

'Yes.'

'Do…do you leave me there?'

Yes, insisted a voice inside him, you do leave her there. Wulf found himself taking her hand. 'I have duties to attend to.' His chest ached. It was harder than he had thought it would be, keeping his plans to himself.

Releasing her, he led them at a jouncing trot through the cathedral close, where a stream of pilgrims was winding around the troops, heading for Saint Swithun's shrine in the Minster. Whichever king sits on the throne, Wulf thought, there will always be pilgrims heading for the shrine. So it had been in the days of King Alfred, so it would be in the future.

Erica had not seen Captain Wulf FitzRobert for a whole week.

Once the horses had been safely stabled, he had marched her through the castle bailey and into one of the towers. He had pushed her through a door at the top of a winding stair. The ladies' bower. And before Erica knew it, she was listening to Wulf's footsteps retreating down the stairs.

The ladies' bower seemed to be the domain of one Rozenn Silvester, a Frankish woman. Rozenn was dark eyed and pretty—a seamstress charged as far as Erica could understand with ordering the wall-hangings for King William's castle. Rozenn had insisted that Erica called her Rose, but, for all Rose's warmth, communication was not easy. Rose was Breton rather than Norman, and her French was delivered with an accent Erica found hard to interpret. Rose had little English.

'I am learning, you understand,' Rose had said, taking Erica's hand and leading her to a window seat, which was almost entirely buried beneath several bolts of cloth.

The shutters were open and the window was glazed with glass, real glass. Erica had never seen a glazed window before. Through it she could see rooks being tossed hither and thither by a gusty wind, yet no wind reached the solar. It was a marvel.

To one side of the room a trestle table had a wide

canvas spread out upon it, along with several sticks of charcoal. There were scissors and shears of varying sizes and half-a-dozen hanks of coloured wool. There was even the luxury of a couple of lighted braziers to draw the chill from the air. 'But it is not—how do you say?—it is not…'

'Easy?'

'*Exactement! C'est trop difficile—oh, je m'excuse!*' And Rose had laughed, brown eyes crinkling at the corners.

Erica—for all that this woman had come in the train of the invaders—liked her immediately.

Rose pushed Erica onto a cushion and tugged one of the fabrics out from the bottom of the pile. A blue worsted, woven from the softest clippings, it was as smooth as silk. 'You like?'

'Yes, it is very pretty.'

'It is not…not…urgh, my English! It is not itchy and it is very warm.'

'I can see that.'

It was only when Rose had held the material up to Erica's face and went on to offer fabric after fabric up for her approval that Erica realised what was happening.

'These…these are all for me?' she had asked, staring at the growing mountain of fabrics which seemed to be in the process of being transferred from the window seat to her feet.

'*Mais, oui*. But, of course. You cannot go to your marriage in this.' Rose's nose wrinkled as she plucked at the muddy green gown that had once belonged to the innkeeper's wife at the White Swan.

'M…my marriage?'

Rose had blinked at her. '*Oui*, you agreed to marry, did you not? And I hear it is soon, very soon. Lord De Warenne will be anxious that your tenants have a leader who answers to him.'

Erica looked away as a wave of nausea took her. What could she say? At the Ely garrison she had agreed to marry Wulf FitzRobert, but William De Warenne had not granted his permission for such a match. She was to marry someone 'fitting'. She stared out of the glazed window, fiddling with her bracelets, blind to the rooks hurling themselves about in the wind outside, deaf to the sizzle of a damp coal in one of the braziers. *I hear it is soon, very soon.* Her eyes stung.

And then some other ladies, Norman ladies, came chattering into the solar, and any chance of private talk was ended. Sick at heart, Erica kept her head high and allowed Rozenn Silvester to take her measure so that the new gowns might be made for her marriage.

In this way a week passed, January was about to turn into February. Outside, in the garths and orchards of England, buds would be forming under the frost. Candlemas was almost upon them.

But Erica scarcely left the solar; she sat alongside Rose, sewing her trousseau with a heavy heart. She ate in the solar and slept alongside the other unmarried ladies, disparagement of any sort was not to be countenanced in Winchester Castle. William De Warenne must hold Wulf in the highest regard. Why else would Wulf have been entrusted with the task of escorting her here?

Erica relished the warmth of the solar after the dank cold of the fens, she relished Rose's company, she relished plentiful food after months of privation in East Anglia. But Erica missed Solveig, she missed Morcar and Cadfael. She missed Ailric and Hereward and could not stop worrying about what had happened to them. She missed Wulf, too. He had said he had duties to attend to. What duties? Where was he? Not that she should permit herself to think of him, not when she was shortly to be married to someone 'fitting'. But she should at least have insisted that Wulf tell her *exactly* what had happened to Ailric and Hereward after that battle in the fens. He had been very vague.

On Candlemas Eve, shortly after nightfall, the dinner bell sounded.

Rozenn smoothed down the heavy silk gown she had just eased Erica into and stood back to examine her with a critical eye. Of darkest midnight blue, the gown fitted her like a glove. Silk lacings at the sides defined her shape, the neck was slashed low at the bosom. Too low? Erica gave it a surreptitious tug.

'*Non, non.*' Rose made a tutting sound and pulled it back. She had embroidered tiny silver stars along the neckline and hem. '*Bien, trés bien.*' Rose smiled and, before Erica realised what she was doing, had clipped a silk girdle about her waist. Out of nowhere Rose produced a gauzy veil, which she secured into place with a headband that flashed when it caught the light. Silver filigree.

'What's this?'

Rose shrugged. 'It is yours, it was brought up to the solar today. A gift.'

'From whom?'

Rose sent her a coy look. 'Your intended, perhaps?'

Erica felt the blood drain from her face. 'It…it's not tonight, is it?'

'What?'

'M…my marriage, it's not tonight?'

Rose sent her a strange look. 'I am sure there is no need to fear. Come, my lady—'

'Please, Rose, do call me Erica. I would like to think we may be friends.'

'*Merci.*' Rose held out her hand. 'Come, Erica. Tonight we dine in the great hall.'

'Rose…' Erica hung back '…it's not tonight, is it? Please tell me.'

Rose gave her one of those careless, Frankish shrugs and led her to the stairwell and Erica could not be sure that Rose had understood her question.

As they stepped through the archway and into the hall, the warmth of the fire came to greet them, bringing with it the smells of roast pork, of mulled wine and mead, of rich spices from some unknown land. Erica and Rose sank onto a bench at one of the tables set at an angle to the high table where the great Norman lords sat. Erica had never felt so ill at ease. Her mouth felt dry as she looked for William De Warenne but she could not see him. Thank the Lord. Her marriage could not take place without the blessing of the new Lord of Lewes. She did, however, recognise the knight that Wulf had greeted on the day they had arrived, Sir Richard of Asculf, the garrison commander.

Breathing more easily, Erica smoothed down the blue gown. Her eyes went in search of Wulf, but she could not see him either. Had he left Winchester? Perhaps he had new orders. If so, she might not see him again. Her throat tightened.

'*Madame?*' A serving girl was offering her wine. Nodding, Erica shifted her cup so that it could be filled.

Noise. She was sitting in the Great Hall in Winchester Castle surrounded by people, Franks, for the most part, laughing and talking in that foreign tongue of theirs. Her father would turn in his grave. So many Franks, she thought, shooting a sidelong glance at Rose, Rose whom she liked. She sighed. It made her head spin, the way the world was changing.

A lute-player was strolling past their table; he was dressed like a prince in a green silk tunic edged with gold braid. Yet more gold braid wound round his hose. Catching Rose's hand as he passed, the lute-player lifted it flamboyantly to his lips, but it was no kiss that Erica witnessed—no, she was certain she saw him nibble at Rose's fingertips in a gesture that was both loving and familiar. Erica's heart twisted with longing for something that would never be hers. The lute-player's eyes were dark and they sparkled in the candlelight. Rose flushed and bit back a grin, and he muttered something incomprehensible in yet another foreign tongue.

'Who is that?' Erica asked as the lute-player continued on up to the top table, tossing easy greetings right and left. 'What did he say?'

'Benedict. My husband.' Her grin escaped her. 'He is something of a…how do you say…of a flirt. He spoke in Breton, but it would not be—' her flush deepened '—seemly to repeat what he said.'

A platter of meat, swimming in its juices, landed on the trestle.

Erica was reaching for her eating knife when an arrival at the top table caught her eye. Wulf! She froze.

Wulf was approaching the garrison commander, Sir Richard. Breath suspended, Erica could only watch as they exchanged greetings. It was good to see him, even if all she could see was that broad back. Blindly, she reached for her wine and took a sip, frowning at him over the rim. He was wearing clothes she had not seen before, a tunic the colour of blackberries and a black belt that matched his hose. She smiled. Blue cross-gartering. Of course. She could not seem to tear her gaze away. It was so good to see him. She willed him to look her way.

So much for will—Wulf did not so much as glance in her direction. He muttered in Sir Richard's ear and the knight looked up to make some reply. Wulf nodded, turned on his heel and those long legs carried him out.

Gone.

Misery filled her. Not so much as a glance.

When Rose pulled the meat platter towards her, Erica shook her head—she had lost her appetite.

'Rose, I...I need some air.'

Rose was busy piling her own platter with meat. She smiled, abstractedly. 'Yes, it is noisy in here.' Waving a boy over, she addressed him in a rapid undertone before jerking her head towards a side door. It was opposite the one that Wulf had gone through. 'I would go that way, if I were you. Ronan will show you the way to the chapel, it is the most peaceful place.'

Erica was ushered down a corridor that ran the length of the hall. Candles glowed in wall sconces and the rich tapestries that were hanging on the walls shivered in stray drafts. Wondering if Rose was responsible for the tapestries, Erica nodded her thanks at the serving boy and continued down the corridor. The boy slipped back into the hall.

With every step down the corridor the hubbub behind her diminished. This was what she needed. Peace. Vespers would be long over, the chapel would be deserted. Erica had been glad of Rose's company, but the solar with its chattering Frankish ladies had been far from peaceful these past few days. She needed to gather her thoughts, to prepare herself for her forthcoming marriage, to whomsoever it was. She needed to find a measure of calm.

She padded past a guttering candle, which made a monster of her shadow, and found herself facing an oak-planked door, the door to the Royal Chapel. It opened silently to her touch. The sanctuary light glowed red, altar candles flickered. The skirts of Erica's blue gown swept the floor as she approached the altar and dropped to her knees. Bowing her head, she put her hands together and tried to pray.

'Erica?'

It was only a whisper, but she knew at once who it was and was on her feet in an instant. *'Wulf!'*

He had been leaning against the chapel wall, a tall shadow half-hidden by a statue of Our Lady. Coming towards her, he reached for her hand and threaded his fingers through hers. He was smiling. She was smiling, too, like a fool, she could not help it.

'Sir Richard does not accompany you?' he asked, glancing at the door.

'Sir Richard?'

'No matter.' Wulf lifted her hand to his lips.

She swallowed—he *had* been thinking of her, she had not been not forgotten! 'Did you want to see me?' Erica knew she should not ask, but she wanted, no, she *needed* to hear him admit it.

Wulf was caressing the back of her hand, sending darts of pleasure shooting up her arm. Nodding, he stepped closer, eyes dark and fathomless, breath warm on her cheek. 'Could you doubt it? *Ma belle*—'

She took a step herself, closing the space between them. When they were standing breast to breast in the shadowed chapel, she found his other hand and clung.

Wulf's head dipped. His scent surrounded her, befuddling her as it always did. Just when she thought he would kiss her, heavy footsteps sounded in the corridor. They moved quickly apart.

The candlelight shivered as the door opened. 'I see you found the chapel, my lady.' Sir Richard's English was heavily accented. 'I was scouring the hall for you.'

'Sir?' Wulf smiled; he had not released her hand and unwittingly Erica shrank closer to his side, blinking up at the knight. Sir Richard was not only commander of the Winchester garrison, he was one of King William's finest, or so Rozenn had told her, a landed knight with acres to his name in Normandy. Was this the 'someone fitting' that De Warenne had mentioned? His eyes were grey, amused. They were looking at her in such a way that she tugged at her veil, wondering if it was awry. Sir Richard was taller than most men, the equal to Wulf in height and build.

Was this the man she would have to marry?

'Erica, may I introduce Sir Richard of Asculf. Richard, this is Lady Erica.'

Richard? Wulf knew this knight well enough to dispense with his title? Heavens, this must indeed be the man De Warenne had in mind for her. Swallowing down a rush of bile, Erica bowed her head in greeting and gripped Wulf's hand as though her life depended on it.

Chapter Eighteen

'Good evening, my lady.'

'G…good evening, Sir Richard.'

'Father Cuthbert will only be a moment,' Sir Richard said, smiling, just as Wulf let go of her hand. She felt as though he were abandoning her. 'Gil is helping him bring the candles ready for tomorrow's mass. Ah, here they are!'

Erica's feet were rooted to the spot. This night was to be her wedding night! But how could this be, when William De Warenne was not yet in Winchester? In a daze, she watched the priest bustle in with the boy Gil on his heels. Both were laden with candles.

'My thanks, lad,' Father Cuthbert said, depositing his candles on the altar and waving at Gil. 'Arrange these, will you?' The priest was Saxon, his voice betrayed him.

Gil nodded, bent his head in brief obeisance at the cross and began arranging the candles.

Married? *Tonight?* Without De Warenne? Erica's hand crept to her bracelets; round and round she twisted them, round and round. She flung Wulf a hunted glance, but he was occupied with greeting the priest.

Sir Richard of Asculf, Sir Richard of Asculf. Saint Swithun help her. Panic was taking hold of her, panic such as she had not felt before, not even in Guthlac's hall.

'Father...' Wulf smiled down at the priest '...I thank you for meeting us.'

The sanctuary light glowed red. As her heart thudded, Erica took several steadying breaths. How strange to feel panic here when back in the fens she had felt...nothing. She had felt quite numb, yet now...how very strange.

'Captain, you are welcome,' Father Cuthbert was saying. He turned to Erica with a smile. 'And this is the lady?'

'Aye, this is Lady Erica.'

'Her father was Thane of Whitecliffe?'

'Yes.'

'And you met her in East Anglia on your recent campaign?'

'Yes, Father.'

The priest nodded. 'Lady Erica, you are in agreement? You are content to marry this man?'

Erica blinked. Father Cuthbert was indicating Wulf, not Sir Richard! The relief was so intense that the words jammed in her throat. Vehemently, she nodded. Marry Wulf? *Yes*, indeed!

And then his warm fingers were on hers, peeling them from her bracelets, and her hand was engulfed in his larger one.

Dizzy with relief, Erica found her voice. 'I did tell De Warenne I would marry Wulf. But I need to have private speech with him first,' she managed.

Wulf led her into the shadows by the statue of Our

Lady. 'Erica? You have not changed your mind since then?'

'No, no, for myself I would have this marriage,' she spoke in a swift undertone. 'I trust you personally, as a man. My instincts told me I could trust you in that regard back in Guthlac's hall, and they have not been proved wrong. But you kept your true identity hidden.'

Wulf grimaced. 'You are saying that politically you are unsure of me?'

'Yes. It….it is the others I am concerned for, the people of Whitecliffe. What about them?'

Blue eyes held hers. 'Trust me, I am working to help them.' His mouth twisted. 'Erica, I need you to believe in me. My aim is to reconcile Saxon and Norman. I do not like this warring, it is as though I am fighting myself. Men on both sides are suffering and there is no need for it to continue. It strikes me that our marriage would be good in many ways.' A hand came up and briefly caressed her cheek. 'It is my belief that you and I, together, will accomplish much. You are wholly Saxon, and I, being half-Saxon, already have something of an understanding of what your people need.' He grimaced. 'If, that is, De Warenne will ever forgive me for breaking ranks and taking you without his permission. My pledge to you is that I will do my utmost for peaceful reconciliation. Trust me.'

Erica cleared her throat. 'And Ailric and Hereward? Are they in prison in Ely?'

'They are not, they are quite safe, Erica, you have my word. I hope you may see them shortly.'

She stared at him for the space of a heartbeat and then nodded. 'Very well.' Praying she had made the right decision, she looked at the priest. 'Father, I am happy to marry Captain FitzRobert.'

Father Cuthbert's face creased into a smile. 'Good, good,' he muttered. 'I would be loathe to risk De Warenne's anger if you were in any doubt.'

Sir Richard stepped into the light. 'I will endorse your judgement, Father, should De Warenne question it. Captain FitzRobert is a fitting match for this woman, his character is exemplary. I am proud to act as witness to his wedding.'

The priest gave a quick nod. 'So be it. Gil, lad, light those candles, will you? This is a wedding, not a funeral.'

As the smell of beeswax filled Erica's nostrils, she began to tremble. Wulf's fingers tightened. Warm, he is always warm. She clung to that thought while they exchanged their vows before a dozen glittering candles. This change of fortune was nothing less than stunning, particularly since she had not seen Wulf since their arrival in Winchester. But she felt as though a great weight was being lifted from her. She prayed her judgement was not at fault.

She was marrying Wulf! Not some unknown Norman noble who did not have a word of English, but Wulf, who, while he was not wholly Saxon, she could not help but like. Like? Admit it, girl, it is not mere liking you feel for this man, you are half in love with him and have been since the beginning.

Blinking, startled by the turn of her thoughts as she had never been in her life before, Erica murmured her vows in a soft, clear voice. Wulf made his responses firmly, standing straight and strong beside her. A man to depend upon. If only his lord were not King William's right-hand man. None the less, Wulf had sworn to help the people of Whitecliffe.

She emerged from her thoughts to find those blue eyes looking into hers. A question had been asked and she had not heard it. 'Wulf?'

'Get on with it, man.' Sir Richard grinned. 'Kiss her and have done.'

Wulf's dark head dipped, his lips pressed fleetingly to hers. He looked at the priest. 'That's it?'

All smiles, Father Cuthbert tucked his fists into the sleeves of his habit and nodded. 'You are man and wife, make each other happy.' His smile lost some of its force. 'Of late I have married too many Saxon noblewomen for reasons of state. It gladdens my heart to officiate over one based on love.'

Erica's cheeks burned and she ducked her head to examine the toe of her shoe, a narrow calfskin shoe that Rozenn Silvester had given her. Was it so obvious? Too embarrassed to meet Wulf's gaze, she nevertheless allowed him to take her arm and lead her out.

She did indeed love him, and he was half-Norman. And if that were not bad enough, she had married him. Willingly...

Wulf had many friends in Winchester Castle, friends who had joined with him in this...this conspiracy to see her wed, Erica realised as Wulf led her along a maze of corridors. He must have been planning this for some time. She could have wished that he had warned her but... Erica emerged from her thoughts to find that they were at the bottom of a spiral stairway in one of the towers. Wulf started up it, taking the stairs two at a time.

'Where are we going?'

'You'll see.'

Half of her was relieved by her sudden change in status, while half of her was angry, enough to hit him. Did Wulf not realise what he had put her through? For a few moments back in the chapel she had been misled into thinking that Sir Richard was to be her husband! Her nostrils flared. And as for Sir Richard, yes, he was definitely part of the conspiracy.

'Rozenn Silvester is your friend?' she asked, kilting up her skirts as she took the stairs behind him.

'Of course.'

'And her husband?'

'Yes, I count Ben my friend, too.' Wulf paused on a half-landing next to a studded oak door. A ribbon trailed from the door latch—no, a bow made from green, white and blue ribbons, plaited together. How strange. Tugging Erica towards him, Wulf dropped a kiss on her nose.

Erica scowled, and tried not to look at his mouth, tempting though it was. 'And Sir Richard?'

'Yes, his endorsement was…necessary. Particularly since some matters remain unresolved.'

Erica drew back, overcome with an urge to hug him to her, as tightly as was humanly possible. She had missed him, she had ached for him, the brute. 'In short, everyone knew but me.'

'Not everyone. Erica, there was—is—still need for secrecy, but—'

A cough floated up the stairwell; someone was coming.

'We'll talk inside.' Sliding an arm about her waist, Wulf lifted the latch and drew her in.

Stars, gold stars. They were in a turret room and the blue walls were covered with thousands and thousands of stars! And candles *everywhere*, more than there had been in the chapel, dozens of them, flickering softly. Beeswax by their scent. Erica halted just past the threshold, jaw agape as she looked about her. Wulf booted the door shut and leaned against it, observing her reaction.

Every surface glittered. The plaster walls and ceiling were painted with blue, one of the costliest of colours, made by the grinding of lapis lazuli. It looked as though the craftsman who had painted the room had taken the stars from the night sky and pinned them there. There was a large bed with a carved bedhead and fat bedposts to match. It had the deepest, most comfortable-looking mattress that Erica had ever laid eyes on and was heaped high with pillows and blankets. The folded-back sheets had the subtle sheen of silk. Candles glowed in wall sconces and, at the bedside, coals radiated heat from a brazier.

Wulf came to stand behind her, she could feel his breath on her neck.

'So much light,' she murmured, her anger against him losing its force. 'You remembered my dislike of the dark. And the stars—like that lantern in the fens.'

'Yes.'

'But a much better resting place than the fisherman's hut.'

'Yes'

'But, Wulf, should we be in here?' Her voice was hushed. 'I would think this chamber is intended for your king.'

Recognising that, while Erica was gently bred, she was as awed by their surroundings as he was, Wulf turned her towards him and lightly touched her cheek.

'I doubt it. Sir Richard found us this room and even Richard would not dare billet us in the King's chamber.'

Gil had found time to bring up their belongings; Wulf's pack sat at the foot of the bed, next to a bundle he recognised as Erica's. It gave Wulf an odd jolt to see their things stowed next to each other, a small outward sign of their marriage. Their *marriage*. They belonged together. It was odd, too, that this thought was not accompanied by irritation, or a longing to break free. On the contrary…

She drifted to the bed and picked up one of the embroidered cushions. 'This is very fine work.'

'Aye.' Wulf stared at her back, at the seductive curve of her hips and waist visible through the filmy excuse for a veil that Rozenn had made her. His wife, Erica was his *wife*.

'I like Rozenn.' His wife's fingers were lingering on a flower worked in gold thread. 'And it was kind of Sir Richard to find us this chamber. Wulf, why did you do it?'

'Hmm?'

'Our marriage—why the secrecy? You disobey De Warenne in marrying me like this.'

Again, he closed the distance between them and ran his finger down her neck and back up to her cheek. So soft. His throat was dry.

'It's my lands, isn't it? You want to secure my lands…'

Slowly Wulf shook his head. Her eyes were wide, great green eyes, staring up at him, reflecting the glow of the brazier, of the candles. 'Not the lands, Erica, *you*. I couldn't risk losing you.'

A tiny crease appeared in her brow. She did not believe him—well, for tonight, she did not have to believe him.

She was his wife and that was what was important. With his thumb he smoothed the crease away and lowered his head. 'You did say you would have me, *ma belle*. And according to law, to *Saxon* law, consent between a man and a woman is enough to make a marriage.'

'You have become an expert on Saxon law?'

He smiled. 'This I know. The priest's blessing was desirable, but not necessary. And as for Sir Richard and Gil—they were present to bear witness to our marriage, but hear this, Erica, our consent alone was enough.'

Flushing, she murmured and made to turn away, but he caught her chin and kept his gaze on hers and gave her the lightest of kisses. Those dark lashes lowered, hiding her eyes from him. So beautiful. His *wife*.

He heard her swallow. The brazier brought the heat of summer into the tower room. 'Erica.'

Shaking her head, she pulled free. Her veil fluttered and her skirts swayed as she crossed to the curved wall. Slender fingers traced the outline of a painted star. Wulf sighed, wondering how the few short yards across the rush matting had become such a vast distance. He wanted to reassure her, but remembering what had almost happened to her in Guthlac's hall, he did not know how to begin. Most likely Erica had been dwelling on that. Yet she had consented to marry him and he was as certain as a man could be that Erica of Whitecliffe would understand Saxon marriage rituals as well as he…

But, brave though she was, Erica's spirit had been bruised in Guthlac's hall and shortly afterwards she had been told she was to marry a stranger. In Erica's mind there was probably little difference between being forced by Hrothgar and into such a marriage.

She would not be human if she had not spent the past few days worrying about her likely fate with an unknown husband. Yes, Erica had consented to marry him, but had it been a *real* choice? Was he the lesser of two evils?

Wulf did not want to be the lesser of two evils, he wanted…

'*Ma belle*, you need never fear me.'

She looked across, smiled. 'Wulf, you have no need to tell me that.'

His heart lifted. 'I need to tell you about my sister, Marie, my half-sister, that is.' Seating himself on the bed, he dragged off a boot and dropped it onto the matting. 'She was a couple of years older than me. I did not meet her until my mother died and my father had me brought to Honfleur, but after that she and I became very close.'

'You love her.'

'Loved. Marie was attacked near the market. A man… forced her and she became pregnant and—'

A rustle of skirts and the chime of bracelets and her hand was on his shoulder. 'She was raped?'

Wulf nodded, staring at the knot in her girdle as that never-to-be-forgotten image of Marie, pale and still on her bier, flashed into her mind. 'Yes, she died giving birth to a stillborn son. She was little more than a child herself.'

'Your sister, yes, I see it. That is why you were so quick to come to my rescue in Guthlac's hall.'

To his astonishment her fingers wandered inside the neck of his tunic and trailed up past his ear into his hair. Wulf held himself very still, trying not to lean into the caress until he could bear no more. Then he glanced up, watching for the slightest change of expression. Was she aware of what she was doing?

White teeth were worrying at that distracting mouth. 'You put yourself at risk for me in Guthlac's hall. These past few days, I have been thinking how hard that must have been. You were in enemy territory and yet…'

She was playing with Wulf's earlobe and his blood was beginning to run hot. Her eyes were dark and dreamy, her lips slightly parted. Wulf's ear burned, his heart thudded. She sighed, sent him a shy smile and bent to remove his other boot.

Bemused, holding his breath to the point of suffocation for fear of startling her, Wulf submitted while she tugged it free. She set it next to its mate, stepped in between his knees and rested her hands on his shoulders.

'I am your wife, Wulf, and I would have you know that if you…if we…it will be no disparagement to me if you…' Rosy colour suffused her cheeks. 'It would be…pleasant, I think. Like your kisses.'

She *liked* his kisses. Desire swamped him. Wulf dragged her to him and buried his face in her belly. 'Erica.' Her name emerged as a croak. Rapidly, he pulled himself together. It would not do for her to realise the effect she had on him. Lord, she nearly unmanned him. He gave her a crooked smile, rose, and was lifting the silver headband from her and setting it safely on the nightstand when she caught his hand.

'Wulf, this…' She indicated the circlet. 'It's from you.'

'Yes.'

'I have never been given anything half so pretty, I thank you.'

He looked at her. It was not gold, which she was used

to, but it had cost him more than he could well afford. Wulf was not comfortable with expressing his feelings, but something in those eyes made him want to try. 'The filigree made me think of you. Beautiful. Delicate, but strong. I am glad you like it.'

Erica unpinned her veil and reached for her braid; Wulf brushed her fingers aside. 'Let me take Solveig's part.'

Green eyes met his. 'You watched us in the cottage, that night Morcar…hurt you?'

Wulf smiled, but did not reply as he tugged at a ribbon and her hair came loose. As it unravelled her scent surrounded him—homely and exotic—and dizzied him.

Sitting down with a thump, Wulf pulled her onto his lap and rubbed his cheek against hers. Her lips hovered but an inch from his, her breast was pressing into his chest.

She was smiling a secret woman's smile he could not interpret, but she was relaxed in his arms and that told him all he needed to know. And then those slender fingers were in his hair, sifting through it, doubtless contrasting his shorn locks with those of her housecarls. It came to him that she might like more than his kisses, that she liked his short, Norman hair.

Erica leaned in, pressing more fully against his chest. *She is a virgin*, he reminded himself. *I must go slowly.* Sharp teeth were nibbling at his earlobe, building the heat in his groin. He was having a hard time keeping his hands to himself. *Erica is a lady, a lady. She may be your wife, but she has been gently bred and she is innocent.*

His innocent lady wife was making it hard to think with her green eyes so slumberous, so dark with desire. And his ear, Lord, she was biting his neck, unlacing the front of his tunic…

'Duty,' he muttered. After what Erica had been through, it was his duty not to frighten her.

She lifted her head and her lips curved. 'Duty? Is that what this is?' Her tongue traced a warm wet path along his chin. 'Not entirely.' Drawing back, she leaned her arms against his chest and looked him straight in the eye. 'Sad though it may be, I find your kisses pleasurable. It is very reprehensible.'

With a groan, Wulf brought his lips to hers. It was a fierce kiss, a kiss of possession, and contained the pent-up longing of that painfully chaste journey from Ely to Winchester. It was hard, and hot.

Erica's lips opened. She fisted her fingers in the hair at the back of his head, as though to prevent his escape. Her tongue stroked his, her nails were digging in his shoulder, she was biting, kissing, licking.

Breathless, he pulled away. Her head fell against his chest and then she was urging his lips back to hers. He slid his hand up her ribcage and closed on her breast, stroking it through the cloth of her gown. She quivered.

'Wulf.' His name was no more than a throaty moan.

Muscles weakening, when he fell back on the coverlet she came with him. Her beauty snatched his breath away. Her hair was shining in the candleglow, her cheeks were flushed and her lips were wet from his kisses. Like him, Erica's breath was coming fast, and what he could see of her breasts through the wool of her gown told him that she was as aroused as he. A lady, he reminded himself. Innocent and gently bred and just look at her. How shocking. A grin tugged at his lips. How delightful. Her hand ran over his chest, bracelets chinked, and he shook his head, bemused. Innocent?

'What?' she demanded even as he levered himself to a sitting position in order to drag off her shoes. 'What's so amusing?'

'You are an extraordinary woman. I thought you might be afraid.' Lying back, he ran a finger down her cheek.

Careful fingers mirrored his gesture, lingered on his mouth. 'Not with you, you great ox, never with you.'

'Ox? *Ox?* I'll show you ox…' Wulf tore the tunic from his back, then his chainse and reached for the ties at the side of her gown. Her fingers were there before his. He kissed her shoulder and they fought over lacings and ties. In moments her gown lay on the matting next to his tunic. Her underskirt followed, then his hose and braies…

And before they knew it they were kneeling somewhat unsteadily on the bed, holding on to each other for balance. They were entirely naked. Wulf might have expected awkwardness, embarrassment, even fear, but there was none of that, just an open enjoyment of each other's bodies.

'Oh, Wulf, your bruises.' Gentle fingers reached for the smudges on his ribs. She bent forwards, hair falling between them as she covered his chest in kisses.

'They are fading.' Wulf swallowed and steadied himself by cradling her head. There was no way he could hide his desire. He was nudging against her and he could not stop himself, she would be afraid, she… Lord, but she was beautiful.

Leaning sideways, she felt back onto the pillows, pulling him with her and the light in those green eyes dispelled the last of his qualms. Erica might not love him, but she did like his kisses and, if Wulf had any say in the matter, she was going to like, to more than like, consummating their marriage.

He let his hands roam over her, worshipping her shape. He caressed her breasts, her flanks, the curve of a buttock. And everywhere his hands went, his lips followed. But it was not easy, because although Wulf was in no doubt that Erica was a virgin, she was not displaying the coyness he might have expected a virgin to display.

In this, the bedding of an innocent wife, a man of some experience might expect to be in control. Control? How could he keep control when Erica was moaning and writhing beneath him and her hands were exploring him *everywhere*, in the most unseemly and delightful manner, emptying his mind of sense, of thought? Her fingers closed over him and he gasped, fighting for air. Control?

A pretty foot kicked the bedding aside. She licked that distracting mouth and showered his cheek with kisses and when he pulled back he saw that her green eyes were as dark with lust as his must be. She muttered his name, 'Wulf', any number of times and each time his senses fired, his blood burned.

'Wulf,' she murmured as a beringed hand streaked fire down his sides.

'Oh, Wulf,' she gasped as his fingers slid between her legs and found to his astonishment that although he had scarcely touched her, she was already ready for him.

'Wulf, my Wulf,' she sighed as she ran her tongue up his neck and towards his ear-lobe and bit him, gently. She liked biting him, it seemed. She wriggled beneath him and muttered his name again and her glossy dark hair spilled over the pillows and tangled beneath them. She hooked a foot over his calves and stroked his leg with it.

It was more than a man could bear, especially a man who, while he was experienced, had never been in the habit of taking his pleasure of women as though they were merely conveniences for his easement. And as for this woman, *the* woman, he cared about her, far more than he ought.

'Wulf, please,' she said, a hint of impatience in her tone as small hands tugged at his hips, nudging him into position.

'Wulf.' She groaned, eyes fixed on his.

They moved simultaneously, and then it was done, they were one. Easy. Wulf slid into her as though they had been lovers for years; there was no barrier that he could feel, no gasp of pain, just Erica's eyes on his and a small hand bringing his mouth to hers.

'Wulf.'

'Erica, *ma belle*…' He ought to ask her if she hurt, but she was moving beneath him in such a way that she could not possibly be in pain and his body was responding to her urging, and they were together, moving together. He had no idea that lying with a woman could take a man so completely out of himself. Her body was tight about him, and, Lord, he only had to reach for her thighs for her to be wrapping her legs about him, and they were moving again, fast, faster.

Her breath was flurried in his ear. 'Erica.'

And then he felt it, that sudden tightening round him as she breathed his name one last time and trembled beneath him. One thrust more and her name was torn from him; it felt as though he were giving her his soul.

About them, the stars on the walls swirled and danced in the flickering candlelight. As their breathing slowed, the stars seemed to settle, and when Wulf rolled to one side he was careful to take her with him.

Chapter Nineteen

The door banged back on its hinges and Erica's eyes flew open. She frowned. It was a rude awakening, after last night she had hoped….

Wulf's boy, Gil, rushed up the bed, panic in his eyes. His hair was awry and he was out of breath. There was no sign of Wulf or of his clothes. *'Madame, madame, venez vite!'*

'Gil?' Clutching the bedclothes to her bosom, her naked bosom, Erica sat up. Icy fingers ran down her back.

'Madame, s'il vous plaît!' Gil groaned, made as if to pluck the bedcovers from her, but the sight of her bare shoulders penetrated his panic. Turning, he made a grab for the discarded blue gown and thrust it at her. 'My lady, please,' he said, finding his English, 'Captain FitzRobert has need of you. *Urgently.*'

Urgently. That last word had been unnecessary; the boy's whole demeanour made her blood run cold. As Gil turned away, Erica thrust back the bedcovers and dragged on the gown and girdle. Otherwise, she made short work of dressing, neither bothering with undergar-

ments nor with brushing her hair; she simply tied it in
a knot and shoved her unstockinged feet into her shoes.
'I'm ready, Gil.' On her way out she snatched up the veil
and the silver circlet Wulf had given her. The door
slammed behind them.

By the time they reached the bottom turn of the stairs
and had gained the corridor, the veil and circlet were in
place, hiding, Erica hoped, her uncombed hair. She, like
Gil, was panting. Dread was a knot in her belly.

'Gil, what is it?'

The boy glanced over his shoulder at her, going so
far as to grab her hand to urge her along. 'The
chapel…the Captain has arranged a rendezvous. I…I
fear for him. He is alone and your men…'

'*My* men?'

'*Oui. Ailric et Hereward et—*'

Erica picked up her skirts so she would not trip as
they rushed down the corridor. Questions pressed in on
her. *Ailric and Hereward? Hadn't they been sent to Ely?
How could they be in Winchester?* She tried to
remember exactly what Wulf had told her in the chapel,
but she had been so pleased to see him that she had had
little space in her head for anything else. At the hall
doorway, Erica dug in her heels. 'Wulf has arranged a
meeting with my men? In the chapel?'

'*Oui.*' Gil tugged at her hand.

'How many…how many of my men?'

'Three. My lady, please…'

Three of them… Saints. The picture of Wulf, tied half
naked to a tree, pushed all other thoughts aside. He had
already been beaten to a pulp by her men. She gritted
her teeth, determined to put her panic behind her. It was

time to take command. 'Very well, Gil, I will go immediately to the chapel. You, however, are to fetch help.
You understand?'

Gil nodded.

'Good.' She gestured towards the hall. 'Get that friend
of his, Sir Richard. And…and…that lute-player if he is
around, he looked strong, and also bring…well, anyone
you can think of.'

'Yes, my lady.'

Gil was halfway through the door. In the hall, heads
turned towards them as Erica called after him, 'They
must bring arms, Gil.'

Candlemas candles left over from mass, Erica thought
as she flew into a chapel that was ablaze with light.

Wulf was sitting on the wall-bench between Ailric
and Hereward. Hrolf was standing a little to one side.
Hrolf? She had sent Hrolf to the Willow! She took a
deep breath to steady herself and looked again.

The four of them were deep in conversation. No one
was hurt, no one appeared to be threatening anyone. It
all looked very…amicable. Amicable?

'My lady?' Rising, Wulf came towards her, arm outstretched. He was not wearing his sword, no one was.
Indeed, there was not a weapon to be seen. Some of the
tension left her. 'Are you well?'

She clutched at him. 'You are safe. I thought…Gil
said…' She shook her head, veil fluttering. She was
aware of her men hovering in the background, but she
only had eyes for Wulf. 'What's going on?'

Before Wulf had chance to answer, a Frankish knight
stalked into the chapel.

The previous evening this same knight had sat at Sir Richard's right hand in the hall. He had dark hair and he was wearing a green tunic with an intricate Celtic pattern embroidered on the hem. In such a tunic the knight could hardly be said to be dressed for combat, but his hand rested lightly on the hilt of his sword and his eyes were alert as they quartered the chapel, missing nothing.

Ailric fixated on the knight's sword and his expression became shuttered, his jaw tightened. Sweet Heaven, Erica knew that look…neither Ailric nor her other men were bearing arms, but…

'Adam?' Wulf lifted an eyebrow. 'I thought you understood these negotiations were…delicate and we were not to be disturbed.'

The knight made an exasperated sound. 'God's teeth, man, I am not a complete dolt. But you should know De Warenne has just ridden in, he will be here any minute. It appears he has been informed of your marriage and—' he shot a swift look at Erica '—it might be time for you to make a strategic retreat.'

'Strategic retreat?' Wulf shook his head. To Erica's surprise he was grinning. 'I am no Breton, to rush to retreat.'

The Frankish knight grinned back, muttering something in French which Erica struggled to catch. It sounded like, 'Strategic retreat saved the day at Hastings', but she could not be certain.

There was no time for more. Raised voices could be heard in the corridor. Erica dug her nails into her palms even as the Frankish knight stuck his head through the door to see who was coming. 'Too late, man, you have left it too late. It's De Warenne.'

'I thank you, Adam,' Wulf said, 'but I shall hold my ground.'

And then the knight called Adam stepped aside to admit the Lord of Lewes.

De Warenne had removed his helm, but he was still mailed and cloaked from his journey and his hair was streaked with sweat. Sir Richard of Asculf accompanied him; he was unmailed but he had buckled his sword belt over his tunic. The lute-player Benedict Silvester brought up the rear with Gil; both were carrying shortswords.

Hrolf swore. For a moment, silence gripped the chapel. It was no longer possible to breathe.

A candle sputtered and Erica felt Wulf's gaze rest briefly on her, before it fastened on De Warenne. He bowed. 'My lord.'

'So, Captain.' De Warenne's face was impassive. 'I came here expecting insubordination, which Sir Richard confirms, though he stands by your action. And I find— what is this? Rebellion?'

'No, my lord.' Wulf's voice was steady. 'I would hope you know me better than that.'

'I thought I did, Captain. But at the very least it would seem that you have contravened a direct order— you have disparaged this woman—'

'No, my lord,' Erica burst out. 'That is not true, Wulf has *not* disparaged me!'

De Warenne's gaze was cold. 'He is not your equal but he married you, did he not?'

'Yes, my lord, but…' Erica reached for Wulf's hand '…it is no disparagement for me to marry him. I…I love him.'

Wulf's hand jerked in hers, his gaze burned. 'Erica?'

De Warenne made a dismissive movement. 'Silence, Captain!' Cold eyes narrowed on hers. 'Lady Erica, you are telling me that you are married in *every* sense?'

Erica's cheeks scorched, not with shame, for she was proud to have married Wulf, and never more so than at this moment. All the while she thought he had forgotten her, he had been fighting behind the scenes for reconciliation between her people and his. But De Warenne's question was embarrassing. What had happened between her and Wulf last night had become public when it ought to be private. But this was 1068 and, because she was a thane's daughter, it mattered that she had given her virginity to Captain Wulf FitzRobert. It mattered because the ownership of her lands was called into question.

'Yes.'

'Hell, Captain, you tread a thin line, you realise that?'

'Yes, my lord.'

'And why have Lady Erica's housecarls come to Winchester Castle?' De Warenne put his fists on his hips. He had not, Erica realised with a puzzled frown, even thought about reaching for his sword. Her heart lifted. Why, all this talk of insubordination, of not trusting Wulf, is just that…talk. The Lord of Lewes *does* trust Wulf; more than that he *likes* him. It is his pride that makes him shout and bluster, De Warenne is angry because Wulf disobeyed his orders.

Wulf stood to attention at her side, a soldier in his bearing except for one tiny but significant detail—he was holding her hand. Erica glanced down at their linked fingers. Not once had Wulf spoken of love, but he had shown it in the way he treated her. From the moment of their first meeting in the bailey at Guthlac's castle he had held her in respect, he had kept her safe. Wulf was one of the most self-contained men she had met, he never gave space for his emotions and yet…and yet…shooting him a swift glance, she intercepted a searching glance from those blue eyes and her lips curved…he had gone out of his way to *ask* De Warenne for her hand.

Wulf *did* care.

Erica did not know if he loved her, but he had said he thought her beautiful and, far more importantly, he claimed that he wanted her and not her lands. Unfailingly, Wulf had honoured her with the truth. She would take him at his word; marriages had been built on worse foundations.

'You, Saxon.' De Warenne cut into her thoughts; he was staring at Hrolf. 'I have not seen you before—are you part of this lady's household?'

'Yes, my lord.'

De Warenne's brow darkened. 'You were with her in East Anglia?'

'Yes, my lord.'

'What of your arms, your other compatriots? I had heard that four, maybe five score men, answered to the Thane of Whitecliffe. Where are the rest of you?'

Wulf released Erica and stepped forwards. 'These housecarls are unarmed, my lord. They came to the chapel under my safe conduct to discuss terms for a peaceful settlement for the entire warband.'

'So, your report was correct, Asculf,' De Warenne said. 'I confess that I doubted it. Captain?'

'My lord?'

'Have you come to terms?'

'Yes, my lord. Provided safe conduct is agreed for my lady's men and no reprisals are made against their families, most of the housecarls are prepared to leave the fens and return to Whitecliffe.'

'*Most?*'

Wulf spread his hands. 'Not all will treat with Normans, my lord, not all will return. But those that do will swear fealty to you provided—'

'How many will remain outside the law?'

Ailric cleared his throat. 'Not above a dozen, my lord.'

'You may give me their names later.'

Ailric flushed and his eyes slid away.

'Saxon, did you hear me?'

'Yes, my lord.'

'Very good.' De Warenne swung back to Wulf and gave him a curt nod. 'There are bound to be a few hardened rebels, but on the whole you have done well, Captain. I confess I did not look for so swift a result.'

'Thank you. My lord, about my marriage—'

De Warenne cut him off with a wave. 'Say no more, Captain, you disobeyed a direct order.'

'Yes, my lord.'

'My lord?' Ailric cleared his throat; there was a decidedly belligerent gleam in his eyes. 'You must know that our loyalty is dependent on you giving your blessing to Captain FitzRobert's marriage with Lady Erica. Should it be annulled, we shall be forced to reconsider our position.'

'You are in no position to threaten me, Saxon.'

Ailric tightened his jaw. 'I do not threaten, I merely state the terms as we have agreed them. Captain

FitzRobert has acted honourably in his dealings with us. He stood out against Thane Guthlac in the matter of the bloodfeud, he protected our lady. And after Guthlac's castle was fired, he trusted Hereward and I to begin negotiations with the rest of our men. He is half-Saxon, he understands us.'

After a moment's silence, De Warenne shook his head and held out his hand. 'Asculf, your sword, if you please.'

Steel rasped as Sir Richard drew his sword. The hilt was pressed into De Warenne's palm.

Erica bit her lip; she could not read Wulf's lord, but cold sweat was running down her back. Her hand crept to her bracelet, twirling, twirling.

'Peace, lady,' De Warenne said. 'No blood will be shed in the King's Chapel. Captain, kneel.'

Wulf's cheeks emptied of colour. He swapped startled glances with Richard of Asculf and fell to his knees. Erica found herself at his side.

De Warenne's lips curved. 'I was not best pleased when I heard you had married Lady Erica. I had intended her to marry someone of her own standing.' He raised the sword, turning it so the flat tapped Wulf's shoulders in quick succession, once, twice, thrice. 'So. You had best be a knight. You have been acting like one in any case, organising treaties with outlaws, marrying their ladies and giving them the confidence to summon our knights on your behalf. But I warn you, Captain, you put the cart before the horse, and, while I understand your motives, I would not wish you to make a habit of it.

'You have got away with it because you have been vindicated by the outcome, and because it is my judgement that England has need of men like you. Understood?'

'Yes, my lord.'

'Oh, get up, FitzRobert. You are made knight.'

That night, Erica was lying alone in the tower room unable to sleep. She was going home!

Whitecliffe! Preparations were in hand, they were setting out in the morning. She could scarcely believe it. Of course, much had changed since she had left her father's hall—her homecoming was going to be nothing like the one she had planned. Wulf would be riding in at her side—her husband—a man who had taught her to trust him in *all* ways, politically as well as personally. De Warenne had gifted him with her father's land.

Erica's forehead creased—would everyone accept him? A Norman knight at Whitecliffe? Who would have thought it? A sound on the stairwell caught her attention. Wulf would win them over, particularly if he continued to deal fairly with everyone. He was a just man and they would appreciate that.

The door opened. Wulf. Candles guttered as he approached the bed, his shadow stretched across the star-painted walls.

'Still awake, *ma belle*?' The mattress dipped under his weight as he sat down beside her. 'I am glad of that, because I have something for you.'

'Oh?'

He pressed a folded cloth into her hands. 'Here.'

Erica blinked. Green, blue and white, like the ribbons on the door latch. Her heartbeat increased. The ribbons had not been a coincidence then, Wulf knew about her father's device. Green, blue and white—the shades were an exact match of the colours her father had chosen for his battle pennon.

'Aren't you going to look at it?'

Carefully, scarcely daring to breathe, Erica unfolded the fabric. Yes, as she suspected, it was a newly made pennon. Her eyes stung. Here was the green of the sea, dancetty with waves; and here some blue silk to represent the sky above the cliffs near Lewes; while the white cliffs themselves…

She opened the last fold and blinked in surprise. 'What's this?' The white cliffs had changed—oh, there was still a broad band of white in the middle of the pennon—but superimposed over them someone had stitched a wolf's head, in profile. A black wolf with a red eye and tongue.

Wulf's expression was guarded, but his mouth went up at one corner. 'It's a wolf.'

'I can see that, but—'

A large finger reached out to trace the outline of the head. 'It is—' his smile enlarged '—an ambiguous device. De Warenne has approved it, by the way.'

Erica's eyes went from Wulf's to the pennon and back again to Wulf's.

'I…see. A wolf's head—outlaws and rebels.'

'That's *you*, my lady, my outlaw wife who bears the wolf's head. And your men, too, the housecarls who went with you into the fens.'

She shook her head. 'But you, your name, it is also *you*, Sir Wulf.' Erica's lips curved as she bent her head over the pennon, smoothing out the fabric. Wulf had just succeeded in dispelling any lingering doubts as to whether he would be accepted at Whitecliffe. 'It is fine work, I like it. Rose?'

'Yes.' Taking the pennon from her, Wulf put it to one side. 'I want you to know I will protect you, Erica. Always.'

She tipped her head to one side. 'That is important to you?'

'It is the most important thing. Ever since Marie died, I have longed to be in a position to be able to protect those I love.'

He leaned over her, and a large hand cupped her cheek even as she reached for him.

'Those you love, Wulf?'

Wulf's cheeks darkened, but before she could question him more closely, his lips were moving over hers and his hand was sliding into the neck of her nightgown, making her feel that sensual tug between breast and womb.

'Wulf?' Managing to draw back, Erica gave him a little shake. 'It is not fair, you had my confession in the chapel, before witnesses. I need yours. You love me?'

'I am not good with words, *ma belle*,' he muttered, tossing his belt aside. 'But I can show you what I feel.' He placed her hand low on his hose. 'See what you do to me. No other woman has ever affected me like this. You only have to enter a room and this happens.'

'Wulf FitzRobert, I need the words!'

'Erica, *je t'adore*, and well you know it. Stop being a tease and let me prove it to you. If, that is—' an endearing look of uncertainty entered his eyes '—you are not…recovering after last night.'

She took him by the shoulder and looked deep into his eyes. 'The words do not frighten me. I love you, Wulf, and I would have you know that I will be proud to return to Whitecliffe with you at my side.' She grinned. 'And as for last night, I was afraid you might chastise me for my unseemly behaviour.'

'I must admit, I was shocked.'

She widened her eyes. 'You were? Truly?'

He nodded. 'I expected much more in the way of maidenly behaviour.'

'You did?'

'Mmm.' Lifting the bedcovers, Wulf slid in next to her and pulled her close. 'And since you are a knight's lady, I think we had better try again.'

'You want maidenly, ladylike behaviour? Are you sure?'

'Indeed, and you must learn to be obedient. Kiss me.'

Meekly, she lifted her lips to his. 'Yes, Wulf.'

In an instant the kiss flashed from meek to intense. Erica moaned and opened her mouth. Wulf pressed close, closer. After a moment, he lifted his head. His eyes sparkled in the candlelight, his mouth curved and he shook his head. 'It's no good, you definitely need more practice.'

'Mmm? What's that?'

Gentle hands swept up and down her length, holding her tightly to him. A dark brow lifted. 'Maidenly modesty, *ma belle*, you really haven't got the hang of it. I can see we will have to try again and again until you get it right…'

* * * * *

MILLS & BOON
Historical

On sale 1st May 2009

Regency

LORD BRAYBROOK'S PENNILESS BRIDE
by Elizabeth Rolls

Miss Christiana Daventry will do anything to keep
from the streets – and the insufferably attractive
Lord Braybrook urgently needs a governess! Headstrong,
tawny-haired Christy is so deliciously endearing that Julian
quickly forgets how scandalous it would be to yield to this
attraction for his penniless governess…

Regency

A COUNTRY MISS IN HANOVER SQUARE
by Anne Herries

Debutante Susannah Hampton is confused by dashing
Lord Harry Pendleton's attentions. Arrogant, but undeniably
attractive, he is not the spouse she had in mind – but this
innocent country miss is determined to inflame her new
husband's passion – and melt the ice around his heart!

MILLS & BOON
Historical

On sale 1st May 2009

Regency
AN IMPETUOUS ABDUCTION
by Patricia Frances Rowell

Moments after stumbling upon a band of thieves, terrified
Persephone Hathersage was abducted on horseback! Trepidation
soon gave way to desire for her brooding, battle-scarred captor.
Phona knew any impropriety with this nameless rogue would
tarnish her reputation – yet appearances could be quite deceiving!

CHOSEN FOR THE MARRIAGE BED
by Anne O'Brien

Elizabeth de Lacy is about to take the veil when she is told she
must wed her family's sworn enemy! A union with the de Lacy
family would serve Lord Richard Malinder well – if only to keep
his enemies close. But Elizabeth never expected to find Richard
so kind, seductive and devastatingly handsome…

WESTERN WEDDINGS
by Jillian Hart, Kate Bridges, Charlene Sands

You are cordially invited to three weddings in the Old West
this May! Three favourite authors, three blushing brides, three
heartwarming stories – a perfect recipe for spring!

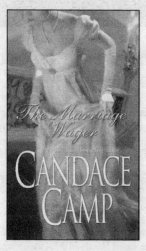
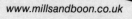

2 FREE

BOOKS AND A SURPRISE GIFT!

We would like to take this opportunity to thank you for reading this Mills & Boon® book by offering you the chance to take TWO more specially selected titles from the Historical series absolutely FREE! We're also making this offer to introduce you to the benefits of the Mills & Boon® Book Club™—

- ★ FREE home delivery
- ★ FREE gifts and competitions
- ★ FREE monthly Newsletter
- ★ Exclusive Mills & Boon Book Club offers
- ★ Books available before they're in the shops

Accepting these FREE books and gift places you under no obligation to buy, you may cancel at any time, even after receiving your free shipment. Simply complete your details below and return the entire page to the address below. You don't even need a stamp!

YES! Please send me 2 free Historical books and a surprise gift. I understand that unless you hear from me, I will receive 4 superb new titles every month for just £3.79 each, postage and packing free. I am under no obligation to purchase any books and may cancel my subscription at any time. The free books and gift will be mine to keep in any case.

H9ZED

Ms/Mrs/Miss/Mr .... Initials ....
BLOCK CAPITALS PLEASE

Surname ....

Address ....

....

.... Postcode..........................

Send this whole page to:
UK: FREEPOST CN81, Croydon, CR9 3WZ

Offer valid in UK only and is not available to current Mills & Boon Book Club subscribers to this series. Overseas and Eire please write for details and readers in Southern Africa write to Box 3010, Pinegowie, 2123 RSA. We reserve the right to refuse an application and applicants must be aged 18 years or over. Only one application per household. Terms and prices subject to change without notice. Offer expires 30th June 2009. As a result of this application, you may receive offers from Harlequin Mills & Boon and other carefully selected companies. If you would prefer not to share in this opportunity please write to The Data Manager, PO Box 676, Richmond, TW9 1WU.

Mills & Boon® is a registered trademark owned by Harlequin Mills & Boon Limited.
The Mills & Boon® Book Club™ is being used as a trademark.